THE RELUCTANT VIRGIN

'Are you going to tie me to the bed in there?' she asked, her eyes imploring him to do just that. He nodded and she smiled happily. She was more than ready to do whatever he asked of her. He unbuckled her restraints and led her, still half-naked, back into the main room. The bacchanalia was still in progress, and it took them some moments to struggle through the mêlée to reach the great bed. He shackled her quickly until she was held in a secure position. That done, he stood and faced the crowd. He clapped his hands loudly.

'Can I have your attention, please?' he shouted. His words made little difference. 'Silence!' he bellowed. A sudden hush descended on the mass of half-naked people littered around the room. 'This lovely young lady has just been introduced to the pleasures of pain,' continued Joseph, 'and she has asked that her initiation be continued in the sight of you all.'

By the same author:

FALLEN ANGELS
DEMONIA
THE CLOAK OF APHRODITE
PYRAMID OF DELIGHTS
THE TRAINING OF FALLEN ANGELS
THE WARRIOR QUEEN

THE RELUCTANT VIRGIN

Kendal Grahame

This book is a work of fiction.
In real life, make sure you practise safe sex.

First published in 1999 by
Nexus
Thames Wharf Studios
Rainville Road
London W6 9HT

Typeset by TW Typesetting, Plymouth, Devon

Printed and bound by
Cox & Wyman Ltd, Reading, Berks

ISBN 0 352 33339 1

One

Karina Devonside stared bleakly out of the window of her bedroom at the rolling lawns of Devon Manor. Yesterday had been the last day of college, and now she faced the loneliness of six weeks of idle pursuits until university beckoned with more years of what she considered to be purposeless studies. But, far worse than this, soon it would be her birthday.

A beautiful young lady's twenty-first birthday should be a very special occasion. When that young lady is the daughter of one of the richest landowners in England and is about to inherit a considerable fortune of her own, the event should be doubly momentous.

But, for the lovely Karina Devonside, it was to be anything but special. The celebrations loomed ahead of her like a sentence of death. In just three short weeks, she would reach that magical age and, to her utmost dismay, she would still be a virgin.

It hadn't seemed so important when she had reached eighteen; indeed, many of her friends at college had still been 'intact', as it were, but as the years had progressed and they had regaled her with their lascivious tales of their countless erotic encounters, her need to experience similar delights had become a matter of urgency. She had even taken the precaution of going on the pill, just in case. She well remembered the excitement that she had felt when she had swallowed the first tablet. Her feelings had been a mixture of nervous apprehension and mounting enthusiasm at the thought that she was preparing herself to become a real woman. Later, as each empty packet was discarded, her disappointment and frustration increased.

It wasn't as though she didn't have the looks and personality to attract hordes of interested suitors. Karina Devonside had the sort of appearance that would cause men's heads to turn and women's expressions to become pained with envy. She was tall and slim with long auburn hair that framed her delicate flawless features. Her eyes were emerald green and shone with youthful innocence, coupled with a hint of mischievous promise. Her mouth was full and her lips were naturally formed into an inviting pout that, even in her adolescence, she had come to realise that men would find irresistible. Her unblemished skin was the colour of the purest amber, thanks mainly to her mother's ancestral influences, and bore a delicate sheen reminiscent of the finest silk.

She modestly considered that her figure, too, was all that most men could desire. Many times in the recent past, she had divested herself of the dour uniform provided by St Jennifer's College and had stood naked before the long mirror in the dormitory to examine her physical attributes. Her breasts were not large but were perfectly formed and very firm, like two ripe apples ready to be harvested. Her nipples were long and deep brown and, for no real reason, appeared to be in a permanent state of erection. Her narrow waist accentuated the smooth sweep of her curves to the special place between her legs. Her mound was unusually prominent, covered by wisps of down-like hair that failed to conceal her most intimate treasures. The lips pouted thickly like those of her mouth, offering a blatant invitation to any who might desire to enjoy their succulent promise.

Once, during a netball tournament at college, she had been forced to borrow a pair of shorts from her best friend, Sandy. Despite being very full-breasted, Sandy was somewhat slimmer about the hips than Karina and the shorts had fitted her extremely tightly. Nevertheless, the game had been played and won, and it was only during the presentation of medals that Karina had realised that there was a problem.

A group of local youths from the village were openly staring at her and making ribald and obscene comments about her crotch and bottom. Their words had cut into her like knives, and she'd rushed from the field in tears. Once in the relative sanctuary of the changing room, she'd stood in front of one of the small mirrors and had been horrified at the image that she'd seen staring back at her. The tight white shorts caressed her fleshy mound like a second skin, every detail clearly visible through the thin material. At first, she had felt both disgust and embarrassment, but the more that she had gazed at herself, the more aroused she had become. The thought of these unwashed, surly yobs not only leering at her private parts but also openly discussing her physical attributes had thrilled her immensely.

She would often think of that day and would touch herself there while staring at her image in the mirror. She would gently caress the hard little bud and stroke and pull at the soft, wet lips as she imagined a lover's fingers delving into her and preparing her for the ultimate joy. In her imagination she would see the youths, all of them, and would picture them standing naked, their cocks hugely erect, waiting to impale the sweet lushness of her hot, virginal pussy. She would invariably come, a sweet release that would ease her frustrations, albeit only for a matter of moments.

Her legs were long and shapely, but it was her bottom that she considered her most attractive asset. Her pert, thrusting buttocks curved in a most sensuous manner, an attribute that had often been remarked upon by her friends. She was justifiably proud of her lovely bottom and had taught herself to swing her hips in a subtle but provocative manner as she walked around her bedroom or along the long passageways of her home. Often, she would make a point of sashaying past one or other of the male servants in the house, before suddenly glancing over her shoulder to see him staring at her rear. Their embarrassment would always both thrill and amuse her, but she knew that she was far too much of a lady to allow any of them to get close to her. That would never do.

On other occasions, she took to parading herself around the small market town near the college in the tightest and most revealing of outfits, and would take great delight in observing the way that the men looked at her. Her favourite garment was a pair of skin-tight white jeans that she invariably wore without the benefit of underwear. As she walked towards them, she would see men's eyes move to stare directly at her crotch and she revelled in the fact that she knew that the shape of her thick sex-lips was clearly visible. The episode at the netball tournament had taught her that.

And yet, despite all this, she remained a virgin. No lips had ever suckled her long nipples, no fingers (other than her own) had probed the lush prize between her smooth thighs and no hands had smoothed their palms over her firm, inviting rear. And now her twenty-first birthday loomed ahead of her and the shameful thought of reaching such a great age without having enjoyed any form of sexual contact with a man horrified her.

Karina turned from the window and slipped out of her silk robe. She allowed the gossamer-like garment to drift silently to the floor and then walked naked into the bathroom. Steam billowed from the already prepared tub and clouded the many mirrors that surrounded the sumptuous room. She slipped into the soothing warmth of the scented water and relaxed in its gentle ambience. She closed her eyes.

She began to think of her friends back at St Jennifer's. She knew that, despite their assurances, she was unlikely to see many of them again and it saddened her. It appeared to her that an important part of her life had suddenly ended. She had lived and laughed with the girls for so many years, and now they were gone.

Not Sandy, though. Karina knew that she would see her best friend again. The two of them had been inseparable, especially during the last years of their studies. Other students had even commented that they had appeared too close, and a malicious rumour had spread that they were lovers. It was not true, of course, although such things were known to go on within the hallowed portals of the old college.

Karina was fully aware, however, that if she had been honest with herself, such an idea would not have been totally out of the question. Sandy was an attractive, tomboyish girl who was almost a year younger than she was. She was barely five feet tall with short, bobbed brown hair and elfin-like features. Her dark eyes shone with mischief and her features were formed into an almost permanent grin. Her breasts were far too large for her small frame but she had always seemed proud of them, often displaying their firm, upward swell under the flimsiest of garments whenever she could.

Karina thought of the day when Sandy had confessed that she had lost her virginity. She had listened enviously as her friend had recounted the occasion in the most graphic detail as they'd sat huddled together in a corner of the sports-field. The lucky young man had been one of the local lads, a strapping youth who had been the object of many of the college girls' fantasies. Karina had pictured her friend, lying on her back with her uniform skirt rolled up to her waist and her knickers thrown carelessly to one side, while the young man had pounded into her. From what Sandy had told her, there had been no pain or discomfort, and this had surprised Karina. Their somewhat old-fashioned biology mistress, Miss Roe, had warned the girls that their first sexual experience, especially if it occurred at a relatively early age, would be an extremely painful encounter. Sandy had happily rubbished this and had told Karina that the event had been the 'most wonderful thing that could ever happen'. She had even admitted that she had allowed him to put his thing into her mouth. In her youthful innocence, Karina hadn't believed her. No girl could do such a thing. Only when other girls at the college confessed during the long nights in the dormitory to enjoying similar delights did she learn that it was all part of the delights of sexual fulfilment.

The young man may have been the first, but he certainly wasn't destined to be the last. Sandy had, as she put it, 'got a taste for it'. Karina had lost count of the number of times her friend had excitedly told of her latest sexual conquests, always in the most lurid detail. They would lie in their adjoining beds in the darkened dormitory and Karina would fondle herself between the legs as Sandy chattered on, and sometimes she would manage to bring herself to orgasm, although she was always careful to do so quietly, lest her friend or any of the other girls in the room realised what she was up to.

Sandy had once confessed that she had had two men at the same time. The mental picture of the busty young girl sandwiched between the thrusting bodies of two handsome men filled Karina's dreams for many nights to come and, as time went on, she began to fantasise about finding herself in such a delightful situation. The thought of having a stiff cock inside her pussy and another in her mouth thrilled her and she vowed that she would enjoy the experience at the earliest opportunity.

But she hadn't even managed to meet just one lover. True, there had been many young men presented to her by her anxious mother at Devon Manor, but they had all been of a most unappealing type. They were invariably the sons of the rich: gutless, spoilt brats with all the personalities of raw vegetables. Her impending wealth was well known among the society frequented by her parents and Karina wisely became suspicious about the sincerity of her host of privileged suitors. Eventually she had pleaded with her mother and father to stop their matchmaking and to allow her to make her own way in the world, at least as far as men were concerned. They had reluctantly agreed, although an occasional young lord or duke would still be invited to their home, ostensibly to join the hunt or enjoy the trout fishing in the fast-flowing stream that ran through the grounds of the manor.

Not that she didn't find some of them physically attractive. It was their inane prattle about their comfortable lifestyles, their cars or their exotic holidays that she found nauseating. She came to dread the holidays and spent most of the days at the manor indulging in solitary pursuits – reading, walking in the grounds or swimming in the pool when the weather permitted it – always waiting impatiently for her return to college.

Now it was all over. Her father had seen to it that she had gained entry to Oxford and she knew that she would, no doubt, find herself once more in the company of the wealthy or the unapproachably studious. She saw the next three or four years as being bleak and friendless, an eternity of loneliness looming ahead of her like a prison sentence. Even Sandy would not be there. Her friend had opted to take up a course in farm management, no doubt in the expectation of enjoying many romps in the meadows with a host of lusty young labourers. She would be happy; she always was.

Karina reached up and turned the hot tap on. She allowed the water to gush noisily for a few moments in order to reheat the bath and then lay back once more and closed her eyes. Her fingers quickly found her soft sex-lips and she caressed herself gently. She thought about the workers on the estate, the young men who laboured bare-chested in the hot summer sun. She rubbed harder against her stiff little bud and breathed deeply as her fantasy began to unfold. It was a favourite daydream of hers.

She would imagine herself walking through a field of swaying corn, with the heat of the sun beating down on her bare shoulders. The birds would be singing and she would spot a deer running towards the woods in the distance. Suddenly, a man would appear, as if out of thin air. He would be tall and muscular with handsome, smiling features. He would be wearing nothing but a simple pair of shorts, and they would be so tight that she would be easily able to discern the shape of his long thick penis.

She would be dressed in a simple summer dress of the purest white, and she would have neglected to put on any underwear. The breeze would cause the flimsy garment to billow up suddenly and he would see her virginal mound and the soft curves of her bottom. He would smile and then take her roughly into his arms and push his hand up her dress as they embraced. They would kiss passionately and she would feel him slipping his fingers between the succulent folds of her sex-lips. She would reach down between them and gently stroke the front of his shorts and would feel *it*, his cock, stiffening quickly under the rough denim.

He would lay her down in the corn and pull off her dress in one expert movement. Sometimes the material would tear; other times it would drift into nothingness. Then he would stand for a moment, just looking at her, before at last slowly removing his shorts. He would then stand staring at her again, displaying his proud erection to her eager gaze. And it would be enormous; they always were, in her fantasies.

The farm-worker would kneel between her legs and she would watch as he pushed his huge cock into her. It would slip in easily; there would be no pain. And she would come, just at the moment that she felt his thick rod throbbing inside her, filling her with his cream.

Karina rubbed herself rapidly as she pictured her imaginary lover until her emotions exploded into blissful release. She breathed the steamy atmosphere heavily and wiped her sweating forehead with a flannel. Her pussy throbbed. It had been good.

The sound of the dinner-gong echoed throughout the old house. Karina checked her reflection in the long mirror. She had chosen to wear an ankle-length black dress that accentuated her slim lithe figure perfectly. The garment was slit at one side to reveal much of her long shapely legs, although at the same time cut in such a way as to conceal the fact that she was wearing stockings. She hated the restrictiveness of tights and had always preferred to go bare-legged or wear stockings.

She shook back her long hair and, after glancing once more at the mirror, she set off for the dining room. As she neared the door to the room, she heard her father's voice, and then another, also distinctly male, and which she didn't recognise. Her heart sank. Her mother had done it again! Another hopeful young man would be sitting at the table, greedily waiting for his chance to get his hands on her millions.

She stood for a moment at the door. For a moment she seriously considered the idea of returning to her bedroom, locking the door and refusing to come out until the stranger had gone, but she realised that such a protest would be considered childish. She took a deep breath and turned the handle. She walked into the dining room swiftly with her head held high and with a deliberately haughty expression on her face. She paused for a moment as the door was closed behind her by one of the servants.

'Ah, Karina,' boomed her father's voice. 'We have a guest.'

'So I see,' she replied in a disinterested tone. She walked to her place without even glancing at the newcomer. The chair was pulled back for her and she took her seat. She looked down at the table as if she were checking the line of cutlery and then busied herself by unfolding her napkin.

'Karina!' hissed her mother. 'This is the Honourable Charles Simons!'

Karina raised her head and looked across at the stranger. Unusually, the man had remained seated when she had entered. He was older than her mother's usual matchmaking attempts – much older, in fact. Nevertheless, he was distinctly handsome and his features were those of one who had travelled and experienced much in life. She nodded politely, determined to ignore his lack of etiquette in not standing when she had joined them at the table.

'I am pleased to meet you, Miss Devonside.' The man rose a little from his seat and offered her his hand. She gripped his fingertips lightly in greeting. Their eyes met briefly and she felt sudden, unexplainable shivers run through her body. His stare was cold and his eyes were unblinking. For an instant, Karina sensed that he was reading her mind. She released his fingers and looked away uncomfortably.

'Mr Simons is something of an adventurer,' chirruped her mother. 'He has travelled all over the world!'

'Really?' replied Karina, determined to maintain her show of indifference, although there was definitely something incongruously appealing to her about their enigmatic visitor.

'He has just returned from the Amazon,' continued her mother. 'Can you believe it?'

'Lots of people go to the Amazon these days, Mother,' said Karina as she took a sip of water from her crystal glass.

'Karina!' snapped her father.

Simons laughed and waved his hand. 'Please, Mr Devonside,' he said, 'your daughter is correct. Brazil is little more than a tourist attraction these days. Once impenetrable forests are now criss-crossed with major highways.'

'Just what do you do, Mr Simons?' asked Karina.

He looked directly into her eyes and she sensed the same strange feeling of unease that she had had before. 'I am a writer,' he answered simply.

Karina raised her eyebrows as though impressed. 'Really?' she said. 'I can't say that I know your name. Do you write under a pseudonym?'

'No, but my subject is very specialised and my readership is limited. I study and write about matters of the occult.'

'The occult? How fascinating!' For once, Karina's interest was genuine. 'Is that what you were doing in South America – researching, I mean?'

Simons smiled, clearly pleased that she was apparently beginning to warm to him. 'Indeed,' he answered. 'I learnt of an ancient people, a tribe that lives close to the foothills of the Andes and who practise a strange form of worship that I wished to study. I gained enough material to write a hundred books.'

'Tell us more,' piped up Karina's mother excitedly.

Simons smiled politely in her direction. 'Perhaps after we have eaten,' he replied. 'It is hardly the stuff of dinner conversation.'

The soup arrived as if on cue and it and the remaining courses were consumed in virtual silence, broken only by the occasional inane comment from Mrs Devonside.

Throughout the meal, Karina constantly felt her eyes drawn to their recondite visitor. She found herself becoming more and more aroused. Her nipples had hardened dramatically and she was beginning to regret her decision not to wear anything under her dress other than the stockings and a tiny pair of panties. He would surely be able to discern her discomfort from the way that her buds had become so prominent under the tight-fitting dress. She began to imagine him taking the place of her farm-worker in the cornfield. Every so often, their eyes would meet and she would look away in embarrassment, convinced that he knew what she was thinking. His eyes seemed to be boring into her very soul. She became hot and it was not long before her panties were soaked.

At long last, the meal was finished and Karina excused herself and left the table. She walked out through the open French windows into the garden and breathed in the relatively cool air of the late evening. She shivered slightly, but it felt good to be outside.

'May I join you?'

Karina suddenly realised that Simons was standing behind her. She turned and regarded him suspiciously. This was par for the course. Her mother and father would have disappeared to the library to take brandy, leaving her to the mercy of yet another ardent suitor.

'If you wish,' she said, resuming her nonchalant tone of voice. Simons moved to stand next to her and rested his hands on the low stone wall that ringed the patio.

'It's a lovely evening,' he said quietly as he stared out into the semi-darkness. An owl hooted somewhere in the distance.

'Tell me about this tribe in Brazil,' said Karina, anxious to steer the conversation towards a more interesting subject than the weather.

Simons turned and half sat against the wall. He looked into her eyes and then seemed to deliberately allow his gaze to travel up and down her body. She shivered again.

'Are you cold?' he said. She shook her head.

'No, no. It was too hot in there, that's all. Tell me about the tribe. Do they worship the devil?'

Simons laughed. 'No, Miss Devonside, anything but.'

'Please call me Karina,' she said softly.

'Certainly, Karina. It is a lovely name for a beautiful young lady. You are very beautiful, you know.'

'Thank you,' she said, with undisguised discomfort. Her nipples were hard again and she knew that he would probably be able to see them clearly through the sheer material of her dress. She folded her arms across her chest.

'Are you sure you're not cold?' he asked with apparently genuine concern in his tone. 'Please, let me go and fetch you a wrap.'

'No,' she snapped. 'I said that I'm perfectly all right. Please tell me about the tribe.'

Simons smiled resignedly. 'The people are called the Atca. They worship just one thing – sex.'

Karina's eyes opened in surprise. 'Sex?' she said, with a nervous laugh. 'How can anyone worship sex?'

'Very easily,' Simons replied. 'There are many people in the Western World who think of little else. It's just that the Atca people have turned it into a religion.'

'What do they do? Do they pray to a giant willy or something?' Karina was surprised at her words and immediately sensed that she was becoming flushed with her embarrassment.

'The phallus is important to them, yes, but there is much more. They believe that they were created to enjoy constant arousal and satisfaction in as many a diverse way as possible.'

'Did you meet them? Did you worship with them?'

'You mean, did I have sex with them? Sadly, no. Their religion forbids outsiders to participate in their ceremonies. But I learnt a great deal from them.'

Karina sat down on a nearby bench and crossed her legs. His eyes fell immediately to the expanse of exposed thigh and she knew that he would be able to see her stocking-top. The knowledge excited her. 'What sort of things did you learn? Different ways to do it?' She was trying to keep her voice calm, but the subject matter and the closeness of this enigmatic stranger made it difficult.

Simons laughed kindly. 'I don't think that I ought to say any more,' he said as he sat next to her. 'I consider that your father may not approve of my discussing such delicate matters with his lovely daughter.'

'I won't say anything,' she pleaded. 'Please, I am genuinely interested.'

Simons reached over and touched her bare knee with the tips of his fingers. Karina trembled visibly. 'You're a virgin, aren't you?' he breathed. She turned her head quickly and glared at him.

'I beg your pardon?' she said angrily.

'You're a virgin,' he repeated. 'It's nothing to be ashamed of.'

Karina thought for a moment. She looked down at his hand, which was still resting on her knee. She knew that she wanted this man, and that she wanted him to take her completely. But how could she, with her parents likely to appear at any moment?

'I'm not,' she lied. 'I've done it lots of times.'

Simons laughed and removed his hand from her leg. 'If you say so,' he said.

'I have!' Karina protested.

'All right, I believe you,' he said, although his expression made it clear that he considered the opposite to be the truth. There was an awkward pause. 'How old are you, Karina?' he said after a few moments.

'Nearly twenty-one,' she replied, glad that he appeared to be changing the subject.

'The Atca women marry when they are sixteen. By your age, they would already have had three or four children.'

'I wouldn't like that. I don't want babies for years.'

There was a long silence as the two of them stared out into the rapidly descending gloom. The moon disappeared behind some clouds and the previously silvery forms of the trees became forbidding dark shadows under the night sky.

It was becoming colder. Karina shivered and Simons slipped his arm around her shoulders. She leant against him and turned her face towards his. His gaze caught hers and she knew that she was lost. Their mouths met. She kissed him gently and inexpertly, never having really kissed a man before in her life. He responded by forcing his tongue between her lips. She parted her teeth almost automatically and their tongues met. He tugged her shoulders and pulled her closer to him. Karina uncrossed her legs and moved her body against his. He slipped his free arm around her waist and she hugged him tightly around the neck.

The kiss was long and passionate, and was as wonderful as anything that she could have ever imagined. She felt a warm but unfamiliar sensation between her legs. It was far stronger and demanding than anything she had experienced before by her own hand. She wanted him to touch her – there, in that secret, virginal place. She knew that she wanted to feel him probing her soaking sex-lips with his expert fingers.

He pulled his face away from hers and she sat back. Her heart was thumping and she was sure that he would be able to hear it. She looked absently out into the night, wondering what to do or say next. She could sense that he was looking at her.

'Are you sure that you're not a virgin?' he said presently.

Karina glanced into his eyes and then looked down at his lap. His trousers were bulging noticeably at the front. She looked back quickly at his face. 'I *am* a virgin,' she said, as though she were confessing to the most heinous crime. 'But that doesn't mean that I want to be all my life.' She was surprised at her bravado, realising at once that she was actually offering herself to him in a blatant and obvious way.

'Shall we go for a walk in the garden?' His words rang melodically in her ears. She smiled and stood up and then held out her hand. He rose and grasped her hand and they headed out into the darkness. Karina glanced back at the house, fearful that her parents might see them. She saw the open doors leading to the dining room and knew, in her heart, that the next time that she entered the house she would no longer be a virgin.

Karina knew exactly where she would take him. The place was close to the main lake, not too far away. It was her special place. When she was a child, she had sat in the shade of the trees and bushes and had daydreamed for hours. As she had got older, she had decided that a handsome lover would one day share her secret. At last the time had come.

She led Simons through the undergrowth at the water's edge until they arrived at her hidden refuge. She sat on the grassy bank and picked up a stone, which she threw nonchalantly into the water. She watched the ripples forming larger and larger circles as the handsome stranger sat next to her. She made to throw another stone but he grabbed her wrist and pulled her towards him. Their mouths met again, and this time she kissed him with a passion that she felt must surely impress him. His hand cupped one of her breasts and she pressed her mouth harder against his. He fondled her firm flesh gently and then pinched her nipple between his thumb and forefinger. She squealed, more from delight than pain, and pulled her face away from his. She grinned broadly. He ran the palm of his hand from one breast to the other and then back again.

'You have beautiful breasts,' he breathed. He pinched the nipple again. 'Do you like that?' he asked. She nodded. 'Wait until I get it between my lips,' he continued. He reached out with both hands and pinched both of her stiff little buttons simultaneously. 'Your nipples are very big and hard,' he breathed. He cupped her apple-firm breasts and held them firmly. 'Take off your dress,' he said suddenly. He sat back to watch her with an almost arrogant expression on his face.

Karina felt her entire body trembling. She couldn't believe what she was going to do. She barely knew this man and yet she was going to strip herself naked before his eyes and let him take her. She turned her back on him and nervously unclasped the back of her silky garment. She felt him draw the zip down and then she pulled the concealing material from her shoulders and down over her arms. Freeing her hands from the material, she turned to face him again and sat back, her breasts now bared to his hungry gaze. He bent his head forward and took one of her nipples into his mouth and began to suckle it gently. She felt his teeth rasp against her hard flesh and the sensation thrilled her. She stroked the top of his head tenderly as he sucked her. The moon broke free from the clouds and she looked down and watched him. Somehow, it all seemed so perfect.

Simons moved his face from her breast and once more gazed into her eyes. His stare seemed to be draining her of her will and yet she knew that she was in control of her emotions. Quite simply, she wanted him to fuck her. He began to tug at her dress. She raised her bottom from the grass and he pulled the garment free of her in one quick movement. She looked down. Her tiny white panties were so wet that they were completely transparent at the crotch. He smiled and touched her mound with the tip of his finger. She gasped.

'You really want it, don't you?' he breathed.

Karina merely nodded, her eyes wide and her mouth formed into a perfect pout. He moved in front of her and gripped her panties at each side of her body. She raised her bottom once again and the last concealing garment was torn off. Now, all she wore was her black suspender belt, matching stockings and her shoes. He seemed content to leave her dressed in this manner.

She lay back, allowed her legs to fall slightly apart and waited for him to make the next move. He looked down at her lovely body, staring at her with abject lust in his gaze. Karina began to feel nervous again. There was no going back now. She was going to be fucked. She couldn't say no. Things had gone too far for that.

He bent forward and suckled her other nipple. She felt his hand move down over her flat stomach and slowly, agonisingly slowly, it traced a path to her aching pussy. She gasped again as he touched her engorged sex-lips with his fingertips and then she moaned softly as he began to rub the soaking flesh gently but rhythmically. She parted her legs as wide as was possible in her awkward position. She felt him delving between her lips, not too deeply but enough to open them into an inviting pout. She closed her eyes to savour the sensation. She imagined his big hard cock slipping into her and she could feel her juices running from within her to soak her bottom and the grass beneath her.

She felt him move his body and then suddenly she sensed something different, a sensation that was so good that she nearly cried out in ecstasy. She opened her eyes and looked down. His head was resting between her thighs. He was licking her! He was actually licking her cunt! She lay her head back and closed her eyes once more. She could feel his tongue circling her sex-flesh, occasionally probing between the lips and then lapping along the full length. She began to breathe in a stilted, haphazard fashion. He moved so that he knelt fully between her legs. She looked down again and was thrilled to discover that she could now actually see his tongue sliding around her soaking flesh.

He glanced up at her and then raised his head. 'Watch,' he said simply.

Karina raised herself to rest on her elbows and drew her legs back slightly. She saw him move his face back to her pussy and then watched in fascination as his tongue flicked rapidly over her throbbing little bud. Suddenly, he gripped her thighs tightly and pressed his mouth hard against her mound. He seemed to part his teeth slightly and she felt him grip her hard little button between them. His tongue began to flutter over it at an incredible rate, up and down and then from side to side. She sensed a familiar churning building up within her loins. She was coming; she was actually going to come in a man's mouth!

She grasped hold of his hair and pressed her crotch against his face. He held his position, his tongue fluttering wildly over her clitoris. Suddenly, her release tore through her lower body and she squealed loudly. The sounds of her cries echoed around the trees and bushes. She was aware that her parents might hear but, for the moment, she couldn't have cared less. She wanted the feelings searing through her virginal body to go on forever.

Gradually, the sensations of delightful release subsided and she began to relax. Simons slowly eased the movements of his tongue until, at last, he raised himself to a kneeling position. She looked at his face adoringly. His mouth and his chin were soaked with her juices and shone in the silvery moonlight. For a brief moment, she felt guilty at having come in his mouth. What must he think of her?

He smiled and moved to sit next to her. A gentle, sensuous silence seemed to fill the air. The owl hooted again, as if to voice its own approval.

'Have you ever seen a man's penis?' Simons asked after a few quiet minutes. She shook her head. It was true that she hadn't, not even in a photograph, but

Sandy's graphic descriptions had made her fully aware of what to expect. 'D'you want to see mine?'

See it? she thought to herself. See it? I want it rammed inside me!

She decided not to give voice to her true feelings and merely nodded again. Simons quickly unzipped his trousers and eased his stalk into view. She stared at the offered prize through wide, excited eyes. She'd wanted him to take all his clothes off so that she could enjoy his nakedness, but for now this was sufficient. His cock wasn't as long as she had thought it would be, but it was nevertheless very hard and erect.

'Touch it,' he said as he lay back on the grass. Karina reached out tentatively with her hand. Her fingertips touched the stiff flesh and she drew them away quickly as if it had burnt her. 'Go on,' he said with a chuckle. 'It won't bite!' She reached out again and slipped her fingers around the bone-hard shaft. It felt strangely wonderful to be grasping a cock for the first time in her life. Simons grasped her wrist and coaxed her to move her hand up and down. She found the way the skin moved within her grip to be strangely arousing. It was as if it were sliding against an oiled surface. 'Move your face closer,' he breathed. 'Have a good look at it.' She bent forward until her head was inches away from the stiff, gnarled flesh. She squeezed his shaft tightly. She couldn't understand how it could be so hard. 'Lick it,' he said suddenly. She looked up at his face in horror.

'Oh, no, I couldn't. I just couldn't,' she pleaded.

'Go on. I did it for you and you know how much you enjoyed it.'

She stared into his eyes and felt her will slipping from her. She turned her head and once more gazed at his thick stalk. Nervously, she bent her head further forward and pushed her tongue out a little between her pursed lips. The tip of her tongue touched the head of his cock and she drew away immediately.

'Go on,' he pleaded. 'You'll get to love it.'

Karina pushed out her tongue again and this time licked across the spongy flesh. To her surprise, she found that it tasted no different than if she'd licked the back of her own hand.

'Take it in your mouth,' he groaned hoarsely.

She took a deep breath and then allowed her pouting lips to envelop the bulbous plum-shaped head. She heard him moan softly. She wanted to give him pleasure, just as he had done for her. Almost instinctively, she began to circle her tongue around his cock while taking as much of his stalk inside her mouth as she could manage. He groaned again and she started to bob her head slowly up and down. He matched her movements with gentle thrusts of his hips. She gripped his exposed stalk and rubbed it in time with the movements of her head. She was enjoying it now, savouring the taste and texture of his wonderful cock in her sucking mouth.

Suddenly, he groaned loudly and she felt his cock throbbing against her tongue. She didn't realise what was happening at first and continued to suckle and caress him. She swallowed hard, and then she knew. His cream descended her throat in a small lump and she pulled from him, allowing his wet penis to flop against his trousers. She swallowed again as though she had taken poison and wiped her mouth on the back of her hand. She couldn't believe what he'd done. She'd heard of it, of course, but somehow had never relished the idea of allowing a man to come in her mouth. She looked at him with a shocked expression on her face.

He grinned guiltily. 'Sorry about that,' he said sheepishly. 'I couldn't stop myself.'

Karina glanced back down at his groin. His cock lay tiny and flaccid in his lap. She reached out and took hold of it and began to rub it gently.

Simons grabbed her wrist to stop her. 'No, don't do that.'

She looked back at his face. 'Aren't you going to . . . don't you want to . . .' she whimpered.

He quickly forced his exposed genitals back into his trousers and zipped them up. 'I'm sorry, Karina,' he said, rather insincerely. 'That's me finished. I'll come to you in the night, if you want.'

Karina's anger grew with each word that he uttered. He had used her, and now he was offering to use her again. Tearfully, she grabbed up her dress and rushed out of the bushes, half expecting him to chase after her. She managed to struggle quickly into the dress and then rushed back to the house. Once inside, she made for her bedroom and hurried through it and into the bathroom. She looked into the mirror and thanked God that her parents hadn't seen her. Her hair was tousled and filled with blades of grass and one of her cheeks was streaked with evidence of her lover's release. She washed herself quickly, brushed her hair and then returned to the bedroom to change into a pair of jeans and a T-shirt. She pulled the clothing over her nakedness quickly and then sat down heavily on the bed and mused over her previous experiences.

She looked down at the floor glumly. It was difficult enough for her to find a man who was interested in her; for some reason, they all seemed to find her unapproachable. On the one occasion when she did manage to arouse someone's interest, something like this had to happen. Still, at least she would have something to tell her friend, Sandy, at long last. And perhaps Simons would come to her in the night, as he had promised.

Karina peered at the clock by her bedside through glassy eyes. The green digital figures proclaimed the hour as being 3 a.m. She turned her head away from the thing and stared at the ceiling. Sleep had been impossible. Simons hadn't crept into her bedroom, of course, although she'd spent the hours of darkness listening with bated breath to every creak and groan that had echoed through the timbers of the old house, hoping for the sound of his footfall.

She was lying under the silk sheets naked and ready for him. Why hadn't he come to her? She knew that she was beautiful; Sandy had told her so many times, as had other friends at St Jennifer's College. And Simons knew that she was available to him and that she was waiting for him in her bed, ready to give herself completely to him and surrender her virginity to his thick, probing cock.

She moved her hand down under the sheets and caressed the soft succulent lips between her thighs. She was still very wet. She'd brushed her teeth twice before climbing into bed and yet she imagined that she could still taste his come in her mouth. She remembered the strangely arousing sensation that she had felt when she had first taken his stiff stalk between her lips and had licked around the thick stem with her long tongue. She felt both angry that he had come so quickly and rather proud that she had aroused him so much that he had been unable to hold back.

She began to rub the hard bud of her clitoris gently. She felt like crying, the need for fulfilment being so powerful. She made a sudden decision. If he wouldn't come to her, then she would go to him. She would demand that he satisfy her hunger. Her parents wouldn't hear; the guest room was in a wing of the house far away from their bedroom.

Karina slipped out of the bed and wrapped her robe around her shoulders. She padded quietly out of the room and headed down the long passageway to where Simons was sleeping. The silence within the house was unnerving. She reached the door to the guest room and stopped in her tracks. There were sounds coming from the other side of the heavy door, the sounds of panting and the creaking of the old bed-frame. She turned the handle of the door and opened it gingerly a couple of inches.

She peered into the room through the narrow gap. The lights were still on and, from where she was standing, she had a full view of the bed reflected in one of the large mirrors on the dressing table. She could see Simons lying on his back, his naked body almost hidden by the pillows and sheets. Sitting astride him, with her back to the mirror, was a woman. She was thrusting her backside up and down on him and Karina could see his stiff cock slipping in and out of her hairy little pussy. She couldn't make out who the woman was, but assumed that she was one of the serving girls. It didn't matter anyway. All she cared about was that this woman was enjoying the pleasures that she herself so desperately needed.

Karina watched them for a few moments and then closed the door quietly and crept back down the long passageway to return to her lonely bed.

Two

Sandy was well aware that shopping for suitable outfits to wear during a short stay at Devon Manor was going to be a nightmare and she hadn't been proved wrong. Harrods had been impossible and the smaller exclusive shops in the arcades of Knightsbridge hadn't proved much better. The problem was always the same for her: size eight from the waist down and size fourteen above.

Having large breasts wasn't always a disadvantage, of course. Boys and men were drawn to her like a magnet. It was as though they assumed that, because she was blessed with a large bust, it meant that she possessed an equally huge sexual appetite. Fortunately, at least in her case, they were right. Their reasons for approaching her were shallow, of course, but Sandy didn't mind. She wasn't looking for anything meaningful – not yet, at least. Relationships were for older women.

She'd become aware of her attractiveness to members of the opposite sex at a young age, but the strictness of her upbringing and the ever watchful eyes of the matriarchal staff at St Jennifer's College had served to ensure that she had remained a virgin until well after her seventeenth birthday. It was at her elder sister's wedding reception that things had changed.

Sandy had reluctantly agreed to be one of the bridesmaids but had regretted the decision immediately when she had been fitted in her dress. The garment was embarrassingly young in style and the cut of the flowery bodice enhanced the size of her full, firm breasts to such an extent that her mother had been forced to order her to wear a lace shawl to conceal her sumptuous curves. Despite her shapeliness, being barely over five feet tall she had appeared to be at least two years younger than she actually was, and she had pleaded with her parents until they had agreed to allow her to wear a pair of shoes with particularly high heels, which gave her another six inches in stature. The dress was suitably altered to hide the shoes and, after a few days' practice, she became confident of walking in the unfamiliar footwear without falling on her face.

The day of the wedding came, and insult was added to injury when Sandy was forced to wear a flower-covered band in her hair to complete her outfit. This time, her protests were ignored. The ceremony had been long and excruciatingly dull, but her sister had looked lovely and everything went without a hitch.

The reception had been held in a giant marquee pitched on the lawn behind her parents' farmhouse. It had been a grand affair with over three hundred guests, most of whom Sandy didn't recognise. She'd found herself sitting alone in a corner, sipping a glass of orange juice, which she'd surreptitiously laced with a large measure of vodka, and willing the time to hurry by.

The stranger had appeared out of the crowd of strangers and had stood for some moments close to her, glancing occasionally in her direction. He'd looked to have been about twenty-five, and was remarkably handsome. Dressed in a formal black dinner-suit, he'd appeared every inch the gentleman, and she'd been instantly attracted to him. Nevertheless, she'd felt nothing but embarrassment at the ludicrous way that she felt she was dressed and had willed him to leave her alone in her misery.

He hadn't gone away, however. Instead, he'd walked over to her and had offered to get her another drink. 'Orange juice?' he'd asked.

'Vodka and orange,' she'd replied curtly.

The stranger had feigned surprise. 'Vodka and orange? Certainly.'

She'd watched him walk over to the bar and had glanced around nervously to ensure that her parents didn't see him add the spirit to the fruit juice. When he had returned, he'd sat next to her and handed her the glass. She'd drained the one that she was holding with one gulp. They'd made small talk, and Sandy had found herself warming to his casual charm. He'd been surprised when she had told him her age, but she had wanted to make sure that he knew that she wasn't the pathetic little girl that she had appeared to be.

'I bet you hated having to wear that dress,' he'd said with a wry smile.

His words had endeared him to her for life. They'd danced and, as the evening progressed and the vodka had begun to take effect, she had actually found that she was enjoying herself.

Later, he'd walked her in the garden and they'd kissed under the moonlight, with the strains of a gentle ballad being played by the band in the marquee wafting through the air. The moment had been magical and the outcome inevitable. Sandy had taken him into one of the barns and they'd lain together on a pile of fresh straw. His kisses had immediately become more passionate and urgent and, when he had touched her breast she'd felt that she would die. She'd felt somewhat nervous at this point, but the wetness between her legs and the incredible urge within her young loins had told her to give herself to this stranger entirely.

Her underwear and the hated dress had soon been strewn across the floor of the barn and he had almost torn his smart suit from his slim body. Naked, he'd looked to her like a god, his muscular body tanned and his hard erection appearing remarkably large to her inexperienced eyes. He'd lain again at her side and had fondled and suckled her breasts, kneading the melon-sized globes and nipping her hard nipples lightly between his teeth, sending waves of euphoric delight coursing throughout her trembling body.

Then he'd fucked her; a long, slow bout of sensuous coupling that had awakened feelings within her that she hadn't thought possible. When he'd come, he'd pulled from inside her and had allowed his cream to soak her breasts in a manner that was to be aped by many of her future lovers. She'd massaged the warm juice into her fleshy mounds, and then they'd rested in each other's arms like true lovers instead of near-strangers. Later, suitably tidied-up, she'd left the old barn as a woman, ready to embark on the new and exciting life that she now knew lay before her.

Sandy struggled through the crowds on Regent Street, carrying at least half a dozen brightly coloured shopping bags, testament to her eventual success in searching out the right outfits for her short stay at Devon Manor. Just one more stop lay ahead of her – shoes. One could simply not spend a full fortnight at such a regal and palatial place without a few pairs of new shoes!

The shop that she had in mind was one of the smaller outlets, tucked down a narrow alley between two department stores. Karina had introduced her to the place some months previously and she had been pleased to find that, although the footwear was extremely expensive, the styles were original and handmade.

She burst through the doorway to Baring and Son, Designer Shoes, and dropped her packages on the floor by the side of a small sofa. Apart from a young male assistant, there was nobody else in the shop. He turned as she entered and smiled politely. Sandy sat down on the sofa and rubbed one of her ankles.

'I think that I should have come here first, Adrian,' she said. 'I expect that my feet will be swollen from trudging around town all morning.'

'I will make allowances for that, madam,' he said. 'Please, rest for a moment. Would you like a coffee?'

'Love one. Two sugars, please.'

'I remember, madam,' responded the young man as he walked through a curtained exit at the rear of the shop. 'Cream and two sugars.'

Sandy smiled to herself. Such old-fashioned courtesy was rare in London in modern times and it was refreshing to receive it. She took off her shoes and caressed the soles of her feet. The bustle of Knightsbridge could just be heard, coming through an open fanlight window set above the door. The city could have been a million miles away, at that moment.

People rarely ventured down the alleyway leading to the shop, which had caused Sandy to wonder how Adrian and his father managed to stay in business. Here it was, however, and she was glad of a little peace and quiet.

Adrian returned with her coffee and set it down on a table beside her. He was probably in his late twenties, slim-hipped but otherwise broadly built and with kind, handsome features that she found most appealing. She had previously visited the shop on a number of occasions, on the pretext of buying shoes, simply in order to try and get to know him better, but his father had always been there, and the younger man had always appeared reluctant to allow the conversation to stray from business. Now it was different. He brought a second cup of coffee and sat down next to her.

'Have you been clothes-shopping?' he asked, eyeing up her pile of purchases.

'Yes,' replied Sandy before she took a sip of her refreshing beverage. 'It's been a nightmare. I'm glad it's done at last.'

'Just shoes to buy, then?'

'Yes, just shoes – but, like I said, I'm not sure that I'll get the right fit. My feet are killing me!'

Adrian knelt down on the floor before her and took hold of one of her feet in both hands. Due to the heat of the day, she hadn't worn tights or stockings, and she found his gentle touch soothing in the extreme.

'Your feet are hot,' he said, in a quiet tone of voice as he massaged her. 'I'll cool them for you.' With that, Adrian got to his feet and disappeared into the back room once more. He returned after a moment, carrying a small, plastic bowl and a piece of white linen.

Setting the bowl on the floor beside her, he soaked the linen with water and then wrapped the cloth around her foot. The water was cold and she found the sensation to be delightful. After a few seconds, he soaked the linen again and repeated the action with the other foot. Sandy felt a strong sense of calm and wellbeing as he held her foot in his strong grip while he playfully rubbed his thumbs under her toes.

He carried on for some minutes, first one foot and then the other, and she began to realise that she was becoming more than a little aroused by his sensuous touch. She relaxed back on the sofa and closed her eyes, her breathing quickly becoming gentle and shallow.

'You have beautiful feet,' he said suddenly.

Sandy opened her eyes and smiled. 'Thank you,' she replied. 'No one has ever said that to me before.'

'That's because not many men realise how delightful and erotic a lady's feet can be.'

Sandy regarded him curiously. He was staring at her feet while he caressed them, the look on his face clearly one of pleasurable admiration. To Sandy, it seemed that he was looking at her feet in the same way that most men looked at her breasts. 'What do you mean, erotic?' she ventured.

'The shape, the feel and, above all, the taste.' Adrian

didn't look up at her as he spoke, and his voice was filled with emotion. His gentle, insistent touch was beginning to have a profound effect on Sandy and she found that she was beginning to experience the more familiar stirrings within her loins. She parted her legs slightly in the full knowledge that, should he glance higher, he would be treated to the sight of the V of her tight white panties. He didn't look up, however. His gaze was fixed on her bare feet, and his hands were beginning to tremble.

'Can I kiss them?' he said suddenly.

His request surprised her, but Sandy didn't hesitate to reply. 'Yes,' she answered, in a hushed voice.

Adrian bent his head forward and kissed each toe lightly. Strange but highly pleasurable tremors seemed to rush up her veins to meet at the point between her legs, the very point where her flesh was becoming more and more wet. She gasped as he took two of her toes into his mouth and suckled them. Adrian moved his mouth from her and looked up at her face. He smiled.

'You like it, don't you?' he said confidently. Sandy nodded. Adrian moved his face back to her feet again and began to run his tongue wetly over each instep, soaking them with his saliva. 'Are you beginning to feel sexy?' he asked, after a few moments of this delightful treatment. Sandy merely nodded in response. 'May I do something else?' he asked.

'You can do anything that you want,' was Sandy's simple reply. She meant every word. The fluttering, sensuous lapping of his tongue against the soles of her feet had aroused her in a way that she would have never considered possible, and her only thoughts were of a deeply salacious nature.

Adrian straightened and let go of one of her feet. As Sandy watched, he unzipped the front of his trousers and quickly eased out a very stiff cock. She glanced nervously at the door to the shop, knowing that someone could come in at any moment. Adrian was clearly unconcerned, however. Gripping one of her feet in each hand again, he held them close together and then moved himself forward until his stalk slipped between them, the wetness of his saliva on her tender skin easing his progress. Sandy felt that she understood his need and parted her knees widely, so that the soft flesh of her insteps gripped his rod as he thrust it back and forth.

'That's it!' he gasped. 'That's perfect!' He began to fuck her feet at a much faster rate and his breathing turned into hoarse grunts of pleasure. Sandy realised that he was going to come soon and she desperately wanted to join him in mutual release. She grasped herself between the legs and began to rub her hot little cunt furiously through the thin, soaked material of her panties. Adrian watched her avidly, never letting up his rhythmic thrusts against the soles of her feet for a second. Sandy felt the surge building up inside her and rubbed harder. 'I'm coming!' she shouted.

It was as if her words were exactly what Adrian needed to hear. With a loud groan, he ejaculated, his white cream streaking over Sandy's inner thighs. The sight of the purple head of his cock spurting his juices brought her over the edge and she came with a gentle sigh, the lips of her pussy seeming to open involuntarily and her juices flowing to join with his.

After a few moments, Adrian looked up at her, his expression a picture of guilt. 'I – I'm sorry,' he spluttered. 'I don't normally treat customers in this way. I . . .' His words trailed off, his embarrassment taking over now that his lust had been sated.

'That was amazing, Adrian,' she said, with a broad grin as she ran the tips of her fingers over the creamy mixture of their juices on her inner thigh. 'But I think I need that cloth and the water again.'

* * *

Sandy sat back in the comfort of the seat in the first-class compartment of the 12.55 to Exeter, glad that she was alone. As the train pulled out of Waterloo, she knew that there would be just one stop at Basingstoke and then the express would plough ceaselessly through the countryside until it reached its final destination.

The carriage was hot, even with the small window drawn fully open, and she was glad that she had chosen to travel in just a pair of lycra cycling shorts and a skimpy T-shirt. Her outfit had drawn considerable appreciative interest from the many commuters who had thronged the marble concourse of the London station, her unfettered breasts bouncing provocatively under the loose cotton of her top and the curves of her bottom clearly defined by the tightness of her tiny shorts. One of the platform attendants had even helped her with her bags, something unheard of in recent times.

Sandy had always been one to revel in the attentions of men and was justifiably proud of her body. Whenever possible, she would wear clothing which accentuated her sexuality. Even at college, she had often been reprimanded for parading herself in the shortest of skirts and the tightest of blouses. Today, however, the brevity of her outfit owed much to the heat of the day.

As the shattered, graffiti-daubed streets of the city finally gave way to the rolling fields of Berkshire, she began to muse over her experience in the shoe shop. It had been the first time in her short but considerably full sex life that she had come without the slightest intimate touch to her body and the idea intrigued her. She had heard that some men found deep excitement in a woman's feet, of course, but it had been the first time that she had experienced such a thing. She had found Adrian's touch incredibly arousing and, when he had come, the sight of his sperm jetting from the purple head of his cock trapped between her soles and spraying over her thighs had been one of the most exhilarating visions that she could remember.

She shifted uncomfortably in her seat and allowed her fingertips to playfully caress her soft mound through the thin material of her shorts. Although she had orgasmed that morning with Adrian, she still felt empty and badly in need of a good hard fuck. What Adrian had done had been delightful, but it had not been enough.

The strong sun was shining directly into her face and, although she was enjoying the heat, she reached into her handbag and retrieved her sunglasses and put them on. She lay back and began to dream of past exploits. After a while, she started to play the game of trying to remember the names of all her lovers, recalling, at the same time, the many and varied adventures that she had enjoyed with them.

The train pulled into Basingstoke long before she had been able to complete her mental list and, to her profound irritation, the carriage door opened and a young couple clambered in. Sandy pulled her hand quickly from between her legs and feigned sleep. She heard the slam of the door and the whistle of the guard and the train was moving again. Without shifting her position, she opened her eyes and looked at the two people who had dared to intrude upon her solitude. Thanks to her dark sunglasses, she knew that they would not be able to tell that she was eyeing them and would probably assume that she was sound asleep.

The girl was blonde, slim and attractive. She was about twenty years of age and her exposed skin was heavily tanned. She was dressed in a short skirt and a simple top that was similar to the one that Sandy was wearing, but her breasts were small and jiggled noticeably with the movement of the train. The man was of African or West Indian descent, his handsome ebony features strong and masculine and his mouth full. He was wearing shorts and a singlet top that served to highlight his muscular body, which the blonde girl seemed to be having difficulty in keeping her hands off.

They kissed and cuddled each other with the passion of new lovers, seemingly oblivious to Sandy's presence.

As the minutes passed, their caresses became more and more intimate. Sandy watched with envious pleasure as the blonde traced the strong line of the man's thigh-muscle, her fingers inching up slowly to the bulge in the front of his shorts. At the same time, the man cupped each of her small breasts in turn, pinching the nipples into hardness through the cotton of her T-shirt. Suddenly, the man pushed the flimsy garment up, exposing her breasts completely, and then bent his head as if he intended to suck them. The blonde pushed him away roughly.

'Stop it, John!' she hissed. 'She'll see you!' She glanced nervously across at Sandy, who merely lay still, anxious that they should ignore her.

'She's asleep,' the man whispered. 'And, anyway, it's fun.'

He attempted to bury his face against her chest again but the girl forced him away once more. 'It was bad enough when you fucked me on the beach outside the hotel, last month,' she continued with a giggle. 'God knows how many people in the bar must have seen us!'

'The waiter certainly did.' His words seemed to stop the girl struggling and a coy smile appeared across her face. She looked into his eyes lovingly.

'That was brilliant,' she whispered. 'I'd never had two cocks inside me at the same time before.'

The man kissed her lightly on the lips. 'I could tell that you liked it,' he breathed. 'I've never known you come so often.' They kissed again, this time with fervent passion as he squeezed and pinched her breast with one hand while raising her top with the other, until he managed to pull it over her head and throw it on the seat behind her.

'Oh, John!' the girl protested, making a grab for the garment. 'What if she wakes up?'

'What if she does? She looks like a sexy little thing, anyway.'

Sandy could see that they were both looking directly at her now. She half closed her eyes in case they could see that she was staring back at them and shifted slightly, taking a deep breath and parting her legs a little.

'She's dead to the world,' said the man.

'Her shorts are very tight,' said the blonde. 'And she's obviously not wearing any panties. You can see everything.'

'Mmm,' was her lover's simple reply.

'And she's got big tits,' continued the girl. 'I bet you'd like to play with them, wouldn't you?'

He laughed and playfully pushed her back so that she was lying under him on the seat. 'Never mind that,' he chuckled. 'I've got plenty to play with here!' He moved his face down and Sandy watched as he suckled one of the young blonde's nipples. At first, the girl attempted to push him away, but then she quickly succumbed to the pleasurable feeling that he was giving her and lay her head back on the seat and closed her eyes.

Sandy could see that her lover had his hand up her skirt and was rhythmically massaging her between the legs. Her own pussy was becoming increasingly damp and she began to worry that her arousal would show through her tight white shorts. She was scared to move, however. She didn't want to startle the newcomers before they had gone much, much further.

She didn't have long to wait. The man leant back until he was in a sitting position once more and then he raised his girlfriend's legs and rested them across his thighs. Then, with a speed that surprised even Sandy, he reached under the blonde's skirt with both hands and deftly yanked her panties down her long legs and pulled them off completely. The girl merely giggled, clearly used to such treatment, although she did cast a wary glance in Sandy's direction.

Moments later, the man had buried his head between the girl's legs and Sandy could hear the wet sounds of his oral lovemaking. The girl moaned gently as her lover suckled her pussy and stroked the wiry hair on his head tenderly.

'God, you're good at that,' she murmured happily. He responded by moving his head rapidly up and down. The girl lowered the leg nearest to Sandy so that her foot rested on the floor and Sandy was now able to see the man's long tongue lapping along the full length of the blonde's shaven cunt. Sandy had to fight the desire to grasp herself between the legs and began to wonder if the two lovers would mind if she let them know that she was watching them. She decided not to, at least for the moment.

The girl came with a suddenness that surprised both her lover and Sandy. She gasped loudly and her small body shook with the tremors of delight that were surging through her; she put the back of her hand to her mouth and bit it in order to suppress a scream of joy. The man sat up with a startled look on his face but she just lay there for a moment, gazing at him through adoring eyes.

Without moving her head, Sandy managed to glance down at her own crotch. There was a definite patch of dampness showing clearly between her legs. She looked back at the couple, but saw that their interest was evidently in each other and each other alone. The blonde sat up slowly and then began to ease her lover's shorts down as he raised his backside slightly in order to help her. Sandy waited with bated breath. She had never seen a black man naked before and thrilled at the thought.

His cock sprang into view suddenly. It was as long and as thick as she had hoped, the stalk jet black and the head a silky brown colour that glinted in the bright sunlight. The blonde knelt on the seat and took hold of her prize, then rubbed it gently for a few moments before moving her head down and taking him into her mouth. As she sucked him, Sandy could see that she was caressing his balls with one hand and rubbing his stem with the other. She felt her own mouth go dry as she tried to imagine the taste and texture of that wonderful fat cock between her lips. She wanted to crawl over to them and kneel on the floor to share him with his girlfriend, but all she could do was watch. She glanced down again. The damp patch had grown considerably and the outline of her pussy-lips was now completely visible. She looked back at the couple, knowing that there was nothing that she could do.

The young blonde was bobbing her head up and down now, fucking her face with her lover's long rod.

'Are you trying to make me come?' he grunted. The girl ignored him, continuing to suckle him voraciously. 'Careful, baby, you'll make me come,' he pleaded.

She pulled her face from him and looked into his eyes. 'I want you to fuck me, right now,' she said. She stood up and unhooked her skirt. The tiny garment fell to the floor and she kicked it away and then spread her long legs on either side of his thighs with her back to their silent and highly aroused observer. Sandy could see the man holding his thick stalk erect as the girl slowly bent her knees and lowered herself, until the bulbous head touched the open lips of her hairless pussy. She paused for a moment, and then let herself slip down so that his entire length disappeared into the succulent wetness. She moaned gratefully as he filled her, falling forward and wrapping her arms around his neck. Her lover gripped her buttocks with both of his hands and pulled them apart, as if to give Sandy a better view of the girl's stretched sex-lips and her tiny, puckered little anus.

At first, the girl seemed content to sit firmly on his lap with his full size trapped completely within her, as they kissed each other passionately. Then she began to move steadily up and down, taking complete control and allowing him to merely sit there while she pleasured herself on his long thick cock. The sight of the ebony pole disappearing and reappearing at such a close proximity was driving Sandy to distraction. The girl began to pump up and down rapidly, her pert little bottom slapping noisily against the man's muscular thighs. She came with a muted squeal and rammed herself down on him, absorbing every inch that he had to offer. He looked quickly across at Sandy, apparently concerned that his lover's cry might have awakened her. She noticed him glance down at her groin and saw his eyes widen.

'You're watching us, aren't you?' he said.

'What's that, darling?' panted the blonde.

'I'm not talking to you,' he replied. 'I'm talking to our friend over there. She's wide awake!'

His girlfriend swung her head round and Sandy froze in terror. 'Are you watching us?' the girl asked. Sandy nodded. 'It's all right,' continued the girl. 'Take your sunglasses off; you'll be able to see better.'

Relieved, Sandy removed her sunglasses and gave them a nervous smile. The girl raised herself from the man's lap and knelt on the floor at his side. She grasped hold of his stiff pole and held it proudly erect. 'It's a beauty, isn't it?' she said, with a grin. Sandy nodded again. 'Would you like to touch it?' continued the blonde. 'Come on, don't be shy.'

Sandy was in no mood to refuse. She moved swiftly from her seat, knelt at his feet and took hold of his cock by the root. The two women rubbed the bone-hard shaft gently. 'My name's Sandy,' she said, awkwardly.

'I'm Jenny, and this is John.' Sandy looked up at John and smiled. It seemed remarkably strange to find herself being introduced to another girl's boyfriend while holding his cock in her hand. 'We like to share occasionally,' continued Jenny. 'John's got such a whopper and he really knows how to use it, so it would be very selfish of me to keep it to myself. Besides, I love to see him fucking other girls; it really turns me on.'

'How long have you been watching us?' asked John as he relaxed back in his seat to enjoy the delicate ministrations of the two lovely girls kneeling before him.

'All the time,' replied Sandy. 'I wasn't asleep.'

'Your shorts are soaked.'

She looked up at him again and smiled coquettishly. 'You're not surprised, are you?' she pouted.

'I just thought that you might want to take them off,' he answered with a broad grin. Sandy got to her feet and quickly slipped her tight shorts down her legs and stepped out of them. John's gaze immediately fell to the thick bush of hair between her legs. 'Very nice,' he muttered. 'Now take your top off.'

'John wants to see your tits,' giggled Jenny. 'You're a big girl, aren't you?'

Sandy said nothing in reply but pulled the top over her head and let it fall to the floor. She stood before them, proudly displaying her sumptuous curves to their hungry eyes. Though large, her breasts were firm and thrust arrogantly forward, as if defying gravity. Her waist was narrow and her hips were slim, but her bottom was pert and inviting. John smiled, a look of appreciation on his handsome face.

'That's quite a body,' he said. Jenny let go of his cock, allowing it to fall heavily against his stomach. She stood up and faced Sandy, her eyes fixed on the mountainous globes of flesh. Suddenly, she cupped them both with her hands. Sandy gasped, but Jenny merely smiled and caressed her breasts as if it were the most natural thing to do.

'You have beautiful breasts,' she sighed. 'Sometimes I wish that mine were larger.'

'There's nothing wrong with your tits, babe,' said John, quickly.

'Oh, but these are so lovely,' continued Jenny. Sandy was finding her gentle touch increasingly pleasant. Her nipples had stiffened and were standing out like little, dark fingers from her creamy flesh. 'You like that, don't you?' purred Jenny. Sandy merely smiled. Jenny bent her head and kissed one of Sandy's nipples lightly. She looked up at her, as if to seek permission. It would have been clear, from the look on Sandy's face, that no permission was needed. Encouraged, Jenny took the stiff little bud into her mouth and began to suckle. Sandy looked across at John. He was happily rubbing his long stalk slowly. Now it would be his turn to watch.

Sandy let her hands slip around Jenny's waist as the young blonde continued to suckle her hard nipple. She ran the palm of one hand over the gently curving globes of her bottom and then ran her fingertips between them. She heard Jenny moan softly.

'She likes that,' said John. 'She's got a very sensitive little bum.'

Jenny gripped Sandy's melon-sized mounds in both of her hands and turned her attention to the other nipple. Sandy felt her juices flowing from her and her pussy ached to be touched. She tickled Jenny's anus with the tip of her forefinger and the blonde gasped, pulling her face away from Sandy's breast.

'Put it in,' she pleaded breathlessly.

Sandy brought her hand to her mouth and soaked her fingers with saliva, then once more stroked Jenny between the buttocks. She quickly found Jenny's little hole once more and gently eased the tip of a finger inside her.

'Oh, God, I like that,' panted Jenny. She took Sandy's nipple into her mouth again and began to suckle her voraciously. Sandy pushed a little more of her finger into the tight sphincter and then eased it out until just the tip remained inside. Pushing forward again, she managed to slip the full length of her finger into the young girl's bottom. Jenny groaned, her moan of happiness muffled by the fleshy mound pressed against her face. Sandy glanced across at John again. His cock seemed to have taken on even greater proportions, jutting almost vertically as he gently massaged the thick rod with his fingers.

Sandy eased her finger from its tight sheath and Jenny moved from her to lie on her back on the long seat where Sandy had previously been sitting. She rested one foot on the floor and raised her other leg high, clutching her heel and pulling it back until her thigh touched her small breast. It was plain what she wanted Sandy to do. Sandy knelt on the floor beside her and ran the palm of her hand along the shapely thigh nearest to her, until her fingertips touched the soaked flesh of the other girl's pussy.

It was the first time that she'd touched another woman in such an intimate manner, although she had often considered it before. Karina Devonside was normally the object of her fantasies, her friend's lithe body and incredibly long legs appealing to her in the extreme. Often, she would watch surreptitiously while Karina changed for games or the gym, enviously eyeing her slim body and her flawless skin while trying to imagine her lying in just such a position that Jenny had assumed.

Jenny closed her eyes and moaned softly as Sandy worked her fingers around the wet fleshy lips of her pussy. Sandy thought it looked beautiful, puffy, red and without a trace of hair. The skin was soft; clearly the girl had shaven herself quite recently. She eased two fingers between the soft pliant lips and pushed them in to the limit. The silky succulence seemed to be drawing her to probe ever deeper. She pushed a third finger into her and pressed her thumb against Jenny's hard little bud, then eased her little finger into the girl's anus.

Jenny opened her eyes and gasped, her expression one of startled delight. 'Kiss it,' she begged.

Sandy had known that it would come to this, but she also knew that she could not refuse. She lowered her head slowly until her face was inches from Jenny's groin.

'Kiss it,' the girl said again. 'Kiss it and lick it.'

Sandy took a long, deep breath. The scent of Jenny's arousal filled her senses. It was a delicate, inviting aroma that she found that she could not resist. She moved her face closer and pushed out her tongue while easing her fingers from Jenny's juicy warmth.

The tip of Sandy's tongue touched the wet flesh and, for a moment, she pulled back slightly. Jenny's response was to force her hips upward automatically. Sandy probed tentatively forward with her tongue once more and, this time, drew the tip along the full length of the puffy flesh.

Jenny groaned. 'Oh, yes,' she breathed. 'Do it, do it!'

Sandy pressed her face down and took the succulent lips into her mouth. She lapped hungrily between them with her tongue, the taste delighting her. Sucking hard, she drew as much of Jenny's sex-flesh as she could between her lips. Jenny's hips began to buck involuntarily and her moans of ecstasy became louder and more demanding.

Sandy moved her mouth slightly upward and began to lap the tip of her tongue rapidly over the prominent bud of Jenny's clitoris. The girl squealed and her body began to tremble. 'Oh, my God!' she gasped suddenly. 'I'm coming! I'm coming!' Her cries were so loud that Jenny felt certain that they would attract the attention of the guard on the train, but she knew that she couldn't stop. She flicked the tip of her tongue as fast as possible over the hard button. Suddenly, she felt Jenny grasp her hair and force her mouth hard against the soaking flesh. She rasped her tongue furiously up and down. Jenny raised her foot from the floor and circled Sandy's neck with her leg, her heel pressing hard against her shoulder, her entire body shuddering as her climax tore through her. Sandy didn't let up for a moment, knowing – as only another woman can – exactly how to please her lover.

Eventually, the spasms eased and Jenny let her foot fall heavily once more to the floor, while her other leg slipped down to rest on the seat. Sandy raised her face and grinned, wiping the juices from her chin with the back of her hand.

'You've done that before,' said Jenny appreciatively.

Sandy shook her head. 'I haven't,' she replied. 'It just came naturally.' She bent over and kissed Jenny lightly on the mouth. The two women gazed into each other's eyes. Sandy's pussy ached for release but, for the moment, she was happy just to caress the other girl's soft features with her fingertips.

Suddenly, Sandy felt the touch of a large hand to her upturned bottom. She turned her head and looked over her shoulder. John was kneeling behind her, gently stroking her pert little globes. He was completely naked now and his blue-black skin shone with a sheen that highlighted his muscular form. His cock was jutting from his hairy groin, the head now tinged with purple and glistening with juice. Sandy turned herself and knelt, facing him. She reached out, intending to circle his thick shaft with her fingers, but drew back quickly and glanced at Jenny nervously.

'You can lick him, if you want,' said the young blonde, with an encouraging smile. 'In fact, you can do anything you like.'

Sandy looked at the girl questioningly. It was one thing to have had sex with her, while her boyfriend had watched; somehow, that had been all right. But this was altogether different. She had been made love to by two or more men on a number of occasions in the recent past, but she had never shared the attentions of one man with another girl. 'Are you sure?' she asked timidly.

Jenny's smile broadened. 'Go on,' she coaxed as she reached out her hand and grasped Sandy's wrist. 'Don't be shy. It won't bite.'

John merely sat back, resting his shoulders against the edge of the seat and with a benign expression on his face. Jenny eased Sandy's hand towards him until it touched the hard, ebony pole that was jutting from his hairy groin. She grasped the rod immediately, her fingers barely able to encircle it.

'Go on,' repeated Jenny. 'Suck him, do what you like. Let me watch you for a while and then I'll join in.'

Sandy needed no further encouragement. She turned her head and stared at the monstrous black cock and she felt her mouth go dry at the thought of what delights were in store for her. She began to slowly move her hand up and down the shaft, pulling the loose skin against the hard flesh with a gentle, teasing rhythm. She glanced up at his face. He was staring at her through half closed eyes, his lips parted and the tip of his tongue licking against his teeth. Sandy bent her head forward and opened her mouth. She held herself motionless for a moment, the wet purple-shaded head barely an inch from her face. It looked almost too big to slip between her lips.

'Suck him! Suck him!'

Sandy turned her face and glanced at Jenny. Her new-found friend was now sitting on the edge of the seat opposite, with her legs splayed wide apart and her fingers probing deep inside her oily pussy. There was an expression of near-manic lust on her elfin features. It was evident that she was taking great pleasure in witnessing her boyfriend's delight. Sandy turned her head again and once more faced the bulbous, mushroom-shaped treat that awaited her. She parted her lips once again and took it into her mouth. Circling her tongue against the spongy flesh, she savoured his taste and breathed in deeply to enjoy his scent. The aroma was fresh and very masculine, and it made her head swim. It was almost as if he had oiled his body with some form of scented aphrodisiac, which was invading her senses and robbing her of her willpower.

Holding her tongue flat under his probing stalk, she moved her face forward and engulfed as much of it in her mouth as she could, while gripping his exposed length with both of her hands. She sensed him throb within her mouth. Easing her head back again, she let him slip from her mouth until just the tip was held between her pouting lips. She licked the end with the tip of her tongue and tasted the salty, creamy-textured evidence of his arousal.

'God, she nearly made me come!' he said, clearly addressing his words to Jenny. Sandy raised his thick stalk and held it against his stomach with one hand, while caressing his balls with the other. He throbbed again and a short stream of clear fluid pumped from the angry end and slipped slowly down the long shaft and over her fingers. Sandy let go of his cock and put her hand to her face, then licked his cream from her fingers.

John stared into her eyes and mouthed, 'Wow.'

She bent her head forward again and put her lips to the heavy sack between his legs. She traced the shape of his plum-sized balls with the tip of her tongue while taking one, and then both of them into her mouth. Grabbing his cock once more with one hand, she rubbed him slowly, anxious not to make him climax before he had fucked her. There was no way that she was going to be denied the feeling of that thick hard rod filling her aching little pussy.

Suddenly, she felt a warm wetness against her buttocks and knew that Jenny was licking her bottom. Arching her back and moving her knees apart a little, she afforded the young girl easier access to her most intimate treasures and gasped as she felt the tongue lap greedily over her soaking cunt-lips and the tight little sphincter of her arse. Sandy allowed John's balls to slip from her lips and then slid her tongue slowly up the heavily veined shaft until she once more enveloped his knob within her mouth. The thought that she now had a lovely big cock in her mouth and a woman's silky tongue probing and prodding at her nether regions thrilled her immensely.

She felt Jenny's fingers stroking against her sex-lips and then sensed them slip inside her. She was so wet and so ready for sex that she couldn't tell how many of them were probing inside her, and she didn't care. Jenny began to push her fingers in and out of her, fucking her with her hand while, at the same time, rubbing her hard little bud with the fingers of her other hand. Sandy engulfed over half of John's superb length within her mouth and felt the tip of the head touch the back of her throat. She swallowed hard and tried to take him further, but his thickness and her position precluded this delight. She moved her head back slightly and contented herself by suckling the hard rod and lapping her tongue against it, while enjoying the expert touch of Jenny's fingers to her hot pussy.

Suddenly, she felt Jenny's tongue prodding against her anus and she knew that she was going to come. The combination of sensations, the feeling of taking a man's cock deep into her mouth and knowing that she was soon going to be fucked by that same magnificent weapon, coupled with the myriad of joyous and electrifying thrills that she was experiencing between her legs, was more than any woman could resist. The orgasm tore through her with a force that startled her and caused her to utter a muffled cry. Jenny instantly realised her need and Sandy felt her probe her long tongue deep into her bottom, while her fingertips rubbed rapidly against her clitoris, sending Sandy into raptures of delightful release.

When it was over, the two girls knelt at John's feet

and gazed at each other. For a brief instant, it was as if he wasn't there, as if he didn't matter. Jenny leant forward and the two women kissed, their tongues immediately probing and circling against each other and their lips pressed hard together in a mutual passionate embrace. Sandy reached out and cupped Jenny's small, firm breasts and thrilled as the young girl did the same to her, raising her heavy globes of flesh as if weighing them in her hands.

The kiss seemed to last an age. At last, they parted and knelt silently for a few seconds. The train rattled noisily over some points and the carriage shook violently, the sudden movement having the effect of breaking the almost ethereal mood. Jenny smiled and stroked Sandy's cheek with the backs of her fingers. 'Now,' she said, slowly and deliberately. 'Fuck him. Fuck yourself on him, use him, do whatever comes into your head.'

There was no need for further conversation. Sandy pulled herself to her feet and turned to face John, who had remained in the same position on the carriage floor, with his back resting against the edge of the seat. He grinned broadly and clutched his cock by the root, holding it firmly erect. Sandy turned her back to him and placed a foot on either side of his thighs, and then slowly lowered herself to a squatting position. Jenny sat again on the seat opposite to her, in order to enjoy the spectacle. The fact that the girl was staring at her pussy made the situation all the more exciting for Sandy. She lowered herself further until she felt the familiar touch of the head of a wonderfully large cock to the succulent lips of her soaking cunt.

'Use him; fuck him!' whispered Jenny, her wide eyes transfixed by the sight between Sandy's splayed thighs. Sandy let her body slip down and gasped as inch after inch of the monstrous length filled her aching sheath. 'God,' breathed Jenny, 'she's taken it all in one go! I've never seen that before!'

Her words reminded Sandy that this wasn't the first time that this amazingly uninhibited couple had engaged themselves in such a lascivious pursuit, but it didn't matter. For her, it was the first time that she had enjoyed herself with a man and a woman at the same time, and it was very special.

She held herself still, both to savour the feeling of incredible fullness within her groin and to get used to his size. She looked at Jenny and grinned. 'He's big,' she said, simply.

Jenny nodded. 'Nice, though, isn't it?' she said, with a gentle laugh.

Sandy's response was to begin to move her body up and down, supporting herself by resting one hand on the seat behind her. John barely moved his hips, seemingly content to let her do all the work. She leant back against him and sensed the power of his chest-muscles as they rubbed against her back. John reached around her and cupped her bobbing breasts with his large hands. His touch was far firmer than Jenny's had been, but no less pleasant for that. She felt him pinch her long nipples hard as she increased the pace of her movements. Using his entire length with each downward thrust, she gasped rhythmically as the head of his big cock thumped against her cervix, sending tremors of pleasure coursing throughout her lower body.

Jenny knelt between the rutting couple's legs and bent forward. At first, she seemed happy to merely stare at the sight of her boyfriend's cock slipping in and out of Sandy's widely stretched cunt-lips, but then she leant further forward and suddenly pressed her wet mouth against the hot mound. Sandy rammed herself down hard against John's groin and absorbed his full length inside her, and then held herself still so that she could savour the delicate touch of Jenny's tongue flicking against her hard bud. She sensed John's thick rod throb inside her and tensed her lower muscles, in order to grip it tightly within her succulence.

He groaned and dug his fingernails into the tender flesh of her breasts. 'Careful,' he gasped. 'You'll make me come! Jenny won't be happy if you do that.'

Sandy relaxed and gave herself entirely to Jenny's fluttering tongue. The feeling of total fullness, coupled with the incessant and rhythmic lapping against her aching clitoris, was rapidly bringing her to the point of no return. John began to move his hips under her, thrusting his long cock in and out of her while he pinched her nipples again between his fingertips. She looked down. Jenny was staring up at her as she licked her hairy little mound, her face soaked with Sandy's juices. The delightful sight was too much. With a muted squeal, Sandy arched her back and stiffened her body and then came, the release tearing through her young body with a force that thrilled her immensely. Jenny sensed her joy and pressed her mouth hard against her and gripped her bud between her teeth, while John pounded heavily up and down. Sandy gasped loudly as the spasms of orgasm ripped through her, until she could take no more. She sighed and leant back against John's superb body. Resting her head on his shoulder, she turned her face to his and they kissed.

Jenny moved from her and, once more, sat on the seat opposite. Sandy looked across at her and smiled weakly, then eased herself from John's lap so that his cock slipped from inside her and slapped against his stomach. She felt her knees begin to buckle and she sat down heavily on to the floor, still panting laboriously. 'That was amazing,' she breathed.

'I've never seen anyone take John in one go like that,' replied Jenny. 'You must be very experienced.'

'I've done it a few times,' answered Sandy, still having some difficulty in speaking as she gasped for air, 'but I've never had anything like that. You two are fantastic.'

'We try,' said Jenny with a broad grin.

Sandy gazed lovingly at the beautiful young blonde. Jenny's face glistened with wetness and her eyes sparkled with lust. Easing herself from her seat, she knelt on the floor of the carriage next to Sandy and turned herself so that she rested her elbows on the seat, with her bottom presented to John.

It became immediately clear to Sandy that her two lovers were not finished yet. John lost no time in moving behind his lovely girlfriend. He knelt on the floor and gripped her by the waist, his long cock pointing directly between her pert buttocks. From her position, Sandy could clearly see the lushness of Jenny's open sex-lips and, for a moment, had the urge to push John out of the way and to plant her mouth against them and suckle for all she was worth. She resisted the temptation, however. She wanted to see him slip his huge ebony rod into the waif-like body of the young blonde, and to hear her squeals of delight as he penetrated her.

John inched himself forward and Sandy watched as Jenny's soaking sex-lips enveloped the thick plum-like head of his cock. The young girl moaned in ecstasy. Sandy immediately put her fingertips to her own pussy and began to gently caress herself, as John slipped more and more of his thick shaft into her new friend. Soon, he was fully inside her, with his groin pressed firmly against her buttocks. Sandy reached out and stroked his strong muscular backside, and he began to steadily fuck his girlfriend. Jenny responded by pushing her bottom rhythmically against him, the two lovers enjoying a perfect unison of practised delight.

Sandy moved behind John and gripped his buttocks with both hands, then bent her head and ran her tongue wetly over the hard globes of shining sable flesh. She slipped her tongue down between them, running the tip up and down over his anus, and then moved lower until she was able to lick his balls. Clearly enjoying the attention, John raised himself to a squatting position, to make it easier for her, without once altering the pace of his steady thrusts. Sandy twisted herself until she was lying on her back, and then moved her head under him. As she lapped her tongue over his balls, she gazed up at the wonderful sight of his massive cock sliding in and out of his girlfriend. Jenny's sex-lips were red and engorged and seemed to be gripping the black pole tightly, as if unwilling to allow him to move from her. Sandy moved her head back and managed to lap the tip of her tongue over Jenny's hard clitoris. The young blonde squealed noisily in response and John took the initiative and began to pump heavily in and out of her, the force of his lovemaking causing her to press her mound hard against Sandy's sucking mouth. Sandy gasped for breath, but continued to stimulate her friend's soaking sex-flesh as best she could, while John's balls slapped over and over again against her chin.

'I'm coming!' she heard Jenny yell suddenly. 'I'm coming!'

The lovely blonde's orgasm seemed to go on forever as both John and Sandy attacked her lush flesh in his or her own way. Gradually, the young girl's cries of delight abated and Sandy knew that she was done. She moved her head forward and once again traced the shape of John's balls with the tip of her tongue. Suddenly, he withdrew his immense length from within Jenny's cunt. Sandy grasped the thick shaft and began to rub him furiously, then forced her face upward and took the bulbous knob into her mouth. He came immediately, his cream jetting to the back of her throat. She swallowed his juices voraciously as if her life depended on it, still rubbing his throbbing stalk until he had no more to give. She let him slip from her mouth, then gave the drooping phallus a few more tender licks. John moved wearily from her and managed to sit back on the carriage seat. Sandy struggled to her feet and then sat down opposite him, while helping Jenny up from the floor. The two women sat together, their arms around each other's waists. They looked at the exhausted, sweating man and then turned to face each other. Their mouths met and they kissed, a long and passionate embrace.

Sandy gazed lazily out of the carriage window as the beautiful Devon countryside sped by. Her body was still trembling slightly and her pussy ached from having accommodated John's magnificent cock. She licked her lips and found that she was still able to taste Jenny's sweet pussy-scent. She looked across at her new friends. Jenny was dozing in John's arms. They had changed into smart attire; Sandy assumed that they were heading for some important meeting in Exeter. She herself had found another pair of shorts in her suitcase to replace the sodden garment that she had worn previously.

'Are you going on holiday?' asked John suddenly. His voice sounded warm and soothing, like chocolate.

'Sort of,' Sandy replied. 'I'm visiting a friend who lives with her parents out in the country.'

'That's nice,' mumbled Jenny, lazily as she opened her eyes. 'We're going to work in the country.'

'What do you do?'

'John is a butler and I am a housekeeper. It's our first job since leaving training college. We're going to work in a really posh house – a manor, would you believe!'

Sandy had a sudden thought. 'What's the name of the house?' she asked, half anticipating the answer.

'Devon Manor,' replied John. 'Do you know it?'

'Oh, yes, I know it,' replied Sandy with a grin. 'That's where I'm going.'

There was a short pause as the truth of the coincidence sank in. 'Looks like we might be seeing much more of you, then,' said John with a wry smile.

'There isn't much more to see!' laughed Sandy. She looked back out of the window. The fields and woodland had given way to the sprawling housing estates that signalled the outer reaches of the city of Exeter. She began to wonder what Karina would think when she found out that her best friend had had sex with two of her family's servants.

Somehow, she found the idea most amusing.

Three

Karina sat on the palatial sun-terrace of Devon Manor, lazily sipping from a long glass of iced tea. The afternoon had been unbearably hot and even now, as the evening approached and the sun cast long shadows across the manicured lawns, she felt comfortable in her shorts and tiny top. She glanced at her watch. Ten past six. Sandy's train would have arrived in Exeter by now, and her friend would have been picked up by Johnson in the Rolls.

A young man was working a few feet away from her, trimming one of the many hedges that bordered the patio area. He was stripped to the waist and his jeans seemed to be unnecessarily tight. Karina placed her glass on a table and took off her sunglasses. The gardener glanced up and smiled. She acknowledged his greeting with passive interest and looked the other way.

She began to think about the Honourable Charles Simons. She couldn't believe that she had been naked with him and yet she had remained a virgin. It had been the closest that she had ever come to losing her 'cherry', as the girls at college called it, and the fact that she had gone so far without achieving complete fulfilment had made her frustration even worse. The familiar ache between her legs returned to torment her. Reaching out, she took up her glass again and took another drink while gripping her thighs tightly together. She could feel that she was damp; but then, she nearly always was, these days. Her young body constantly hungered with lust and the seemingly uncontrollable feelings were driving her mad.

She looked again at the gardener, who was still busily pruning the old hedge. She savoured the sight of his slim suntanned torso and his tight buttocks and wondered whether he was wearing any underwear. There didn't seem to be any telltale line under the tight denim. He turned slightly and she was treated to the sight of the bulge in the front of his jeans. The outline of his cock was plainly visible and she was surprised that she hadn't noticed it before. She licked her lips and squeezed her thighs together again. The ache was becoming unbearable.

She surreptitiously tipped the remains of her drink into a nearby plant-pot. 'Raoul,' she called. 'Have you a moment?'

The young man set down his shears on the grass and walked quickly over to her. 'Yes, miss?' he answered dutifully.

'Raoul, please will you get me another drink?' She handed the empty glass to the young man and found that she couldn't stop herself from gazing at the delightful shape in the front of his jeans. Raoul paused for a moment before taking the glass, as though allowing her a little time to enjoy the view. It was evident that he was fully aware of what she was looking at. 'Iced tea,' she said curtly, in an attempt to regain some dignity.

'Yes, miss,' he replied quickly and he hurried towards the house. Karina turned and watched him go, once more savouring the sight of his slim bottom. She'd seen him many times before, of course, and he had often been the subject of her numerous fantasies. She'd lost count of the number of times that he had had her in her dreams, fucking her in every conceivable position: sometimes alone, sometimes accompanied by other men.

He returned quickly, carrying a newly filled glass. Karina glanced again at the front of his jeans and noticed, to her great satisfaction, that his shape appeared, if anything, to be much larger than before. He stood in front of her and handed her the drink, which she took from him and rested on the table. She looked up at his face and smiled. 'Thank you, Raoul,' she said, in a voice that she considered was suitably seductive.

'You're welcome, miss,' he replied.

She glanced down at his crotch. His cock had lengthened and thickened considerably and the shape of the big head was clearly visible. The young man was quite obviously attracted to her; all she had to do was reach out and touch. She wondered what her parents would say, if they learnt that she had had sex with one of the gardeners. It would not do, of course; but, well, they didn't need to find out.

'Is there anything else, miss?' Raoul's voice was slightly hoarse, as if he were nervous.

'Sit a while and talk to me,' she replied.

'I can't, miss. Mr Latham will have my ears if I don't finish the hedge before I go.'

'Have you got a girlfriend?' asked Karina, totally ignoring his protests.

'Er, yes, miss,' he stumbled. 'I'm seeing a girl called Sally. She works behind the bar at the Bull in the village.'

'Do you love her?'

The young man coughed nervously. 'Yes, miss,' he managed to say.

'She's a very lucky girl,' purred Karina. 'You're very handsome.'

'Yes, miss; er, thank you, miss.' Raoul turned to go.

'I said, sit for a while,' she said angrily.

'I really have to finish the hedge,' he replied, moving away from her. 'Mr Latham will –'

'Bugger Mr Latham,' she snapped suddenly. The

young man looked at her in surprise. 'I told you to sit,' she continued in an arrogant tone. Raoul shrugged and sat on the edge of a low wall next to her. Karina glanced again at his bulging jeans. His shape was smaller. 'You're not wearing underpants, are you, Raoul?' she asked, in a matter-of-fact tone.

'Miss?' he answered.

'You heard me. I can see everything.'

'I – I'm sorry, miss.' Raoul crossed his legs quickly, in an effort to hide his bulge from her sight.

Karina reached over and touched him lightly on the knee. 'Don't apologise,' she breathed. 'I like it.' She moved her hand slowly up his thigh, surprised at her sudden brazenness.

Raoul brushed her hand away. 'Please, miss,' he protested. 'I'll get the sack.'

'Nobody need know. Come on, let's go into the house.'

'No, miss. I'm not allowed in the house. Anyway – Sally – she would never forgive me.'

His feeble excuses were beginning to annoy her. He was no longer the bright and confident individual that she had always supposed him to be. She sat back angrily and folded her arms. 'Go to your Sally, then,' she barked. 'But make sure that the hedge is trimmed properly before you do.' Raoul stood up quickly but Karina grabbed him by the wrist and held it firmly. 'Be assured, Raoul,' she hissed, 'if you say one word about this you will be looking for another job!'

The young man nodded obediently and then turned and scurried away, clearly relieved to have escaped her clutches. Karina felt wretched. It had been the first time in her life that she had had the courage to make a direct play for a man and it had blown up in her face. She felt degraded and humiliated and knew that she would never be able to look the young gardener in the face again.

Her first impulse was to go back into the house,

rather than have to sit on the sun-terrace so close to where he was still working. After a moment's thought, however, she decided to remain. After all, she mused, this was her house and he was merely an employee. She lay back on her seat and watched him pointedly. Occasionally he glanced nervously in her direction as he clipped the hedge, but she didn't turn her head away; she wanted him to know that she was watching every move that he made. In a strange way, she found that she was exuding a sense of power over him, knowing that he had to finish his task under her unwelcome gaze, and it made her feel good.

He moved closer to her until he was only a few feet away. Karina watched as he shaped the bush expertly, using the shears with deft, fluid movements. The muscles of his upper arms rippled as he worked and there were beads of fresh sweat on his strong back. He turned slightly and she noticed that the bulge in his jeans had once more grown considerably, the thick shaft of his penis clearly outlined under the heavy denim. He glanced at her and smiled briefly. Karina purposely maintained an aloof expression, determined not to allow him to embarrass her a second time. She looked down at herself. Her nipples were firmly erect and were clearly visible through the thin material of her top. She parted her legs and rested her hand on the top of her thigh, with her fingertips just touching her shorts. Raoul stopped working and apparently seemed to be trying to adjust a nut on the shears. He was standing directly facing her now and Karina could see that his cock appeared to be fully erect under the restricting cover of his jeans, the thick head pushing against the cloth as if it were trying to burst out into the open. Staring directly and shamelessly at the inviting sight, she ran her fingertips between her legs and traced the shape of her pussy through the thin, damp material of her shorts.

Raoul set the shears down on the grass and moved

towards her. Karina continued to blatantly caress herself, her eyes now fixed on his. 'Miss,' he began.

'Yes, Raoul?' she asked casually as she opened her legs even wider and rubbed herself rapidly.

'Miss, I –' His words were interrupted by the sound of a car's wheels crunching against the gravel of the drive behind him. Karina sat up quickly. The Rolls-Royce had arrived, no doubt bringing her friend Sandy from the station. She looked back at the young gardener. He stood for a moment with a desperate and confused expression on his face then he turned, picked up his shears and hurried away.

Karina stood up and watched him go. Although the arrival of the Rolls had frustrated the moment, she felt that she had won. Despite his misgivings and his love for his precious Sally, it was clear to her that he had been about to proposition her. There would be other times, other opportunities. Perhaps it would be Raoul who would rid her of her hated virginal state.

The limousine drew up close to the terrace and stopped. Johnson, dressed in his smart grey chauffeur's uniform and peaked cap, stepped quickly out and held open the rear door as Karina walked over to greet her friend. To her surprise, a tall coloured man was the first to emerge, followed by a young and exceptionally pretty blonde girl. Sandy clambered out of the vehicle behind them and rushed over to her. The two friends flung their arms around each other and they hugged tightly.

'Sandy! It's great to see you again!' said Karina happily.

'And you, K,' replied Sandy.

'Who are your friends?' asked Karina as she watched the two strangers helping Johnson to lift the suitcases from the boot of the car.

'That's John and Jenny. I met them on the train. They're coming to work here.'

Karina looked at her friend with a horrified

expression on her face. 'You mean to say that Johnson allowed servants to ride in the Rolls? Whatever was he thinking of?'

Sandy laughed. 'Oh, dearest K,' she said. 'You never change! I invited them to travel with me. What was the point of them getting a taxi when they could ride with me?'

Karina leant forward and whispered in her friend's ear. 'Sandy, you must never fraternise with the servants; it just isn't done.' As she said the words, she thought about what she had so very nearly done with the gardener and she felt suddenly cold.

'It's a bit late for that,' giggled Sandy.

'What d'you mean?'

'I'll tell you later. Come on; let's go in. I'm dying for a bath.'

Karina watched her friend unpack her belongings while the maid busied herself in the next room, preparing Sandy's bath. 'What did you mean when you said it was too late not to fraternise with the servants?' she asked.

'We made friends on the train,' replied Sandy as she hung her clothes on the hangers that she took from a large pile on the bed. 'They're really nice people. I got to know them really well.'

'How well?'

Sandy looked at her guiltily and Karina noticed her friend begin to blush slightly. 'We just chatted,' was the simple and unconvincing response.

'Oh, come on, Sandy. I know what you're like! What did you do?'

'We fooled about a bit, that's all.'

'What, kissing and cuddling and things like that?' Karina was beginning to feel quite hot, despite the fact that it was early evening, the windows were wide open and she was wearing very little.

'A bit more than that,' replied Sandy with a grin.

Karina sat down on the bed and crossed her legs excitedly. 'Come on, Sandy,' she pleaded. 'Tell me: what did you do?'

Sandy put down the dress she was arranging on a hanger and looked directly into Karina's eyes. 'Everything,' she pouted.

Karina gasped. 'On a train?' she exclaimed. 'You let that guy do it to you on a train? Where was his girlfriend while this was going on?'

'She was there. We all did things together.'

Karina paused for a moment, words eluding her. On the one hand, she was angry that her friend had had the temerity to have sex with the servants but, on the other, she was intensely envious that Sandy had made yet another conquest and was so blasé about it. 'The girl,' she said eventually. 'Did you – did you touch her, you know . . .?'

'Touched, kissed, licked, everything.' Sandy resumed her task of hanging her clothes in the large wardrobe as if she had said nothing untoward.

Karina could scarcely believe what she was hearing. 'You mean that you actually licked her, between the legs?' she said, her eyes wide with astonishment.

Sandy sat down on the bed beside her, smiling broadly. 'It was my first time, you know, with a girl. I'd thought about it before, of course, but I'd never had the opportunity. I'd often wondered whether I really could lick a girl's pussy or whether I'd back off at the last moment, but it just happened. It seemed so natural and it was wonderful.'

'And the guy – did he make love to you?'

'He fucked both of us,' replied Sandy in her usual, crude manner of speaking. 'And he came in my mouth.'

'Wow,' said Karina wistfully. 'Why doesn't anything like that ever happen to me?'

Sandy chuckled and began to remove her clothing, in order to bathe. 'It's not the sort of thing that happens every day,' she laughed. 'And besides, I'm sure you've had your moments!'

Karina said nothing in reply but watched as Sandy removed her trainers and then her shorts. There were no panties, of course. Sandy rarely wore underclothing unless she was out shopping for clothes or shoes. Karina couldn't stop herself from glancing at her friend's hairy little pussy and thought about the manservant pushing his big black cock into the tiny hole. 'Was it different, doing it with a black guy?' she said suddenly.

'Not really. I mean, he was big, but I've had bigger.'

'Does size matter?' Karina was beginning to enjoy the conversation and wanted it to continue.

'It does to me. I love the feeling of being really full inside and, when they start pumping into me, I love it when the end thumps against my roof – it really sends me wild. It hurts some girls, but I can't get enough of it.' Sandy got to her feet and headed for the bathroom, her large breasts bouncing heavily as she walked.

'You've got a lovely body, Sandy,' said Karina.

Her friend turned her head and smiled coyly. 'Thank you,' she answered before disappearing into the bathroom.

Karina followed her. 'Can I sit and chat while you're having your bath?' she asked.

'Sure, why not?' Sandy slipped quickly into the foaming water of the bath and Karina sat on a small stool close to her. 'Mm,' murmured her friend. 'This is the life.' She soaped her arms and then spread the cream liberally over her breasts, paying particular attention to her nipples.

'You are lucky,' said Karina, 'having such large breasts.'

Sandy examined her fleshy mounds, as if to confirm her friend's statement. 'I think that they're too big,' she answered. 'I'd rather have a figure like yours. I tell you, it's a nightmare, trying to find clothes to fit me. You're the lucky one. You always look so elegant, whatever you wear.'

Sandy had meant it as a compliment, of course, but her words cut into Karina like a knife. She didn't want to look elegant – she wanted to be sexually attractive. Somehow, to her the two things were miles apart. 'You know you were saying that size was important to you –'

'It's not vital,' interrupted Sandy. 'But it does make a difference.'

'What's the biggest one that you've ever had?'

'Karina!' chided Sandy with a grin. 'You shouldn't be asking me things like that!'

'Go on,' Karina urged. 'I'd really like to know.'

'That's easy,' replied her friend as she lay back in the hot soapy water with her head resting on a small, plastic cushion. 'It was Martin Knowles.'

'Martin Knowles!' gasped Karina. 'The caretaker's son at St Jennifer's?'

'That's him.'

'I didn't even know that you went out with him. All the girls fancied him.'

'He was quite a hunk, wasn't he? I didn't actually go out with him. I'd left my gym-shoes in the sports pavilion and went back to get them, after classes were over for the day. He was in there, sorting out some equipment, and we got chatting.'

'And?'

'And he fucked me,' said Sandy with a suppressed laugh.

'Oh, right,' replied Karina sarcastically. 'One minute you were chatting and the next he was doing it to you?'

'Not quite,' answered Sandy as she wiped the flannel over her forehead. 'I love the way that you say, "doing it". Why don't you say "fucked", like anybody else?'

'I don't use words like that: not often, anyway.'

'You should. There's nothing a guy likes more than when a girl begs him to fuck her or lick her cunt. You should try it.'

'I don't think I could.' Karina was beginning to feel a little embarrassed but, at the same time, her discomfort was soothed by a strong sensation of arousal. She was still damp from her close encounter with the young gardener and Sandy's conversation wasn't helping. 'Anyway, go on; tell me what happened with Martin.'

'OK, but I'll have to use those words that you don't like; I can't help myself when I'm talking about sex. Like I said, we were chatting, sitting on one of the benches. He was really amusing, making me laugh over and over again, and the way that he kept looking at me with those big, green eyes of his was making me melt. I was still quite inexperienced at that time. I think I'd only had sex with two or three other boys and I was still unsure as to how to make a play for someone like Martin. I knew that he'd been with loads of girls and his manner was brimming over with self-confidence.

'He told me one joke that made me laugh so much that I got hiccups. I felt such a fool, I can tell you. Anyway, he was very nice about it and rubbed the top of my back firmly until they went away. Then he suddenly said, "You're not wearing a bra." My heart nearly stopped. He asked me if I ever wore one and I told him that I didn't, then he said that he'd often seen me around the college and had admired my lovely tits. He actually used those words.

'He asked me if he could feel them. I wasn't going to say no, was I? He caressed them through my blouse, at first, and then unbuttoned it and took them out. He held them in his big hands for a moment and just stared at them. I still had my college tie on and he rested it between my breasts, which I thought was silly but he said that it made them look even sexier. That made me laugh and calmed my nerves a little.

'He bent his head forward and sucked one of my nipples, while he kneaded the other breast with his strong fingers. Suddenly, he moved his hand down and I felt his fingers touch the inside of my thigh. Almost immediately, he began to move his hand slowly upward, under my skirt, while he continued to suck my nipple. I wasn't wearing panties and my juices were beginning to flow. I had a pretty strong feeling that when he touched me there, I would probably come.

'I opened my legs wide and he moved his hand further until his fingertips brushed against my soaking wet sex-lips. He took his face from my breast and looked deep into my eyes, then eased two or maybe three fingers inside me. "You really want it, don't you?" he said. I can't remember whether I answered or not – there was hardly any need. I was saturated down there.

'He made me lie on the bench and pushed my little skirt up to my waist. He gazed at my pussy for a few moments and then looked me up and down. I must have presented quite a picture, lying there in my uniform, my blouse open and my big tits sticking up in the air with the tie still lying between them, my skirt rucked up to my waist and my legs wide open, showing everything that I'd got! He knelt in front of me on the floor, put his head between my legs and then he licked me. God, he was good at that! Until then, other boys had made the effort, but it had never really done much for me. Martin really knew what he was doing. He lapped and suckled at first, and then he found my clit and he began to flutter the tip of his tongue over it. I came in an instant and had to stifle a scream, in case someone passing by heard me.

'Martin got to his feet and just stood looking at me, with a silly grin on his face. My whole body was trembling and my pussy felt like it was on fire. I mouthed the words "fuck me" and his smile disappeared. He unzipped his trousers and pulled out his cock. It was half hard, but was already bigger than anything I'd seen before – not that I'd seen that many.

I reached out and grasped it and then rubbed it gently up and down. It hardened almost immediately. I couldn't believe the size of it! It was as big as a rounders bat and just as thick! I sat up and gripped the stalk with both of my hands and then took the huge end into my mouth. I began to rub my hands up and down the long thick shaft while I suckled the head. I sensed him throb in my grip and I tasted his cream. For one horrible moment, I thought that he had come, and I didn't want that – not until I'd had that monster inside me.

'I moved my face away from him and let go of his cock, then lay back on the bench with my legs wide open. Martin squatted across the bench with one foot on either side and then he aimed the thing at my open little pussy. The end went in quite easily but, as he pushed forward, it felt like I was being split wide open. It hurt slightly and I told him to go easy. He was obviously used to girls having problems accommodating him, because he was very gentle. He moved very carefully, slipping two inches or so in me at a time, until I felt the head touch the back. I looked down. There were still at least four inches to go. I couldn't believe it. In a way, I felt a little sorry for him, not being able to get it all in.

'He fucked me slowly, helping me to get used to his size. The more he did so, the more my juices flowed and I found that I was able to relax. Occasionally, he circled his hips slightly and his cock prodded and probed in all directions, opening me even more. Suddenly, he pushed forward heavily. I glanced down again and saw, to my amazement, that I had taken the lot! Our pubic hairs were meshed together, soaked with my juices.

'He held himself still for a moment. I raised my legs and dug my heels against his bottom and gripped his shoulders with my fingers. "Fuck me!" I said. "Fuck me hard!" My words certainly stirred him into action, because he started to thrust in and out of me wildly.

Every time that he plunged forward, the head bashed against my roof. It was heavenly! I came again, and this time I shouted out. I couldn't help myself.

'He held himself still and we both listened hard, but there were no sounds coming from outside. Deciding that all was well and that we were safe, he started to fuck me again like an animal. Suddenly, he grunted something about me being on the pill and I said that I was and then he rammed his massive prick right up inside me and his expression turned into a grimace. I felt his thick shaft throbbing inside me and I knew that he was filling my cunt with his cream. I came again and clawed and scratched his back frantically. My pussy ached and I could feel my juices soaking the bench under my bottom.

'Martin pulled from me and offered his still quite hard cock to my mouth. I licked and suckled it as though my life depended on it, swallowing as much of our combined juices as I could. It had been over too quickly but, in view of his size, perhaps it was just as well. My pussy ached for most of the remainder of the day, as it was. God knows what I'd have felt like, if he'd given me a marathon session!'

'Did you see him again?' asked Karina, her voice sounding hoarse.

'Not in that way, no. If you remember, it turned out that he was seeing Miss Benson, the geography teacher, on the quiet. I think they actually ended up getting married. I recall that I used to look at her in class as she stood there, looking all prim and proper in those awful grey suits that she always wore and I used to think, 'I know what's been up you, last night!'

The two girls laughed at this and then Sandy made to clamber out of the huge bath. Karina held a towel up for her and wrapped it around her body. She held it close around her for more than a moment and could feel Sandy's sumptuous curves pressing against her. Their eyes met briefly. Sandy held the stare but Karina pulled away and walked back into the bedroom.

She sat on the edge of the bed and looked down at the floor as Sandy followed her into the room. 'I needed that,' said her friend.

'Hm?' replied Karina as she looked up at the other girl.

'The bath. I needed the bath. What did you think I meant?'

'Oh, nothing,' answered Karina, trying to avoid looking directly into Sandy's eyes. 'My mind was wandering.' She watched as Sandy busily towelled herself dry. There was no doubt about it. She was becoming sexually aroused, watching her lovely friend rub her sumptuous body with the towel. Whether it was the thought of Sandy having so recently had sex with both a man and a woman, or whether it was sheer animal attraction, she didn't know: but the urge was as strong as anything that she had felt before. 'You really have got beautiful breasts,' she said eventually, her voice dry with emotion.

Sandy stopped drying herself and stood motionless, as if posing for her. She smiled kindly. 'So you said,' she answered quietly.

'Do they ever hurt? I mean, do you get backache or anything like that? They're so big, while the rest of you is tiny.' Karina was genuinely interested in her friend's answer. Often, in the past, she had watched Sandy running around the gym or playing field, her huge orbs bouncing as though with a life of their own, and she had considered that such attributes must surely be uncomfortable.

Sandy dropped the towel and stood naked in front of her. She cupped her breasts with both hands and raised them slightly. 'Not really,' she replied. 'I'm very lucky. My tits are really firm. I've been told that when I'm older, they may be a bit of a nuisance, but not if I look after them.'

'How d'you mean?'

'I massage them twice a day with baby oil. Jenny Panton showed me how to do it. Do you remember her?'

Karina nodded. How could she forget Jenny Panton, head girl at St. Jennifer's? Her breasts were every bit as big as Sandy's but she was tall and of strong, athletic physique. Many of the girls in her class would gaze at her adoringly, admiring her perfect body and impeccable deportment.

Sandy opened her suitcase and retrieved a small plastic bottle. She poured a little of the contents out on to the palm of her hand then set the bottle down on a table. 'This is what she showed me,' she said as she smoothed the oil over her fleshy mounds. Karina watched, dry-mouthed as her friend gently but firmly massaged the viscous fluid into her breasts. Sandy's nipples darkened and became elongated almost immediately. 'You just rub them, especially underneath,' she said. 'It strengthens the muscles and stops them sagging in later life.' She arched her back and leant her head to one side and Karina saw her pinch her nipples simultaneously between the thumb and forefinger of each hand. She felt a sudden stab of arousal between her thighs.

'You're really enjoying doing that, aren't you?' she said.

Sandy looked across at her and grinned. 'My tits are really sensitive,' she answered. 'A guy has only got to touch me there and my juices start to flow.' She stopped caressing her magnificent orbs of flesh and sat down on the bed next to Karina.

'Have you had a lot of guys, you know, all the way?' asked the latter, nervously. The closeness of her friend's naked body to her, coupled with the gentle scent of freshly bathed skin and the baby oil, was having a marked effect upon her senses.

'A few,' Sandy replied coyly. 'I like sex. There's nothing wrong with that, is there?'

'Nothing,' responded Karina, feeling herself beginning to blush.

'What about you?' asked Sandy. 'You're always very secretive about things like that. How many guys have you made love with?'

The question cut into Karina like a knife and she regretted her curiosity about her friend's exploits immediately. She looked down at the carpet, her mind racing. She wanted to lie and to invent a host of fictitious lovers to impress Sandy, but they had always been straight with each other and she felt that she had to tell the truth.

Sandy rested her hand lightly on her shoulder. 'Come on,' she said with a girlish laugh. 'Don't be shy. We're friends, after all.'

Karina felt the waves of unstoppable emotion build up inside her and the tears suddenly began to flow. She sobbed uncontrollably, her body trembling visibly. Sandy curled her arm around her shoulders and hugged her tightly. 'Oh, Karina,' she said in a soft, caring tone. 'What is it? Please tell me.'

Karina looked into her eyes and took two deep breaths in an effort to regain her composure. She felt weak and stupid, but was also intensely aware of her friend's naked closeness. One of Sandy's breasts was crushed against her bare arm and she could feel the hardness of her erect nipple. 'I'm a virgin,' she said suddenly. The words slipped from her lips like the foulest curse known to mankind.

Sandy looked at her in genuine astonishment. 'I don't believe you!' she said. 'You're nearly twenty-one and you're so gorgeous! Come on, you're kidding me?' Karina shook her head sadly and began to cry again. Sandy hugged her tightly and planted a gentle kiss on the top of her head. Karina allowed her arms to circle around her friend's naked waist.

'It's nothing to be ashamed of,' continued Sandy. 'Lots of girls choose to save themselves for the right man. I hear that it's all the rage in America at the moment.'

'But I don't want to save myself,' wailed Karina. 'I'm desperate to have sex. Sometimes, I think my body is going to explode if I don't get it soon! I even propositioned one of the gardeners this afternoon – can you believe it? My parents would die if they found out!'

Sandy stroked Karina's thigh softly to comfort her. Karina shivered slightly, relishing her friend's gentle touch. 'Why d'you think it is?' she said eventually as she struggled once more to control herself. 'Why don't men want to know me?'

There was a short pause and then Sandy moved back slightly from her and looked her directly in the face. 'Do you want me to be honest with you, Karina?' she said, her tone becoming suddenly quite serious. Karina nodded unhappily. Sandy wiped a tear from her friend's cheek with the tip of her finger. 'I think that there are two reasons. One of them is the fact that you really are gorgeous.'

'How would that stop men? Surely they –'

'That's precisely the problem,' interrupted Sandy. 'A lot of guys are reluctant to approach really lovely girls, assuming that they will get turned down. It's an ego thing, I suppose.'

'So, what am I supposed to do?' asked Karina tearfully. 'Make myself look ugly?'

Sandy smiled and stroked the back of her hand against Karina's cheek. 'You couldn't do that if you tried,' she said. 'Anyway, it's more about attitude.'

'What do you mean?'

'That's the other problem. I'm afraid that you often come across as very aloof and unapproachable when you're talking to guys. I've noticed it before.'

'I don't mean to be like that.' Karina's words

sounded weak, like those of a small child caught out by a parent or teacher.

'You need to lighten up,' continued Sandy. She began to stroke her fingers through Karina's long auburn tresses. 'You're great when you're with me and the other girls, but you seem to be a completely different person when there are guys around.'

'That's just nerves, I suppose.'

Sandy laughed and squeezed Karina's thigh. The sensation caused a sudden surge of warmth to course throughout her lower body. 'There's no need to be nervous of men,' said her friend. 'Let them do the worrying.' She moved her hand up Karina's thigh a little, until it was less than an inch from her crotch. Karina looked down at her legs. In her mind, she knew that she desperately wanted her friend to touch her in that hot special place. She began to tremble again, this time from lust and anticipation.

Sandy took her hand from Karina's thigh and put it to her chin, turning her face to hers. They looked deeply into each other's eyes. Sandy moved her head forward and kissed her lightly on the forehead. Karina raised her face and closed her eyes, while forming her mouth into what she considered to be a sensuous pout. The touch of Sandy's lips to her own was the most magical thing that had ever happened to her in her young life. She responded by wrapping her arms tightly around her friend's neck and pressing her mouth hard against Sandy's fleshy lips.

Sandy suddenly pulled from her and Karina sensed that she had gone too far. She felt wretched and ashamed. She put her hand to her mouth and bit hard against her finger. 'Oh, Sandy,' she wailed. 'I'm sorry, I –'

'Shall I lock the door?' interrupted the other as she looked into her eyes with a meaningful stare. Karina nodded and watched as Sandy moved quickly from the bed and walked across the room. Returning, her friend knelt on the edge of the bed and smiled lovingly. 'Let me watch you undress,' she breathed. Karina immediately removed her flimsy T-shirt and then kicked off her shoes. She stood up, unbuttoned the top of her shorts, pulled down the zip and let the tiny garment slip down her long legs to the floor.

Sandy gazed at her, her eyes shining with lust. 'You are so beautiful,' she said, her voice scarcely above a whisper. 'Let me take your panties off.'

Without waiting for an answer, Sandy slipped from the bed and moved to kneel in front of her. She hooked her thumbs under the lacy material of Karina's panties and slowly tugged them down. Karina felt her juices suddenly flow as her pussy was exposed to her friend's hungry gaze. 'God, you're soaking!' gasped Sandy. She felt a little embarrassed at this, sensing contradictory emotions running through her mind as her panties were pulled down to her feet. She stepped out of them and then sat back on the edge of the bed.

Sandy rose to her feet and stood for a moment, looking down at her. Karina glanced down between her friend's legs. The thick bush of hair was wet and matted. She reached out gingerly and touched the fleshy lips with the tip of her finger. Sandy suddenly grasped her hand and pressed her fingers hard against her soaking mound. 'God,' she gasped, 'you've no idea how long I've wanted you to do that.'

Karina looked up. 'Really?' she said, in genuine surprise.

Sandy moved to kneel next to her on the bed and then wrapped her arms around her, forcing her to lie back on the soft duvet. 'I've had a thing about you for years,' she confessed. 'It started as a crush but, as we got older, it became more than that.'

'I wish that you'd said something,' said Karina. Sandy was almost on top of her by now and her nipples were brushing lightly against Karina's breasts. Their mouths met again and, this time, their kiss was long and passionate, their tongues playfully darting against each other and their lips suckling greedily. Sandy rolled over on to her back, pulling Karina with her. Karina straddled the small frame of her friend's body and pressed her groin against the wet, fleshy mound of her pussy. Sandy responded by gripping her buttocks tightly with her fingers and rubbing her crotch firmly against Karina's hot cunt. Karina moaned and then raised her head high. 'Oh, my God, I'm going to come!' she gasped, suddenly.

The waves of orgasmic delight tore through her with the violence of an electric shock, causing her to rub her pussy frantically against her friend's hot sex-lips. They crushed their bodies together, Karina feeling the mountainous globes of Sandy's huge breasts pressing against her own smaller, but no less firm, mounds. They kissed again, the kiss of two lovers, and she felt Sandy's fingertip tickling the tight sphincter of her anus. She pressed her pussy hard against the other girl's crotch and the finger wormed its way in slightly. 'Ooh, I like that,' she said.

'I thought that you would,' replied Sandy with a broad grin. The finger probed deeper, working in and out of her like a tiny cock. Karina's second orgasm came with equal suddenness as the first and she cried out loudly, then clamped her mouth shut, fearing that the sound would bring the servants rushing to the room. Sandy began to rub her lower body furiously against her and uttered a number of short, muted moans as she joined Karina in blissful release. The two girls pressed their mouths hard together and Karina slipped her tongue between Sandy's lips as the euphoric spasms of joy began to abate within her trembling body.

Eventually, the two women fell apart and lay together on the big bed, staring at the ornately carved ceiling above them. Their breathing was heavy and their naked bodies were coated with sweat. They turned their heads and looked into each other's eyes. 'I don't know what to say,' said Karina breathlessly.

'There's nothing to say,' replied Sandy, with a grin. 'That's only the start.'

'What d'you mean?'

Sandy rolled over on to her side and stroked Karina's flat stomach gently with her fingertips. 'I want to lick you. Would you like to lick me?' The words were spoken with such tenderness that Karina barely had the will to refuse. But it was a big step, and was something that she'd never even considered before.

'I – I'm not sure,' she said.

Sandy moved to lie on her stomach beside her with her face close to her groin. 'Let me do it to you,' she said sweetly, 'and we'll see how you feel later.' She inched herself forward and kissed Karina's stomach. Karina held herself rigid, scarcely able to believe what was happening. She felt Sandy's hot breath brushing against her pussy and parted her legs involuntarily. At first, there was just a gentle kiss to her wet flesh, and then she felt her friend's tongue slipping sensuously up and down the crease. The sensation caused the nerve-endings between her thighs to become alive with desire. Sandy drew her fleshy lips into her mouth and sucked hard, while probing her long tongue between them. Karina responded by arching her back slightly and forcing her mound upward.

Sandy began to concentrate on her hard little bud, flicking her tongue lightly and rapidly over it. To Karina's delight, her friend's finger snaked once more into her bottom. She was amazed how sensitive she was in this place, never having touched herself there before: at least, not in a sexual manner. Sandy's tongue fluttered and teased and her finger moved in and out of Karina's anus with a steady, determined rhythm. She was kneeling at her side by now with her thigh touching Karina's cheek. Karina reached up and stroked her friend's pert bottom gently. Her fingertips found the open lushness of her pussy, and she knew what she had to do.

Grasping Sandy's leg by the heel, she raised it and almost dragged her across her until Sandy's bottom was above her face. The sudden movement had caused the finger to slip from inside her anus, but Sandy continued to suckle her as she slowly lowered her pussy towards Karina's waiting mouth. Karina breathed in deeply and found the scent of her friend's arousal almost intoxicating. She raised her head and pushed her tongue forward slightly, still unsure that she could do it. Sandy's hole looked so tiny and vulnerable and yet Karina knew that, just hours before, it had been invaded by the coloured servant's cock and had, no doubt, also been licked by his girlfriend's tongue.

Sandy managed to slip her finger inside her bottom again and Karina sensed yet another orgasm building up within her loins. She pushed her tongue forward again and the tip touched the fleshy wetness of Sandy's hot pussy. She heard her friend groan with pleasure, the sound muffled by her own pulsating sex-lips. She traced the shape of her pouting labia with the tip of her tongue and then pressed her face against the oozing cushion of flesh and probed deep inside. Lapping hungrily at the juicy succulence of Sandy's cunt, she tasted the creamy delight of her arousal and she came. The orgasm ripped through her with an intensity that she had never thought possible. She pressed her mouth firmly against Sandy's hot mound again and suckled her voraciously, drawing the lips between her teeth and probing deep inside her with her tongue. Sandy groaned and Karina's face became soaked with her juices; she knew that her friend had joined her in another wonderful release. She sucked hard at her friend's lush flesh as if she were trying to devour it, drinking in the delicious creamy fluids and swallowing hard and knowing that she had never tasted anything quite as delightful before.

Lying once more on their backs and staring at the ceiling, the two girls held hands while they cooled their sweating bodies in the slight breeze that wafted in occasionally through the open windows of the bedroom. Karina licked her lips, finding that she could still taste Sandy's delectable flavour on her tongue. 'I don't think that I'm going to bother with men,' she said eventually.

Sandy laughed. 'Don't be silly,' she said. 'What we did was nice, but it's nothing compared to the feeling of a big hard cock going inside you, believe me.'

'What if I never get the chance?'

'You will; of course you will. It's just that you're not in the right place. You're never going to meet the right sort of guy, stuck out here.'

'I had a near thing, the other day,' said Karina, anxious to regain some measure of self-respect.

Sandy sat up quickly. 'Really?' she said, excitedly. 'Tell me about it.'

Karina recounted the story of her experience with the Honourable Charles Simons, encouraged by Sandy to go into every minute detail. Afterwards, her friend shook her head sadly. 'He sounds like a complete bastard,' she said sympathetically.

Karina shrugged. 'He may be, but there was something about him. He had incredible eyes.'

Sandy stroked Karina's left breast gently. 'Forget him,' she said, softly. 'There's plenty more fish in the sea, as the saying goes. Why don't you come back to London with me? I'll introduce you to some new friends and you'll meet a few of the girls from college. We'll have a great time, I promise.'

'London? But you're supposed to be holidaying here with me!' Karina tried to make her protest sound convincing, but in truth the thought of spending some time in the capital interested her greatly.

'Your parents won't mind; they're never here, anyway. Come on, K, it'll be great!'

Karina thought hard. It was true that her parents wouldn't mind – they were already jetting off on their way to Sardinia and wouldn't be back for a month. For once, the thoughts of lazing about on the terrace or wandering aimlessly around the countryside didn't appeal to her in the slightest. 'OK,' she said, after a brief moment. 'Let's do it.'

Sandy clapped her hands and giggled like a small child. 'Great!' she said. 'We'll have a ball, and I promise you that you'll get laid!'

'That isn't the only reason,' responded Karina sourly. 'I'd like to meet the girls again, and just have a good time.'

'Of course,' replied Sandy in a deliberately sarcastic tone of voice. 'Now, let's have some more fun.'

'More? What are you going to do now?'

'Pass me that bottle of baby oil,' replied Sandy, with a grin. Karina handed her the bottle, curious as to what she intended to do with it. 'Now, put a couple of pillows under your tummy and lie on your front,' her friend continued. Karina obeyed, excitedly awaiting whatever lay in store for her. She felt the oil drip on to the small of her back and then sensed it slipping down along the cleft between her buttocks.

'What are you going to do?' she asked sultrily.

'You'll see,' was the simple reply. She began to feel Sandy smoothing the thick oil between her buttocks, her friend's fingertips concentrating their attention on her anus. Her pussy throbbed. The sensation was exquisite. Sandy pushed her finger into her and it slipped easily inside the tight sheath to the knuckle.

'Oh, I really do like that,' Karina said, breathlessly.

'You said that you did. Here, try two.' The pressure of two fingers sliding up her bottom was, at first, a little difficult to accept, but soon Karina found that she was able to relax and enjoy the delightful feeling of fullness within her anus. 'Do you like that?' asked Sandy.

'Yeah.'

'D'you want me to try three?'

'Yeah.'

Sandy eased her fingers out and Karina felt more oil being poured over her cleft. Some of it seeped down to soak her already saturated pussy and the pillow beneath her. She wondered what the servants would think when they discovered the stained bedclothes but, for the moment at least, she couldn't have cared less. There was a slight stab of pain in her rear as three fingers were pushed gently into her, but she fought against the overwhelming urge to push out the intrusion with her inner muscles and soon they were deep inside her tightness. 'God, that's amazing!' she moaned.

'I've got something that'll be even better,' her friend said.

'What?'

'You'll see.' Sandy pulled her fingers out of her and slipped off the bed. Karina watched her open her suitcase and take out a small plastic bag. Opening this, she retrieved something that Karina had only ever seen depicted in the adult magazines that had circulated around St Jennifer's College. It was a phallus, about eight inches long and perfectly formed in every way.

'Where did you get that?' she exclaimed, her eyes wide with astonishment. 'You'll never get that thing in me!'

Sandy merely grinned and dripped more of the oil along the full length of the implement.

'I won't hurt you, I promise,' she said as she crawled back over the bed and positioned herself behind her. 'Pull your cheeks apart, so that I can see what I'm doing.' Karina obeyed immediately but felt distinctly uncomfortable in displaying herself to her friend in this way, and was more than a little apprehensive. More oil was poured on to her and then Sandy worked her fingers in and out of her bottom again. Karina felt the heat rising in her pussy and knew that she was close to coming yet again. She felt the thick knob-end of the phallus pressing against her anus and was certain that it was too big to enter her. Suddenly, it was inside her and the muscles of her sphincter were gripping it tightly under the ridge.

'Go easy, Sandy,' she begged. 'It's too big!' Sandy stroked her bottom and then began to move the thing gently in and out of her, gradually easing more and more of its length into the tight orifice. Karina sensed her inner muscles relax as if they had given up the fight and, eventually, she felt Sandy's fist touching her bottom where she gripped the root of the phallus. Realising that she had accommodated the entire length, she felt somewhat proud of herself. Sandy started to move it in and out of her expertly.

'Oh, that is *so* nice,' moaned Karina.

'Is it?' replied her friend. 'I've never done it.'

'Really? You've never done it at all?' Karina was having difficulty in talking, the sensations caused by the steady pumping of the hard dildo in and out of her bottom driving her to distraction.

'Honestly. A lot of the girls have done it properly, you know, with a guy, but it has never really appealed to me. I get the impression that you might not be averse to such a diversion, though.'

'It really is nice,' said Karina, slowly. 'God, I can't believe what I'm doing!'

'Get used to it, K. You'll be doing all sorts of things like this, when we get to London!' Karina immediately pictured the sight of a man doing this to her, thrusting his cock in and out of her behind. Her pussy felt as though it were on fire. As the surge within her loins rose inexorably to the point of release, she imagined a second lover with his cock pushing simultaneously into her cunt and then, just at the moment that her orgasm tore through her, she conjured up an image of a third man, with his stiff rod in her mouth.

The evening meal had been a casual affair, taken on the terrace. Sandy had flirted outrageously with John, the new butler, and Karina had found herself experiencing pangs of envy at her friend's total lack of inhibitions. Later, as she lay alone in her bed, she thought again of the wonderful sex that she had had with Sandy. Her fingers strayed between her legs to fondle the wet flesh. She glanced at the clock. Two a.m. Surely Sandy wouldn't mind if she awoke her?

She slipped from her bed, pulled a short dressing gown over her naked shoulders and headed out on to the landing. She moved quickly down the corridor to the guest room. Opening the door quietly, she peered inside. The room was illuminated with bright moonlight and she could see every detail. Sandy was lying naked in the centre of the bed, fast asleep. At her sides were the sleeping forms of John and Jenny.

Karina closed the door and returned to her room. She had to get away from Devon Manor, she mused. This kind of thing was becoming something of a habit.

Four

Throughout the long journey to London, Karina could barely keep her eyes off Sandy. Her friend sat opposite her in the carriage and, for most of the journey, had been fast asleep. Karina had tried to doze, but memories of her delicious encounter with Sandy the previous day filled her thoughts. She recalled the wonderful sight of her friend's open sex-lips so close to her face and the luscious taste of her creamy flesh as she'd probed and suckled her, while her own pussy had been stimulated in the same, delightful manner. The thought of making love with another girl had barely occurred to her before and yet it had been so perfect. In a way, she felt that it had been deliciously sinful, like tasting forbidden fruit.

She glanced down. Sandy's legs were slightly parted and the short pleated mini-kilt that she'd chosen to wear for the journey had ridden up a couple of inches, revealing most of her milky-white thighs. Karina licked her lips. She knew that her friend wouldn't be wearing any panties and that all she needed to do was to inch the hem of the skirt just a little further up, and she would be treated to the sight of her bushy mound. She had a strong urge to kneel on the floor of the carriage between Sandy's legs and lick her there, in that hairy little heaven, and to taste her once more. Unfortunately, there were two other people in the carriage: an old woman and a young child. Karina had cursed them mentally when they had burst through the door, just moments before the train had moved off from its last stop at Basingstoke. The woman had managed to immerse herself in some trashy romance novel while the child chewed gum consistently and kept staring at Karina through cold, arrogant eyes.

She tried to ignore the young girl and, instead, looked out of the window to watch the dismal scene of London's suburban sprawl begin to unfold before her. She glanced back at Sandy. Her friend had shifted slightly in her sleep and the skirt had ridden even further up her legs. Tiny wisps of pubic hair were just visible, peeking out from under the hem. Karina looked across at the old woman. She was still engrossed in her book but it was likely that, should she look up, she would be able to see Sandy's embarrassing predicament. Karina reached forward and reluctantly tugged her friend's skirt down, her action causing Sandy to wake from her slumber.

'What, what is it?' she asked sleepily. 'Are we there?'

'Nearly. Did you have a good sleep?'

'I needed it. I didn't get much, last night.' Sandy sat up and stretched herself, her large breasts straining against her tight blouse. Karina made a point of not looking at them, lest either of their companions noticed, and she glanced out of the window. The train was moving slowly and, for no real reason, she tried to make sense out of the graffiti-strewn walls of the sad old buildings close to the track. She looked back at her friend.

'I looked in on you last night,' she said. 'But you were all asleep.' She stressed the word 'all' on purpose, and Sandy glanced down at the floor sheepishly.

'Oh,' said her friend guiltily.

Karina looked at her and grinned. 'Don't worry,' she laughed. 'I'm sure that you had a good time. You must tell me about it some day.'

Sandy looked up, seemingly relieved that Karina wasn't angry. 'I will,' she said, with a wide grin.

'I'm really looking forward to meeting the other girls again,' Karina said.

'It'll be great,' replied Sandy enthusiastically. 'There are six of us, all living close to each other in Knightsbridge. We party all the time. There'll probably be something going on tonight.'

'I do hope so,' replied Karina as she glanced out of the carriage window again. The train was beginning to brake and the grim portals that heralded the entrance to Waterloo Station slipped by. Rising from her seat, she tugged her suitcase from the luggage rack above her. 'We're here,' she said. 'Come on; if we're quick, we'll get a cab.'

By choosing to travel on the afternoon train, the girls had arrived in London at the height of the rush hour and were forced to fight their way through the milling crowds to get to the taxi rank. Luckily, they were able to find an empty cab and were soon on their way to Knightsbridge. The traffic, as usual, was horrendous and the taxi made slow progress.

'We should have used the underground,' said Sandy as the cab shuddered to yet another stop.

'Oh, no,' replied Karina. 'I can't stand the tube in the rush hour. All those people pressing against you.'

'I would have thought that you would have liked that,' teased her friend.

Karina ignored her and checked to see that the glass partition between them and the driver was closed. 'Did you really enjoy yourself with John and Jenny last night?' she enquired in a hushed voice.

'Yes,' replied Sandy. 'That John's quite something.'

'Did you lick Jenny?' asked Karina, feeling strangely jealous.

'Yeah,' was the simple reply.

'Did she taste as nice as me?'

The two girls looked into each other's eyes and it was clear from Sandy's expression that she realised that Karina's questions were based on envy rather than curiosity.

'You tasted absolutely beautiful,' she replied tactfully. She smiled lovingly and stroked Karina's cheek with her fingertips. 'Beautiful,' she repeated.

The momentary silence was shattered by the sound of the partition sliding open.

'Nine Keller's Drive!' called the driver.

The girls struggled from the cab and Karina retrieved their suitcases while Sandy paid the driver. Pushing their way through the hordes of scurrying commuters that crowded the pavement, they approached an old building.

A uniformed man opened the door for them. 'Afternoon, Miss Harrison,' he said in a cheerful voice.

'Good afternoon, Rogers,' replied Sandy. The girls put their cases down once they had entered the ornate hallway. 'This is Miss Karina Devonside,' continued Sandy. 'She will be staying with me for a while.'

Rogers touched the peak of his cap. 'Pleased to meet you, Miss Devonside,' he said warmly. Karina merely smiled. 'Do you want me to take your cases?' he asked.

'No, we'll manage,' replied Sandy. 'Come on, Karina. We'll not bother with the lift; it's only one flight.'

Karina glanced again at the doorman. He was about forty, quite handsome and fit-looking. She wondered if Sandy had had sex with him. It wouldn't have surprised her; after all, her friend saw nothing wrong in sleeping with servants.

Once inside Sandy's small but comfortably furnished flat, the two girls dropped the cases on to the floor and collapsed together on a sofa. 'That was not one of our best ideas,' laughed Sandy. 'Arriving in London at this time of day.'

'Never mind,' answered Karina. 'We're here now. How about a coffee?'

'No milk, I'm afraid. You'll have to take it black.'

'I always take my coffee black.' Karina said the words as if taking coffee any other way was unheard of.

Sandy gave her a sidelong glance and then rose to her feet. 'There's only one bed,' she said as she made her way to the kitchen. 'We'll have to share.'

Karina felt a warm feeling coursing through her loins. The thought of spending entire nights in her friend's arms thrilled her incredibly.

'I'll ring Usha,' Sandy called from the other room. 'She'll know if there's anything happening tonight.'

Karina thought about Usha. She was about Sandy's age; a small-built girl who hailed from Mauritius, and her father was something very important in their country's embassy. As far as she could remember, Usha was a painfully shy girl who seemed to spend most of her time alone, apparently content with her own company. 'What's she doing, these days?' she asked.

Sandy returned from the kitchen, a cordless phone pressed to her ear. She held her hand up to signal for silence.

'Hello, Usha? It's Sandy. No, I'm back in London. I've brought Karina with me from the sticks to show her a good time. Is there anything doing tonight?' There was a long pause while Sandy listened attentively to the reply. 'Yeah? Right. At your place? OK, we'll be there. See you.'

'I take it that something's happening?'

Sandy set the phone down on a table and returned to the kitchen. 'The crowd is going to be at Usha's flat tonight. Apparently she's met this really nice guy who's into all sorts of stuff and she wants everyone to meet him.'

'What sort of stuff?'

'She didn't say,' replied Sandy as she returned to the room, carrying two mugs of coffee. Handing one to Karina, she sat down beside her and sipped from the steaming liquid. 'Usha's really come out of her shell since moving to London,' she continued. 'She's one horny young lady!'

Karina gasped, almost spilling her coffee. She set the mug down on the table in front of her. 'Usha?' she said, astonished. 'She was always so quiet and reserved.'

'It just shows that you can't judge people until you really get to know them. I mean, I never expected to end up in bed with you, but I did; and I certainly would never have believed that you were still a virgin.'

Karina frowned and took up her mug of coffee again. She sipped the liquid thoughtfully. 'You won't say anything about that to the others, will you?' she asked, after a moment.

Sandy stroked her bare thigh gently. 'Not if you don't want me to,' she said softly. 'Anyway, with a bit of luck, it'll be taken care of tonight.'

'D'you think so?' asked Karina nervously.

Sandy nodded, a broad smile playing across her lips. 'Usha's parties always end up as orgies.' She drained the remains of her drink and then got up quickly to her feet. 'Right,' she said. 'I'm going to unpack and then take a shower.' She looked coyly at Karina, who was finishing the last of her coffee. 'Would you like to shower with me?' she pouted. Karina nodded and quickly put her cup back down on the table, then followed Sandy into the bedroom.

The powerful jets of hot water sprayed over the naked forms of the two girls as they laboriously soaped each other's bodies. Rivulets of creamy bubbles ran down their skin, accenting their shapely curves. Karina rubbed a bar of soap between her hands and then, placing it back in the dish, ran her palms smoothly over Sandy's sumptuous breasts. Her friend responded in a similar manner and then slipped one of her hands between Karina's legs.

'God, you're soaked!' she exclaimed. 'And not with water!'

Karina said nothing, but returned the compliment, slipping her fingers into the silky purse of Sandy's hot pussy. 'You're not so dry yourself,' she said, with a girlish laugh. It was an understatement. Sandy's sex-lips were running with creamy juice.

'I think I'm going to come!' she moaned suddenly. Karina pushed all four of her fingers inside Sandy and pressed her thumb hard against her bud. Sandy gasped out loud and fell heavily against her, almost knocking her back against the wall of the shower. Karina rubbed Sandy's pussy furiously until her friend grasped her wrist to stop her. They pulled apart and Sandy turned the shower off. They looked at each other for a moment, then suddenly burst into fits of laughter.

'They'd better watch out at the party tonight,' laughed Sandy, 'or the two of us will eat them alive!'

Usha greeted Karina and Sandy at the door to her flat. Karina was surprised in the change in her college friend's appearance and demeanour. Gone was the innocent little-girl look. She was brimming over with confidence and her eyes, which in the past had always seemed to be looking down at the ground, now shone happily. Her manner of dress was very different to what Karina remembered her wearing in the past, as well. Instead of a pair of scruffy jeans and a baggy jumper, the woman before them now wore an elegant tight-fitting dress of gossamer silk, which clung to her small lithe frame like a second skin.

'Karina!' she exclaimed happily. 'It's good to see you! Please, come in, both of you. The others are already here.'

They were led into a large darkened room in which were seated about twenty people, most of them in their late teens or early twenties. Karina knew most of the girls, of course. They were all products of St Jennifer's and were people whom she was already missing greatly. The room erupted into a cacophony of girlish chatter as old friends greeted each other, while Usha took Karina and Sandy's coats. She returned after a moment, carrying a couple of drinks, which she handed to the two newcomers.

'Where's this mysterious new man of yours, Usha?' asked Sandy.

'He'll be along in a minute,' their friend answered. 'He went to pick up his brother from the station.'

'He's got a brother?' said Karina, with a laugh. 'Ooh, that's handy!'

Sandy managed to perch herself on the arm of one of the sofas and began to sip her drink.

Karina looked around. There were about a dozen young men in the room and she considered all of them to be quite attractive. After what Sandy had said about Usha's parties, she had decided that tonight was the night her virginity would go, and she couldn't help but excitedly wonder to herself which of the young men would be the one to take her first.

The door from the hallway opened and two men entered. The first, a young man in his early twenties, smiled nervously as he walked in. He was carrying a small overnight bag, which he tossed into a corner of the room. When the second man entered, however, Karina gasped and almost dropped her glass.

'Coo, he's gorgeous!' exclaimed Sandy as she stood up from her seat.

'Yes,' replied Karina solemnly. 'I told you he was.'

Her friend looked at her quizzically. 'What d'you mean? Do you know him?'

'That's the guy that I told you about, the one who was a guest at my house.'

Sandy looked puzzled for a moment, then suddenly realised what it was that her friend was talking about. 'That's him?' she gasped. 'The one who . . .'

'Yes,' said Karina slowly. 'The Honourable Charles Simons.'

No sooner had she spoken than Simons noticed her standing there and walked briskly across the room. He held his hand out in greeting. 'Miss Devonside,' he said. 'This is indeed a coincidence.'

'Isn't it?' she replied coldly.

He appeared not to notice her attitude and turned to face Sandy, who was gazing at him like a besotted puppy. 'My name is Charles, Charles Simons,' he said as he shook Sandy's hand firmly. 'May I know yours?'

'Sandy Harrison,' she replied weakly.

Karina turned and walked away, determined not to engage in conversation with the man who had so cruelly tempted her and let her down. She moved over to stand next to the other new arrival.

'You are Charles' brother?' she asked, smiling sweetly.

The young man looked startled. 'Yes, yes, that's right,' he answered nervously. 'My name is Piers. Do you know Charles, then?'

'He visited my parents' home in the West Country last week.'

'Oh, right.' There was a long pause. Piers was clearly attempting to think of something to say but wasn't having any luck. Karina decided to try and lead him into conversation.

'Have you been away?' she asked. 'I heard that Charles was picking you up from the station.'

'I'm just back from university,' he replied, his tone becoming a little calmer. 'I'm up at Oxford.'

'Really?' she said, pretending to be impressed. 'But surely it's the holidays?'

'Oh, yes, it is. I was doing some extra research for Charles. He's recently back from South America and he asked me to look up some information for him.'

'On the Atca people, by any chance?'

Piers looked surprised. 'You've heard of them? Oh,

yes, of course you have. Charles will have told you. They really make a fascinating subject for research.'

'Indeed,' replied Karina. She was trying to sound friendly but her words seemed aloof, even to her, and she began to understand just what Sandy had been talking about regarding her somewhat supercilious manner. She decided to lighten the conversation. 'I understand that the Atca worship sex,' she said, with a grin that was perhaps too broad.

The young man's face coloured noticeably and he looked down at his shoes. 'Yes,' he said, in a hushed tone. 'So I understand.'

Karina grabbed his arm and squeezed it playfully. 'Well,' she laughed, 'who doesn't?'

Piers stiffened and she regretted her attempt at humour immediately. It was plainly the wrong thing to say, especially to such a shy and self-conscious person as Piers appeared to be. 'I'm sorry,' she said, gently, 'I was being silly.'

'Oh, no, please,' he replied, looking at her face again. 'It is I who should apologise. I'm not very good at meeting new people.'

'Well, you've met me now. I'm sure that we'll get on famously.' Karina glanced across at his brother, who was still in deep conversation with Sandy. Her friend was gazing up at him with an expression that would have suggested to him that she was hanging on to his every word. Karina smiled to herself. Her friend was good, very good.

She looked back at Piers. There was some similarity with Charles, as far as bone structure and facial expression were concerned, but otherwise they couldn't have been more different. Piers was fair-skinned with light-brown hair cut short in the style college boys wore in the fifties. He was tall, possibly an inch taller than his brother, and was very slim. But it was his nervous and unassuming manner that endeared him to her.

'Let's get ourselves some drinks,' she said. She slipped her arm through his and led him to the kitchen, ensuring that the two of them walked directly in front of Charles. He glanced at them, but then nonchalantly continued to talk to Sandy. Karina heard him use the phrase 'sexual delights' as they passed by, and assumed that he was talking about the Atca people. She smugly decided that he was a man of limited conversation.

Piers poured Karina a glass of white wine and then took one for himself. For no particular reason, they remained in the kitchen and their chat became more and more amiable and relaxed as the evening progressed. Music blared from the main room and the sounds of laughter and squeals of amusement soon indicated that the party was in full swing.

'I wonder what's going on in there?' said Piers, with a gentle laugh.

'D'you want to go in?' asked Karina, hoping that he would say no.

'I'd rather stay here with you,' he replied. He laughed, suddenly realising that he'd made a joke. 'I mean, I'd rather that *we* stayed in here.' He looked confused, evidently still not sure whether he'd said the right words. Karina smiled and made a grasp for his wrist. Instead, she missed and knocked his glass clean out of his hand. The contents went flying, most of it landing on the front of her dress.

'Oh, bugger,' she said, then looked at Piers guiltily. 'I'm sorry, I don't normally swear. It's just that this dress is new on today.'

'D-don't apologise,' he stuttered. 'Here, let me see if I can find a cloth.' He searched around the untidy room and eventually found a dishcloth, which he soaked liberally with water from the hot tap. He went to wipe the wine from the front of her dress but stopped short and coloured up again.

Karina smiled and took the cloth from him. 'I'll do

it,' she said, with a wry smile. She dabbed the soaking cloth over her chest and suddenly realised, to her horror, that her actions had caused the material to become virtually transparent. She saw Piers looking wide-eyed at her breasts, her nipples and the dark-brown areolae now plainly visible through the wet garment. He swallowed hard, his gaze not moving from her apple-firm mounds for a second.

'Oh, dear,' she said, and she bit her bottom lip with amusement. He looked up at her face and was plainly pleased to see that she wasn't angry or upset. There was a short pause.

'You're very beautiful,' he said, suddenly.

'Do you like my breasts?' she answered, the wine that she had drunk giving her the courage to say something so brazen. He nodded. She took hold of his hand. 'Come on,' she said. 'Let's go and find somewhere private.'

Karina led Piers back into the lounge and the two of them stopped short. The group of guests was arranged in a circle like an audience at a boxing match. But it was not a fight that they were watching; quite the reverse. Holding centre stage was the lovely Usha. Her elegant dress had been discarded and all she wore now was a pair of white hold-up stockings. She was kneeling on her hands and knees, sandwiched between two totally naked young men. One of them, the younger of the two, was steadily pumping his not insubstantial cock in and out of her pussy from behind, while his colleague was feeding Usha's tiny mouth with his own hard length.

Karina glanced around at the seated audience. Many of them were openly caressing each other and a couple of the girls had bared their breasts, while she saw that at least three of the men were having their exposed erections fondled by the nearest young lady.

'Sandy told me that Usha's parties always end up as orgies,' she whispered to Piers. 'Now I can see why!'

She looked around for Sandy, but couldn't see her. She also noticed that the Honourable Charles was absent as well. She glanced up at Piers. His eyes were wide, his stare fixed on the sight of Usha and her two lovers performing less than three feet away from him. Karina looked in the direction of his stare. The man behind Usha was really hammering into her now, causing her petite little body to shudder with the force of his unrelenting assault, while she seemed to have managed to accommodate the entire length of the other man's cock in her mouth. Another young man stood up and began to remove his clothing, clearly intent on taking over from one of Usha's lovers. Karina wasn't sure if she wanted to stay in the room. The scene excited her, but she wanted her moment with Piers to be a private one. She took hold of his hand. 'Come on,' she said.

Piers seemed reluctant to move at first, but eventually gave way and followed her out of the room and into the hallway. There were a number of doors ahead of them. Karina tried one gingerly. It opened. Still clutching Piers by the hand, she led him into the darkened room. She switched on the light and gasped. Sandy was lying naked on the bed, gently sucking the long hard erection sported by the Honourable Charles. She let Simons' cock fall from her mouth and grinned.

'Hi, K,' she said breezily. 'Come and join us.'

Karina shook her head. 'No, no,' she stuttered. 'It's all right. I'm sorry.' Feeling more than a little embarrassed, she almost dragged Piers out of the room, carefully closing the door behind them. She stood in the hallway for a moment, regaining her composure. She wasn't angry, neither with her friend nor with Simons himself. In fact, she felt envious of both of them. She remembered the taste and texture of his thick cock when she had held it in her own mouth and she also recalled the lush sweetness of Sandy's pussy, something which he, no doubt, was enjoying at that very moment. For a brief instant she was tempted to take up Sandy's invitation and return to the room, but thought better of it. Instead, she resolved to give herself completely to Piers. It would be he who would take her virginity.

She moved further down the hall and tried another door. She opened it cautiously and peered into the gloom inside. There were no sounds coming from within the room. Nervously, she flicked the light-switch. There was a large bed in the centre of the room, strewn with guests' coats.

'Come on, it's OK,' she whispered.

Piers followed her into the room and closed the door quietly behind him. Karina turned to face him. The two of them stood nervously for a moment, each unsure what to do or say. She glanced down at the front of her dress. The material had dried a little and her breasts were no longer fully visible, but the garment felt distinctly uncomfortable. She looked up at Piers, who smiled nervously back at her.

'Would you like to kiss me?' she said. He nodded and moved towards her. He took hold of both of her hands and inched his face towards hers. Karina arched her neck and closed her eyes. Their lips met. It was a gentle, brief touch which, nevertheless, she found to be almost magical. They moved apart, still holding hands. 'That was nice,' she whispered. 'Do it again.' She let go of his hands and circled his neck with her arms, pressing her body against his. His torso felt slim and firm against her and she could sense the distinct pressure of his erection crushed against her groin. He was hard for her! He was already aroused!

They kissed again and, this time, she pressed her lips hard against his and forced her tongue into his mouth. She felt him slip his hands around her narrow waist. She drew back from him. 'I'm going to get your shirt wet,' she said.

'It doesn't matter.' Piers pulled her back to him and kissed her again. Taking the initiative, he slipped his tongue between her lips and she felt his hands slip down until they cupped her buttocks. She wondered if he would realise that she wasn't wearing panties. He began to stroke her bottom as he became more confident and she rubbed her lower body gently against his crotch, thrilling to the feel of the bone-hard erection in his trousers.

Their lips parted and Karina gazed for a few moments into his eyes. Piers was certainly handsome in a gentle and kind way: unlike his brother, whose good looks were of the lantern-jawed, hero-of-the-hour variety. She stroked his hair and the back of his neck with her fingertips. 'Would you like to make love to me?' she asked sweetly.

'Yes.' His reply was barely audible and he licked his lips nervously after he spoke. Karina could barely contain her excitement. Her pussy throbbed and she could already feel the dampness between her thighs. She moved away and turned her back to him.

'Unzip my dress, please,' she said. She thrilled as she felt his fingers fumbling with the catch at the top of her dress and shivered slightly with nervous excitement as he drew the long zip down all the way. Karina peeled the tight-fitting garment from her body and let it slip down her legs to the floor. She was naked now, save for her high-heeled shoes. She turned to face him. Piers stared immediately at the wispy curls between her legs and his breathing became shallow and laboured.

'You are beautiful,' he repeated. Karina stood motionless for a moment, enjoying the way that he was savouring the sight of her nakedness. She could see that his hands were trembling and wondered if this was going to be the first time for him also. She walked slowly over to him and took his hands in hers. She clutched his fingers tightly and kissed him lightly on the lips.

'Make love to me, Piers,' she said, in a half-whisper. 'And please be gentle with me. It's my first time.'

He looked shocked. 'Really?' he said, his eyes wide with surprise. 'But you're so – so . . .' It was evident that he was struggling to say the right words. Karina kissed his lips again and then let go of his hands, turned and walked over to the bed. She pushed the pile of coats on to the floor and then lay on the bed, adopting what she thought was a seductive pose with her legs slightly curled and one arm resting across her stomach. She felt her juices slipping from her hot pussy to dampen the crease of her bottom. This is it, she thought, I'm going to be fucked.

She had to wait a good half-minute before Piers at last began to remove his clothing. She watched with amusement as he fumbled with his tie and his shirt buttons, the look on his face a picture of excitement and terror. He threw his shirt on to the floor, kicked off his shoes and wrenched off his socks. She opened her legs wide and he stared at the glistening prize between her thighs. Fingers shaking, he managed to unzip his trousers and, with some difficulty, took them off, casting them on to the floor with his other clothing.

Now all that he wore was a pair of silk boxers. They were quite tight, and Karina could plainly see the outline of his stiff erection, the tip just reaching the waistband of his shorts. Unable to resist the urge, she touched herself between the legs. She was soaked, her sex-lips puffy and pliant, ready to be impaled. The aching need to be penetrated burned within her loins. Piers nervously slipped his pants down his legs and stepped out of them. His erection thrust forward, the near-purple head coated with a sheen of shining clear fluid. It was both longer and thicker than his brother's was and Karina remembered what Sandy had said about size being important to some girls. She felt more than a little nervous, wondering if it would hurt her. It seemed far too large to slip easily into her tiny hole, despite the fact that she was so incredibly aroused.

Piers moved over to her and knelt beside her on the bed. He reached out and tentatively cupped one of her breasts in his hand. 'So beautiful,' he said, yet again. He bent his head towards hers and their mouths met. Their lips parted and their tongues darted forward, slipping and sliding against each other as they suckled each other's mouths in a passionate frenzy. He squeezed her breast firmly and she responded by reaching out and taking hold of his thick erection. It felt as hard as bone. She rubbed it gently, moving the loose skin up and down the long shaft within her grip. Piers released his grasp of her breast and she felt him slip his hand down her body, over her stomach, until his fingertips found the soft wet lips of her pussy. He caressed her inexpertly and she responded by pushing her hips upward, encouraging him to delve deeper. She sensed him slip a finger inside her and she suddenly felt a slight stab of pain which caused her to cry out, the sound muffled by his mouth against hers.

He pulled back and took his hand away from her, although Karina continued to stroke his cock rhythmically. 'Are you all right?' he asked, evidently genuinely concerned.

She nodded. 'I told you that I was a virgin,' she pouted.

'You mean, you're not now?' he asked.

'Technically, I don't suppose I am,' she replied. 'But I still want the real thing.' She squeezed his hard rod tightly, recalling something that Sandy had told her, about using coarse words at the right moment. 'I want you to fuck me,' she breathed. She was surprised at how easily she had mouthed the obscenity, never having used it before unless in fits of anger. To say it in this sort of situation thrilled her immensely. 'Come on, Piers,' she whispered. 'Fuck me.'

He moved to kneel between her legs, his long cock jutting forward ludicrously. She glanced down at the monster. It looked so big; so utterly enormous. Piers gripped it by the root and aimed the head at her virgin hole. Karina raised her legs high and gripped her ankles tightly, not once taking her eyes off the beautiful thing that was about to enter her body.

There was a sudden noise behind them as the door crashed open and a young couple burst into the room.

'Oh, sorry,' a girl's voice was heard to say and the door was quickly closed, but the damage was done. Piers gasped and a stream of hot, white fluid jetted from the angry head of his cock to soak Karina's stomach and breasts. He grasped hold of his stalk as if trying to stop the orgasm but more and more of his cream spurted from him.

'Oh, no, I don't believe it!' he panted.

Karina lowered her legs and just lay there, confused and angry. Piers moved away and stared at her, his expression one of total embarrassment. Karina put her fingertips to her breasts and ran them thorough the thick cream. 'I – I'll get a towel or something,' he stuttered. He looked around the room and found a box of tissues on the dressing table. He handed the box to her. She looked down at his groin. His cock was hanging limp and flaccid, a mere shadow of its former glory.

Karina used the tissues to clean herself up while Piers quickly dressed. 'You don't have to go,' she pleaded. 'I'm sure you'll be able to get hard again!'

He shook his head sadly. 'It's the wrong sort of situation,' he said, as he buttoned up his shirt. 'I'll be afraid someone else is going to come charging in. Perhaps I can take you for dinner or something?'

Karina was about to reply when the door was opened again and Sandy walked in. She was fully dressed and her manner was confidently nonchalant. She looked at Piers and smiled knowingly. 'Hi,' she said cheerfully.

Piers said nothing in response, but picked up his tie and hurried out of the room. Karina watched him go, her mind racing. Sandy sat on the edge of the bed. 'What a team we make,' she said, with a girlish giggle. 'We've had both brothers at the same time. I bet they'd do a foursome with us if we asked them. D'you think you'd like that?'

'I –' began Karina.

'You've got sperm on your face,' interrupted Sandy. 'Did he come in your mouth?' Karina shook her head sadly as her feelings of arousal rapidly turned into ones of sheer frustration.

'Charles did with me,' continued her friend, clearly bursting to tell her tale. Her expression suddenly became clouded. 'You don't mind, do you?' she asked. 'I mean, I know you quite liked him.'

Karina sighed. 'Of course I don't mind,' she said. 'After all, I've just been in bed with his brother.' She wanted to tell Sandy the truth and, in a way, what she did say wasn't exactly a lie, but she also wanted to hear what her friend had been up to, feeling that it might compensate in some way for her own lack of success.

'It was brilliant, honestly,' Sandy enthused. 'He's really kinky. He even wanted to put it in my bottom, but I wouldn't let him.'

'You should've done,' interrupted Karina. 'When you did that to me, you know, with that vibrator thing, it felt really nice.'

Sandy made a face and shook her head. 'Like I said before, I really don't fancy it,' she continued. 'Anyway, what we did do was enough.'

'How did you get to go to bed with him? Last time I saw you, you were just talking.'

'That's right. He was going on and on about this tribe in South America and all the weird things that they did. It was interesting but, to be honest, the more that he talked and the more that he looked at me with those lovely hypnotic eyes of his, the more that I wanted him.

'All of a sudden, he stopped talking, took hold of my hand and led me out of the room. Usha was going at it like mad with a couple of blokes but nobody was taking any notice, least of all me. Charles took me into one of the bedrooms and, the minute that the door was closed, he had his arms wrapped round me and his tongue in my mouth. I just melted. I knew that he could do anything that he wanted to me.

'He started to stroke my bottom with both of his hands as we kissed and I could feel his hard cock pressing against my belly. He lifted up the hem of my dress at the back and clutched my bare buttocks. He whispered something about liking girls who didn't wear panties and then started to finger my pussy from behind. Needless to say, I was absolutely soaking!

'He pushed me away after a few seconds, and I thought that I'd done something wrong. I just stood there, like a stupid little schoolgirl who was about to be told off while he stared at me through those magical eyes. Then he sat on the bed and ordered me to take my clothes off. He just said, "Strip," as simple as that. When I was naked, he smiled and said that I was a very naughty girl and that I deserved a good spanking.'

'He didn't!' Karina was warming to the story by now, and the thought of having her own bottom spanked very hard had often crossed her mind in the past. 'Did he do it? Did he spank you?'

Sandy nodded. 'He made me lie across his knee with my bum sticking up in the air. I was a bit nervous: I mean, I'd never done anything like that before and I wasn't sure that I'd like it, but there was something about him that made me obey. He seemed to exude a strange power that demanded instant obedience.

'I lay there for what seemed like an age, waiting for the first slap. When it came, it stung like hell. I yelped, and he told me to be quiet. He smacked me again, his big hand whacking against both of my buttocks at the same time, and I gritted my teeth so as not to cry out. After about the sixth or seventh stroke, I realised that I was beginning to enjoy what he was doing to me. I was loving the feeling of being at his mercy, and I was enjoying the pain.

'After a couple more slaps, he stopped and started to stroke my skin softly. "You've got a very red bottom," he said. He asked me if I'd ever had a cock inside it and I told him that I hadn't, and that I didn't want it. He said that was OK; he wouldn't force me to do anything that I didn't want to. He helped me up and then told me to lie on the bed while he undressed. My bottom was stinging and my pussy was saturated. I could feel my juices slipping down between my buttocks. I don't think that I've ever been so wet and ready for sex.

'When he was naked, he lay on the bed next to me. I went to kiss him but he pushed me away and forced my head down. It was obvious what he wanted. I moved myself around and gripped his hard cock and then took it into my mouth. That was when you came in. I really meant it, by the way, when I said that you could join us.'

'I wish I had,' said Karina with a pout.

'Oh, come on, I bet you had a lovely time with his brother! Anyway, after you'd gone I carried on sucking him, but I remembered what you told me had happened when you did it to him, so I was careful not to do it too well. I moved across him so that my bum was in his face and he started to lick me. He lapped away at my pussy and my arse – I know I said that I'm not into anal sex, but I do love having my arse licked!

'I felt his cock throb in my mouth and tasted his cream. Not wanting to make him come, I let it fall from my mouth and moved from him. I got astride him and grasped his stalk, then guided it into my cunt.'

'Oh, Sandy!' protested Karina. 'Must you use words like that?'

Her friend glared at her. 'Yes, I must,' she said sharply. 'Anyway, I sat down hard on him, taking the full length into me. He reached up and pinched both of my nipples between his fingers. It really hurt, but it was a nice pain. I began to move myself up and down while he pinched me again and then kneaded my breasts. You know how sensitive I am there. I came within seconds, and I could feel my juices running from me like water from a tap. I thumped myself up and down as hard as I could, until it was over. It was beautiful.

'Charles lifted me up and then made me lie on my back again. He stood by the side of the bed for a moment, just looking at me. I remember that I was trembling, I was so hot for him. His cock was glistening with my come and his pubic hair was soaked. The nerves in my pussy were throbbing; I was desperate for more. I looked him directly in the eye and told him to fuck me, as hard as he could. I would have done anything that he asked at that moment, even let him take me in the bum.

'He turned his back on me and bent down to pick something up from the floor. It was his tie. I thought he was going to whip me with it. I wouldn't have minded. Instead, he curled it round one of the bars at the top of the bedstead and then tied my wrists together, so that my arms were stretched above my head. I was helpless, and the feeling of being so completely vulnerable and at his mercy was incredibly arousing.

'He knelt on the bed between my outstretched legs. Gripping my ankle, he raised one of my legs and rested my foot over his shoulder, and then aimed his hard cock at my open sex-lips. He plunged into me with a wild thrust, the full length going all the way inside me. I gasped, both with shock and pleasure. He began to bang away at me as though I was some kind of whore, using me purely for his own pleasure. Strangely, I found it exciting, to be abused in such a way. Our groins slapped together loudly as he hammered into me, and I knew that he wouldn't be able to keep up the pace for long. Suddenly, he pulled out of me and moved quickly across my body so that his cock was close to my face. I opened my mouth, but he didn't move any further forward. I held my tongue out and he came, his semen spraying over my face and into my mouth. I raised my head and managed to lick the end of his cock as the final drops of juice slipped from him and then I lay back. My face was covered with sperm; in fact, I think I've probably still got some in my hair!'

'It sounds like you had a great time,' said Karina wistfully.

'It was good. I really needed it, particularly after watching Usha's antics. That girl never ceases to amaze me. You'll have to get her to tell you about some of her adventures; they'll make your toes curl.'

Karina slipped from the bed and retrieved her dress. Sandy watched as she pulled the garment on over her head and smoothed it down over her shapely body. 'You really have a lovely body, K,' she said. Karina merely smiled. 'D'you want to go back into the lounge and join in with the others?' continued Sandy. 'There'll probably be a full orgy going on by now.' Karina shook her head. 'Yeah, I suppose you've had enough, it being your first time. Did you enjoy it? Tell me what happened.'

Karina sat heavily down next to her friend on the edge of the bed. She suddenly burst into tears. 'Nothing happened,' she wailed.

'What d'you mean?' asked Sandy, startled at her friend's sudden admission. 'I saw you!'

'He came before he could do it,' Karina sobbed. 'Someone burst into the room and it made us both jump and he just came all over me.' She was in floods of tears now, and Sandy slipped her arm around her shoulders to comfort her.

‘It happens,’ she said. ‘Don’t worry – there’ll be plenty more chances. You should’ve tried to get him hard again.’

‘He was too embarrassed. Oh, Sandy, I was so certain that it was going to happen this time.’

Sandy kissed her lightly on the cheek. ‘Let’s make love,’ she whispered. ‘You and I.’

Karina looked down at the floor. ‘I don’t know, Sandy,’ she said. ‘I don’t know if I want to.’

Her friend hugged her tightly. ‘Come on,’ she said. ‘Let me make you come with my tongue. It’ll make you feel a lot better, I promise.’ Without waiting for an answer, she pushed Karina back and moved to kneel on the floor between her legs. She raised the hem of her dress and quickly pressed her mouth against Karina’s soaking cunt. The feeling of her friend’s tongue flicking rapidly over her clitoris quickly brought Karina to the point of no return. She came with a muted squeal, wrapped her legs tightly around the other girl’s neck and thrust her groin against her sucking mouth.

‘Oh, Sandy, I do love you,’ she panted as the last waves of delightful spasms faded into a memory. Just at that moment, the door to the bedroom was opened yet again. Karina looked up. Piers was standing in the doorway, a look of abject shock on his face.

‘I – I’m sorry,’ he said, and he turned and left the room, closing the door behind him.

Karina fell back heavily on the bed again and put her hands to her face. She felt like rushing after him to try and explain, but knew that what he had seen defied any form of vindication. He’d seen her lying on her back with her legs spread wide open and with another girl kneeling between them, licking her pussy. There was nothing that could be said.

Five

The sound of the doorbell woke Sandy from a deep and satisfying sleep. She slipped quickly from the bed, grabbed her dressing gown from the back of a chair and hurriedly put it on while heading into the lounge. The bell rang again. 'Just a minute!' she called as she tied the cord of her gown.

She opened the door to find Usha standing there. Her friend was dressed in a tiny pair of red shorts and a skimpy white top, which only just covered her small breasts and did nothing to conceal the shape of her long nipples. 'Hi,' said the girl, walking into the flat. 'Are you still in bed? It's past noon!'

Sandy rubbed her eyes and then stretched herself, rubbing the small of her back with her hands. 'Karina and I had a heavy day yesterday,' she replied sleepily. 'What with the journey up from Devon and your little do last night, we were both shattered.' She stretched her arms high above her head. The front of her dressing gown parted and her breasts became fully bared.

'I wish I had tits like those,' laughed Usha.

Sandy brought her arms down quickly and covered herself. 'They're nothing compared to Karina's,' she chuckled. 'Hers are so beautiful; not too big and so pert. D'you know, mine measure more than forty inches?'

Usha moved to stand next to her. 'I don't think that's too big; it just seems so because the rest of you is so small. I prefer ones like yours.' She reached up with both hands and cupped one of Sandy's breasts through the thin material of the gown. 'See,' she said, 'it fits perfectly into both of my hands.' She squeezed the firm mound lightly and Sandy felt a sudden surge of warmth rushing through her lower body. She brushed the hands away.

'Behave yourself, Usha,' she laughed. 'Didn't you get enough last night?' She moved over to the window and pretended to look out into the busy street.

'What happened to you last night?' asked Usha as she sat down on the sofa. 'I looked everywhere for you both, but you were gone.'

'We left at about two. We came to say goodbye, but you were otherwise engaged.'

Usha grinned. 'Oh, right,' she said, sheepishly. 'I suppose that I did get lucky last night. What about you? Somebody said that you disappeared into one of the bedrooms with Charles.'

Sandy walked into the kitchen and switched the kettle on. 'Yeah,' she called. 'You don't mind, do you? I mean, you were busy with those two guys at the time.'

'No, of course I don't mind. He's not a boyfriend, as such. I just like his conversation.'

Sandy got two mugs out of the cupboard and dropped an Earl Grey teabag into each of them. 'Have you slept with him?' she asked, pretty certain of the reply.

'A couple of times,' was the expected answer. 'He's good, but he isn't looking for a relationship, and neither am I.'

Sandy returned from the kitchen. 'I'm going to have a quick shower and brush my teeth. Sort the teas out, will you?' Without waiting for a reply, she returned to the bedroom. Karina was still sound asleep, dead to the world. Sandy moved quietly into the bathroom and closed the door behind her before turning on the shower. She and her friend had talked for ages when they had gone to bed and Karina had been particularly upset about what had happened with Piers. They'd cuddled close and, later, they'd made each other come with their tongues before falling asleep in each other's arms. Sandy thought lovingly about her beautiful, shy friend. It was clear that, unless she lost her virginity soon, she would be distraught. Something had to be done, but for now she decided to let her sleep.

Fully showered and refreshed, she donned her dressing gown again and returned to the lounge. Usha was sitting by the window, staring out at the mêlée in the street below and sipping her tea thoughtfully. Sandy took up her mug and perched on the wide window-ledge beside her. 'Has Charles talked to you about his trip to South America?' she asked, after a moment.

'You mean about the Atca people? He's told me some of it. He's coming round to my place tonight to tell us all about them. That's one of the reasons why I came round, to invite you and Karina to come along.' She glanced around the room. 'Where is Karina, anyway?'

'Still asleep. She's exhausted.'

Usha grinned. 'She went off with Charles' brother, didn't she? Lucky girl – he's gorgeous.'

'Yes, she is a lucky girl,' replied Sandy, purposely not looking Usha in the eye. She decided to change the subject. 'What was the other reason?'

'Huh?'

'You said that inviting us over was just one of the reasons why you came round here today.'

'Oh, yes.' Usha set her mug down on the ledge and fumbled in her small handbag. 'I've got some complimentary tickets for that new Sauna Centre, just off Regent Street. I thought that you and Karina might like to come with me.'

'What, now?' said Sandy. She was still exhausted, but nevertheless found the idea quite appealing.

'Yeah, it's a special lunchtime session, supposedly for stressed-out business types. I hear that it's really luxurious, and you get free food and drinks.'

Sandy drained her mug and stood up. 'Why not?' she said as she headed back towards the bedroom. 'I'll get dressed. I don't think that Karina will be up to it, though; she's out cold.' She moved quietly into the bedroom and quickly slipped on a short, pleated mini-kilt and a plain white T-shirt. Picking up a pair of trainers, she returned to the lounge. Usha was in the kitchen, washing the mugs. Her friend returned just as she was lacing up her shoes.

'Aren't you going to wear any panties?' Usha said, glancing between Sandy's legs. 'That skirt's a little short.'

'You know I hate wearing panties,' replied Sandy nonchalantly, making no effort to conceal her bushy mound from the other's gaze.

'Suit yourself,' Usha giggled. 'Let's hope it's not too breezy out there!'

Sandy scrawled a quick note for Karina and the two girls left the flat. They hurried down the stairs towards the entrance hall. Rogers was there, as usual. He looked up and a small smile appeared on his face, which indicated to Sandy that he had noticed, as she'd skipped down the stairway, that she was not wearing anything under her kilt. She liked that. She enjoyed teasing Rogers.

He opened the door for them and touched the peak of his cap politely as they exited into the busy street. As they hurried down the pavement, Sandy wondered if any of the hundreds of people that they passed had managed to get a fleeting glimpse of her curly bush or her bare bottom. There was only a slight breeze, but the hem of her skirt fluttered provocatively as they walked, and she found the idea quite exhilarating. By the time that they reached their destination, she was wet between the legs and her nipples were as hard as buttons.

The entrance to the centre was nothing more than a plain, heavy door, bearing a small gold plaque which had the simple words SAUNA CENTRE, MEMBERS ONLY embossed on it in black lettering. Usha rang the bell and a tall, swarthy-looking character in his mid-forties opened the door. Usha showed him their passes and he stepped to one side, allowing them to enter. They found themselves in a small, dimly lit waiting room. Sandy began to get a bad feeling about the place. It was anything but luxurious. The man moved behind a counter and retrieved a pair of thick white towels. He handed them to the girls, a vestige of a smile playing across his lips.

'You realise that it's a mixed session today?' he asked. Sandy glanced at Usha, who merely shrugged. Although a little concerned about the rather seedy atmosphere of the waiting room and the somewhat menacing appearance of the doorman, Sandy was feeling so aroused, following their short walk, that she couldn't have cared less. They were shown through another door and stood for a moment, surveying the scene before them. In stark contrast to the shabby room that they had just left, they were now faced with a sumptuous chamber that resembled a Greek temple. The walls were decorated with mock pillars and arches and in the centre of the large room was a small swimming pool, oval in shape and with a couple of fountains gushing high into the air from under the surface of the water.

There were about ten people in the pool, all naked and cavorting like children. Sandy turned to Usha and grinned excitedly. 'I think I've died and gone to heaven,' she laughed. A young couple walked past them, their arms entwined and their naked bodies heavily tanned. The girl was giggling and Sandy noticed that the young man's cock was partially erect.

'The changing rooms are over there,' said the man who had admitted them, with a cursory wave of his hand. 'And the sauna is through the glass door on the other side of the pool. Food and drink will be provided on request.'

Sandy looked in the direction of the changing rooms and then towards the door to the sauna. It was evident that, once they had stripped, they would have to walk most of the way around the edge of the pool to get to the sauna. Normally she wouldn't have minded, but there were a couple of rather elderly gentlemen in the pool and she didn't relish revealing her charms to their already leering gazes. At least they had the towels.

The two girls headed for the changing rooms and found that there was in fact just one room. A partially dressed young man was towelling his hair while a woman was sitting, naked, on a wooden seat, casually sorting through her clothes. The two seemed to be totally oblivious to the other's presence.

'This is quite a place,' said Usha.

'I like it,' replied Sandy. 'No rules, no inhibitions. This is how it should be. People should be much more relaxed about sex.' As she spoke, the young man who was changing out of his clothes removed his trousers and shorts, and made a pretence of searching for something in his kit bag. He glanced at them and both girls saw that his erection was thickening rapidly.

Undaunted, both she and Sandy stripped off quickly and stored their clothes in one of the small lockers set against one of the walls. Usha locked it and took the key, using the elastic strap to fix it to her wrist. Sandy wrapped her towel around her body but her friend merely picked hers up and headed for the door.

Outside, it seemed to Sandy that Usha was walking deliberately slowly around the edge of the pool as they headed for the sauna. It was quite apparent that she was posing for the bathers. Usha was justifiably proud of her slim, lithe little body and the golden tone of her smooth skin, and was also something of an exhibitionist. She had once admitted to Sandy that she had a penchant for making love in public places and that she relished the thought of being observed.

They reached the glass door to the sauna and entered quickly, anxious to avoid letting the heat out. A solitary young man was sitting on one of the slatted wooden benches, his towel spread under him. Usha gave him a friendly, 'Hello,' and sat on her towel opposite him. He smiled in response and then stared down at the floor, as if embarrassed to gaze at her nakedness. Sandy unhooked her towel from under her arms and laid it on the bench. Turning to face the young man, she happily noticed his eyes widen as he looked directly at her breasts. She leant back, her shoulders burning on the hot wood of the wall behind her. The effect of the sudden heat was to cause her nipples to become instantly erect. She crossed her legs and relaxed.

The young man was gazing absently through the glass door by now but she saw, to her profound delight, that his cock was showing signs of stiffening. She nudged Usha and nodded in his direction. Her friend saw his predicament and the two of them clamped their hands over their mouths like naughty schoolgirls, in an effort to stifle their laughter. Fortunately, their companion didn't appear to notice their amusement.

Usha leant back and parted her legs. 'This is the life,' she said. 'I don't know about you, but saunas always make me feel really horny.'

The young man looked across at her immediately and she raised one of her legs so that her heel could rest on the bench. Sandy knew that he would be able to see her pussy quite clearly now. She glanced down between his legs. His cock was stretching noticeably, the stalk thickening and the head beginning to rise. She decided that she would join in the teasing game.

'I agree,' she said. 'I always feel incredibly turned-on after a session in one of these places.' She uncrossed her legs and parted them slightly, then emulated her friend by raising one of them until her heel rested on the bench in the same way. She sensed the lips of her pussy opening and knew that the stranger would be able to see what was happening to her. He stared between her legs and his cock rose to full erection.

Usha rose from her seat and moved over to him. She sat down on the bench beside him and then jumped up suddenly. 'Ooh,' she gasped, 'I've burnt my bottom!' She turned her back to him and bent forward slightly. Sandy grinned with amusement. 'Am I marked?' her friend asked, looking over her shoulder as she bent forward provocatively.

The young man shook his head.

Usha turned to face him, stroking her buttocks with both hands. 'D'you mind if I share your towel?' she said. He stood up and rearranged his towel, spreading it across the seat so that she could sit next to him in comfort. That done, the two of them sat down together with their hips touching.

There was a short pause. The heat was stifling, but it was as nothing compared to the burning sensation that Sandy was feeling between her legs. The young man leant back. His cock was firmly erect and pressed against his stomach. Usha reached across him and grasped the hard stalk. She began to caress it gently up and down and smiled as she looked into his eyes. Sandy watched enviously as his hand snaked between Usha's legs and his fingers began to delve into her tiny hole. She allowed her own fingers to fondle her moist sex-lips, content to watch her friend's antics, at least for the moment.

Usha moved along the bench a little and then bent herself down until she was able to take the stranger's cock into her mouth. Bobbing her head up and down, she deliberately made slurping sounds, which Sandy found especially arousing. She rubbed her hard little bud rapidly. Sweat was pouring from her, running in little rivulets down her body. Her breasts bounced heavily as she rubbed herself, something that was not lost on the young man. He stared avidly at the shuddering globes of flesh while Usha continued to suckle his stiff erection.

'Don't make him come,' said Sandy suddenly. 'I want some.'

Usha raised her head and let his stalk slip from her mouth. She grinned and held the stiff flesh forward as if offering it like a sweet to her friend.

Sandy moved across the sauna and crouched on the floor between his legs. Still gripping the young man's thick cock tightly by the root, Usha aimed the head towards Sandy's open mouth. She took over half of his length between her lips and lapped the hard stalk with her tongue. She heard Usha moan. Moving her head slightly to one side, she looked across at the other girl. The stranger had his hand between her legs and he was rubbing the top of her pussy rapidly, while Usha had all four fingers of her free hand firmly forced inside her succulent sex-lips.

Sandy concentrated on sucking his cock, using all the expertise that she had developed over the past few years. She felt his shaft throb between her lips and drew her head back, freeing his tortured flesh from the soft, wet cushion of her mouth. A trickle of clear fluid seeped from the end and slipped down his gnarled flesh to soak his balls.

She rose to her feet and then squatted across him, lowering herself slowly until she could feel the familiar touch of the spongy tip of a stiff cock against her hot cunt. She reached behind her and gripped hold of the shaft, then guided it into her waiting opening. She sat down quickly on his lap, absorbing the full length inside her burning sheath. He began to move against her, thrusting upward. Sandy matched his movements and her big breasts slapped rhythmically against his face.

Usha moved behind her and, after a couple of seconds, Sandy felt the warm wetness of her friend's tongue licking her between the cheeks of her bottom. She came instantly, her juices flooding from her to soak the young man's groin. The spasms tore through her loins and she shuddered with delight, so much so that his cock slipped from within her oily grip.

'My turn!' cried Usha; she almost pushed Sandy off balance in her enthusiasm to get to him.

Sandy staggered to one side and watched as Usha assumed a similar position to the one that she had used and the stranger's cock disappeared into her pouting little pussy. Sandy crouched behind Usha and snaked the tip of her tongue down her bottom between her buttocks. She lingered a while as she prodded her tongue in and out of Usha's anus, and then moved further down so that she could lick the young man's shaft as it thrust in and out of the other girl's hot flesh. She could taste her friend's delicious juice on his bone-hard stalk. She ran her tongue up again and soaked Usha's anus with saliva, then moved her head back and deftly inserted her forefinger into the girl's tight little sphincter.

Usha moaned happily. 'That's it, Sandy,' she groaned, 'get me ready.'

Sandy knew exactly what she meant, and what she intended to do. She wanted to take him in her bottom. This was something that Sandy knew her friend delighted in. She prodded her finger in and out of the girl's bottom and then licked her middle finger, before carefully pushing both fingers into the slightly less tight orifice. She could feel the young man's hard cock inside Usha's other sheath, moving steadily in and out of her. She pressed her fingers against his stiffness and felt it rub against the tips.

It was evidently the wrong thing to do, at least as far as Usha was concerned. The stranger groaned, clutched her tightly by the waist and rammed his hard weapon deep into her. 'I'm coming!' he moaned.

'I'm not there yet,' gasped Usha desperately. Sandy pulled her fingers from her bottom and Usha forced her small body up and down with alarming speed, clearly trying to make herself come while the stranger was still inside her. It was to no avail. His rapidly drooping phallus slipped from within her and hung sadly between his legs. Sandy bent her head forward again and took it into her mouth. She suckled the softening flesh greedily, enjoying the taste and texture of the remainder of his cream and the scent of her friend's arousal. Above her, Usha was rubbing herself frantically, her fingertips a blur as she coaxed herself towards an orgasm. She came at last with a satisfied sigh and gradually slowed her self-caress to a stop.

The two girls sat back on their bench and regarded their shared lover coyly. He smiled nervously and then rose to his feet, picked up his towel and opened the door. After a brief glance at them, he was gone, the door clanging shut behind him. Sandy watched him walk over to the edge of the pool and saw him slip into the inviting water. It occurred to her that, not only had they both made love to a complete stranger, he had barely said a single word to either of them. Somehow, this made the event rather special.

Karina lay on her back on the bed, staring absently at the ceiling. She noticed a single strand of spider's silk stretching from the light fitting above her head to the curtain-rail over the window and wondered how such a tiny creature could perform such a feat. It seemed miraculous, somehow.

A car-horn blared outside the open window, the noise snapping her out of her daydream. 'This won't do,' she said to herself and she rose from the bed and walked into the lounge. She'd read Sandy's note after she had showered earlier and had been a little disappointed that her friend hadn't woken her. Not knowing where this Sauna Centre was, she'd returned to lie on the bed, enjoying the gentle warmth of the sun on her naked body. She'd thought about Charles and Piers, and had fantasised about them both taking her at once, fucking her cunt and mouth simultaneously. The fantasy had become compounded, and she'd imagined a queue of handsome young men forming at her bedside while she lay there submissively, ready to allow them to do anything that they wanted to her.

She glanced at the clock on the fireplace. Three-fifteen. The day was nearly gone and she'd done nothing. She noticed Sandy's bag next to the clock and had a sudden idea. Feeling a little guilty, she opened the bag and rummaged inside. Her heart leapt as her fingers circled the unmistakable shape of the dildo that Sandy had used on her. She pulled out the phallus and gripped it tightly, recalling the wonderful feelings that it had given her when Sandy had deftly slipped it in and out of her bottom.

She examined it closely. It looked and felt almost like the real thing, long, thick and with a slight curve. The ridge under the head was sharply defined and the head itself was bulbous and smooth. She gripped it by the base and rubbed her free hand up and down the shaft slowly. She put the end to her mouth and traced its shape with the tip of her tongue. It had a slight rubbery taste that was not unpleasant. She opened her mouth and took in as much as she could. Closing her eyes, she remembered the feel of Charles' cock between her lips and the strange sensation when it had throbbed suddenly against her tongue and she had tasted his cream in her mouth. She felt a warm sensation between her legs and wished that he were in the room with her.

A sudden thought came into her head. She returned quickly to the bedroom and then walked through to the bathroom. There was a bottle of baby oil on the shelf by the bath. Retrieving it, she also picked up one of the towels from the rail and went back into the bedroom. She set the oil and the phallus on the bedside table, laid the towel neatly in the centre of the bed and then lay on top of it.

She took hold of the dildo and put it once more to her mouth, closing her eyes. She imagined this time that it was Piers' cock slipping between her wet lips. She licked around the bulbous head and traced the line of the ridge, while the fingers of her free hand quickly found their way to her already damp sex-lips. She slipped her middle finger between them, coaxing them to open, while sucking on the hard rubber phallus. She crooked her finger and eased it into the soft pliant flesh, then moved it rapidly in and out. Her juices began to flow and her breathing became laboured.

She swallowed as much of the dildo into her mouth as she could, then withdrew it and examined it closely, to see just how much of its length was wet with her saliva. She was disappointed to see that barely half of the long thick implement was glistening in the afternoon sunlight. This was something that she needed to practise. Sandy had once told her that men liked to have the full length swallowed, but this would mean actually taking much of it down the throat, and Karina couldn't see how this was possible. Still, she thought, she would learn.

She put the phallus on to the bedside table for a moment and moved her hand down further between her legs, so that she could ease her middle finger into her anus. It felt tight and resisting and she was barely able to get much more than the tip of her finger inside herself. Taking hold of the bottle of baby oil, she soaked her fingers liberally and then tried again. This time, her finger slid with comparable ease all the way in to the knuckle. She moved the finger in and out and then circled it in the way that she remembered Sandy doing. After a few delightful moments, she sensed the muscle of her sphincter relaxing as it surrendered to her insistent probing.

Pulling her finger out of the tight sheath, she poured more oil over her fingers and then carefully eased both the middle and forefingers inside. Her pussy juices mingled with the cool oil as she finger-fucked her arse, the feelings of discomfort fading quickly as more pleasurable sensations took their place. She managed to slip a third finger into her increasingly pliant hole and knew that she was ready.

Taking her hand from herself, she took hold of the phallus and coated it liberally with oil. Holding the bottle in one hand and the gleaming dildo in the other, she drew her legs right back until her thighs rested against her breasts and then poured more oil directly on to her anus. She felt it trickling down her buttock-crease to soak the towel that she had wisely laid beneath her. She managed to set the bottle down without altering her position, and then tugged one of her buttocks in an attempt to open herself. She pressed the head of the phallus against her anus. She pushed hard. The thick head seemed bigger than when Sandy had used it on her and, for a moment, she wondered whether it would go in. She pushed again and suddenly she felt the cock-head slip into her. She gasped. It felt enormous. Moving it backward and forward almost imperceptibly, she gradually eased more and more of the length of hard rubber into her bottom until, at last, she felt the base touch her buttocks. Karina felt a sense of triumph at having accommodated the not inconsiderable length of erotically shaped rubber again. She held it still for some seconds, savouring the delightful feeling of fullness within her body.

She heard a noise, like the sound of the door to the flat being opened and shut. Sandy was back. Karina's first thought was to leap from the bed and hide her sin, but thought better of it. Sandy would no doubt be delighted to find her engaged in such abandoned pleasure and would, hopefully, be more than ready to join in. Karina began to move the dildo in and out of herself as she waited with excited anticipation.

The door to the bedroom opened slowly. Karina licked her lips and thrust the dildo rapidly in and out of her bottom. 'Hi, Sandy,' she panted, not wishing to shock her friend by her sudden unexpected presence.

But it was not her friend who entered the room. Instead of Sandy, a young black girl, dressed in the short white uniform of a maid, came in. The girl stood stock-still when she saw Karina lying there, her mouth and eyes open wide. Karina froze. There was a silent pause that probably lasted only a second or two but, as far as she was concerned, it could have been an hour.

'Pardon, madam,' the girl said at last, in a voice laced with a strong French accent. Karina lowered her legs and eased the dildo from inside herself. The maid's eyes widened even more and a smile appeared across her face. '*Il est très grand*,' she said appreciatively, as she took a couple of steps forward into the room.

Karina watched her close the door, unsure of what to do or say but feeling distinctly embarrassed.

'Would you like me to do it for you?' said the maid, her dark eyes twinkling.

'What?' Karina looked at the girl, shocked at her suggestion.

'Would you like me to do it for you?' repeated the maid. 'It's so much nicer if someone else does it.'

Karina's pussy throbbed. The girl was certainly beautiful, and her words had helped to ease her feelings of embarrassment. But the situation was bizarre. To be found by a complete stranger in a position of such wantonness was one thing, but to be propositioned in such a way was something else entirely. Karina looked at the girl for a moment, her mind racing.

The maid smiled broadly. Her mouth was incredibly full and her lips were remarkably prominent. She exuded an aura of sexuality that Karina knew she could not resist.

'I'd like that,' she said, breathlessly at last.

The maid moved towards her slowly. She unzipped the front of her uniform and slipped it from her shoulders, letting it fall to the floor. All that she wore now, apart from her trainers, was a pair of white panties and Karina saw that both of her long black nipples were pierced with tiny gold rings. 'My name is Michelle,' said the girl as she slipped off her panties and kicked them across the room.

'I'm Karina, I . . .' She stopped short when she glanced down between the maid's legs and saw that not only was her mound completely shaven, but each of the outer lips of her pussy was pierced with two more gold rings. The sight both shocked and thrilled her. She had heard of nipple-piercing, of course, but had never believed anyone would have the courage to adorn her most intimate parts in such a way.

Michelle noticed where Karina was looking and raised one of her legs so that she could rest her foot on the edge of the bed. Reaching down with both hands, she tugged at the rings, blatantly pulling her sex-lips apart. The outer lips were as dark as the maid's sable complexion but the inner flesh shone pink, glistening with juice. Karina felt her mouth go dry. It was the most beautiful sight that she had ever seen.

Michelle moved on to the bed and knelt beside her, resting her hand on Karina's stomach. 'You have a beautiful body,' she said, her strong accent making the words sound like music to Karina's ears.

'So have you,' she breathed. 'Gorgeous.' Michelle leant over and took one of Karina's nipples in her mouth. Her lips felt like a thick warm cushion against her flesh. Karina closed her eyes to savour the moment and, seconds later, felt the other girl's fingertips brushing lightly against the hot succulence of her pussy. The ache within her loins grew rapidly, the more that the maid teased her, and she knew that she would climax very soon. 'I'm coming,' she whimpered. 'I'm coming!'

Michelle rubbed her little bud rapidly while, at the same time, she slipped two or more of her fingers between Karina's soaking sex-lips. The orgasm ripped through Karina like a thunderbolt and she gasped with joy as she was transported to the pinnacle of sexual delight. She opened her eyes and saw that Michelle was staring at her, her expression one of sheer unbridled lust.

Michelle reached over and picked up the dildo. She examined it closely. 'I will use this on you in a moment,' she said suggestively, 'but first I must taste you.' Setting the phallus back on the table, the maid moved quickly down the bed until she was kneeling between Karina's outstretched legs. She looked into Karina's eyes and smiled, then pushed out her tongue slowly. Karina took a sharp intake of breath. The tip of the other girl's tongue was pierced with a small gold stud. Michelle licked her upper lip and Karina saw that there was another stud underneath.

Karina's first though was how painful it must have been to be pierced in such a way, but such thoughts were quickly dismissed from her mind as Michelle bent down and pressed her mouth to her pussy. She sensed the maid's tongue slipping inside her. It felt remarkably long, and Karina knew that if Piers hadn't split her hymen with his fingertip, then Michelle's probing tongue would certainly have done the job.

She ran her fingers through the wiry hair on Michelle's head and tugged her face against her groin, wanting her to delve even deeper. Instead, she sensed the tongue slip from inside her and suddenly felt it flicking rapidly over her tender bud. The difference that the studs made was unbelievable. Sandy's tongue always felt good, of course, but this new sensation was out of this world. Michelle had her sumptuous lips pressed hard against her and Karina could feel her mouth sucking the juices from her, while the maid's tongue fluttered incessantly over her clitoris. She came with a yelp and forced her hips even harder against Michelle's face, rubbing her cunt against the wide, suckling mouth. Michelle's tongue fluttered and circled around her sex-lips and then she sucked them between her teeth and nipped them playfully. Karina couldn't believe it – she was coming again! Her whole body shuddered and she reached up and squeezed her own breasts, pinching the nipples hard. The second orgasm hit her, and she threw her head back and gasped with joy.

Eventually, she collapsed back on the bed and Michelle sat up and gazed down at her. The maid's ebony features were coated with a sheen of sex-fluids and saliva, which made her look even more desirable. Karina took a deep breath in an effort to stop her body trembling. 'Wow,' she said, her voice barely a whisper.

Michelle reached over and picked up the dildo once more, along with the bottle of oil. Karina watched her with a look of excitement on her face. The maid tipped the bottle and poured the oil on to the head of the phallus so that it slipped slowly down the full length. Setting the bottle down, she smoothed the oil sensuously along the surface, evidently adept at the task. She moved to kneel at Karina's side and Karina raised her legs and pulled them back as far as she could, presenting herself submissively to her new lover.

'*Dans ton derrière?* In your bottom?' asked the French girl sweetly. Karina nodded. Michelle leant forward and Karina felt her fingertips touch her anus, before slipping inside her with remarkable ease. Michelle pulled back and then replaced her fingers with the phallus. She eased it in cautiously, but Karina found that her inner muscles gave no resistance whatsoever and the long thick dildo slid into her to the hilt. She once more experienced the wonderful sensation of total fullness as Michelle held the rod deep inside her for some moments, twisting and turning it in a way that sent pleasurable spasms coursing throughout Karina's lower body.

After a short time, Michelle began to move the phallus in and out of her, fucking her bottom with practised expertise. Karina raised her head and watched the implement appearing and disappearing in and out of her. It looked so big, and yet she was accommodating it easily. Each time that Michelle pulled it from her, her sphincter pulsated in an effort to draw it back inside and then, when it was slipped back fully into her welcoming sheath, the stiff rod appeared to touch something deep inside her that caused spasmodic waves of pleasure to emanate from within her, making her pussy throb with a hitherto unknown yearning.

Michelle bent forward and, while still plunging the dildo in and out of Karina's bottom, she started to lick her cunt, drawing the lips between her teeth and nipping them slightly then slipping her tongue deep into her soaking lush flesh. Karina reached down and fingered her little button, knowing that she was about to come yet again. At the same time, Michelle allowed her free hand to wander upward, over her flat stomach, until she cupped one of Karina's firm breasts. She nipped the hard nipple tightly, causing Karina to gasp with pain and delight, and then began to flutter the tip of her tongue rapidly over her throbbing clitoris. The studs did their work well and Karina came with a long low moan, the euphoric sensations making her feel that she was floating on air. Slowly, very slowly, Michelle withdrew the long phallus from inside the tight grip of her arse. When the head appeared, she moved it up slightly until it touched the open lips of Karina's pussy.

Karina grasped hold of her wrist. 'Please don't,' she pleaded. 'I'm a virgin.'

Michelle raised her head and looked her directly in the eyes, her expression showing that she plainly didn't believe her. 'Surely not,' she purred as she teased the outer lips of Karina's sex with the end of the implement. 'You are so beautiful. You must have had many cocks in there.'

'I haven't, honestly.'

'Do you only like women?'

The question stabbed into Karina's mind like a knife. In truth, following her experiences with Sandy and the intense desire that she felt for the maid, she was beginning to doubt her own sexuality and it worried her. 'No, no,' she protested. 'It's just that – er – I haven't met the right man.' She knew that her excuse probably sounded weak, but it would have to do.

'Let me do it for you, then,' said Michelle, her eyes imploring her to agree. 'Let me take your virginity. I will not hurt you, I promise.' She moved her face back so that it was inches from Karina's pussy and slid the head tantalisingly up and down the long slit between her sex-lips as she repeatedly kissed and lapped her tongue over the top of her mound. Karina's mind raced. Her desire to lose her virginity tore at her very soul, but this wasn't how she imagined it happening. Nevertheless, the flicking of Michelle's studded tongue against her hard little bud was forcing her to submit to whatever this beautiful ebony creature desired of her.

'All right,' she breathed, 'do it.'

She felt Michelle ease the thick bulbous head into her. There was a slight feeling of discomfort and she tensed herself, which made it worse. She began to breathe quickly and bunched her fingers tightly against the palms of her hands. 'Ow! It hurts!' she wailed.

Michelle stopped licking her and raised her head. 'Relax,' she said, in a warm Gallic tone. She bent her head again and resumed her delightful lapping at the top of Karina's pussy, then sat up to concentrate on the job in hand. Karina did her best, remembering how much easier it had been to take the phallus up her bottom when she had become less tense. She glanced down. The head of the dildo had all but disappeared into her glistening flesh. It looked remarkably similar to Piers' lovely big weapon to her, except that he hadn't even managed this much.

She lay back again and closed her eyes. 'Do it,' she repeated breathlessly. 'Please do it.' She sensed Michelle pressing the thing hard against her, and knew that it was sliding into her. She raised her head and looked down again. Over half of its length had disappeared, the distended lips of her cunt gripping the rod as if anxious not to let it go. The sight was so arousing that she relaxed completely. The remaining four or five inches slipped into her welcoming sheath effortlessly, as though her body had surrendered to the inevitable.

Karina looked into Michelle's eyes as the maid moved the phallus gently, barely allowing more than an inch to slip from within her before forcing it back again. 'God, that feels so good,' she purred.

Michelle smiled and began to move the rod faster. 'You like that? You like being fucked?'

'Yes,' gasped Karina. She began to move her hips in unison with the maid's insistent thrusts.

'Say that you like it, then,' demanded Michelle.

'I do! I do like it!'

'Like what?'

Karina suddenly realised what she wanted of her. 'I like being fucked!' She almost yelled the obscenity, not caring whether she could be heard through the open window of the room. Michelle started to ram the phallus in and out of her at an alarming rate, at the same time rubbing her clitoris with the fingertips of her free hand. Karina knew that she was coming, and that it was going to be a good one. The warm surge began to build up within her ravaged loins until it became a crescendo of nerve-tearing spasms, shooting throughout her lower body and down her legs. She screamed out loud and Michelle forced the dildo all the way inside her. Karina shuddered and trembled, tears running down her face as she sobbed with delight.

'Michelle! Are you in there?' The voice was harsh and distinctly male. Before the girls could move, he had entered the room. It was Rogers, the door attendant, and he looked furious. He glanced at Karina, who was lying spread-eagled on her back with just the base of the dildo protruding from her pussy. He glared at the maid. 'Michelle, I told you what would happen if I caught you doing things like this again!' he barked.

Karina moved to the edge of the bed and managed to slip the rubber rod from inside herself quickly. 'Please, Rogers,' she pleaded. 'Don't be angry with her. It was my doing.'

'If you please, miss,' the doorman replied, his powerful voice booming around the room. 'I have caught this slut on no less than four other occasions, although this is the first time I have found her with another woman. Nevertheless, she must be punished!'

'Are you going to dismiss her?' asked Karina.

Rogers grinned cruelly. 'No,' he said. 'There is no need for that. Michelle knows what to expect, don't you, Michelle?'

'Yes, sir,' the maid said in a strangely meek tone.

'Position yourself, then,' ordered Rogers. Michelle moved to kneel on her knees and elbows on the bed, with her superbly curvaceous bottom high in the air. Karina glanced nervously at Rogers and saw that he was removing his leather belt. She sprang to her feet.

'No, please, Rogers,' she implored. 'Don't hurt her!'

'It's all right,' mewed Michelle softly. Confused, Karina looked at her and noticed vestiges of a smile appear on her face. 'Honestly, miss, it's all right,' she repeated.

Karina stepped back from the bed, not knowing what to think. She watched as Rogers gripped the buckle and curled the belt once around his hand, before raising it high in the air. He paused momentarily and then brought the strap down forcefully. The crack of leather on bare skin rang out like a gunshot, causing Karina to jump. Michelle gasped, but otherwise made no protest. The belt swished through the air again and lashed across the maid's buttocks, making them quiver. Still she made no sound. Karina couldn't understand how anybody could withstand such pain without crying out.

Three more strokes were administered in quick succession. Karina looked at Michelle's face. She was wincing with pain, but at the same time she was grinning broadly. At last, Karina realised that she was actually enjoying the beating! Four more searing strokes lashed across Michelle's beautiful bottom, the sable skin now turning dark red. The last was administered with particular force and she gasped again, the only other sound that she had made during the course of her punishment.

There was another short pause. Suddenly, Rogers dropped the belt on the floor and wrenched at his trousers, tearing them down along with his underpants. His cock stood stiff and proud. Michelle glanced over her shoulder and then parted her thighs and forced her bottom up even higher. It was obvious that this was a game that the two of them regularly played. Rogers moved to stand at the foot of the bed and pulled her towards him by the waist. Karina watched in astonishment as his cock slid into her without the slightest effort. Michelle moaned happily as Rogers thrust wildly in and out of her, her body shaking with the force of his assault.

Karina touched herself between the legs. The sight of

the maid being so savagely impaled was arousing her to the point of distraction. She moved to stand next to Rogers, unsure of what to do or say but knowing that she wanted to join in. She watched, fascinated for a moment, as his groin slapped noisily against Michelle's bottom, the other girl's position being such that Karina could see every detail of Rogers' stiff cock ploughing through her new friend's dark silky sex-flesh.

Her own pussy ached and throbbed and her juices began to flow copiously once more. She grasped Rogers by the arm, but he seemed oblivious to her presence, so intent was he on hammering in and out of Michelle's pliant body as though his life depended on it. Karina ran her hand down his back and stroked his thrusting buttocks. He glanced at her, but his face showed no emotion other than rampant uncontrolled lust.

Karina glanced at Michelle and then looked back at Rogers. She realised that, although the maid had pleasured her in the most delightful and varied of ways, her real desire was for the man. She reached between his legs from behind and cupped his sweating balls. Suddenly, Rogers forced Michelle forward so that she fell on to her stomach with a gasp and his cock sprang from her, glistening with her juices and clearly as hard as steel. For a brief, marvellous moment Karina thought that he was going to leap on her and give her the same superbly rough treatment, but she was wrong. With a long, guttural moan he came, his cream shooting from the head of his cock to streak across Michelle's supine form. Karina's heart sank.

It was just at this moment that the door to the bedroom opened and Sandy walked in. 'Hi,' she said, in her normal nonchalant manner. 'Has Michelle been misbehaving again, Rogers?'

Six

'The freedom to enjoy sex without inhibitions or interference is a basic human right.'

The Honourable Charles Simons had been addressing the group for well over an hour, but certainly, as far as Karina was concerned, he might have been talking for mere minutes. She and her young friends had hung on to his every word as he expounded his theories of the continuation of the modern sexual revolution, based on the practises and beliefs of the Atca people of South America. The group were all sitting on the floor of Usha's flat like a bunch of schoolchildren, wide-eyed and fresh-faced, eager to learn more. Simons was sitting on a chair, delivering his talk in a stern and humourless manner, which underlined his firm conviction in his dogma. At times, his presentation had bordered on the evangelical, as though he were earnestly trying to convert his youthful audience to his way of thinking.

'The pursuit of sexual gratification and excellence must know no boundaries,' Simons continued. 'You must destroy any barriers that society and your upbringing may have inflicted upon you.' He paused for a moment and looked around at the seated group. 'Now, I want to conduct an experiment,' he continued. He leant forward in his chair and gently took hold of the hand of one of the girls, a newcomer to the group whom Karina did not recognise. 'Amanda, stand up, please.'

The girl got to her feet. She was of average height, slightly chubby with large breasts and a superbly rounded bottom, the shape of which was accentuated by the skin-tight jeans that she was wearing. Her face was pretty, her large eyes shining through owl-like glasses that were perched on the bridge of her small nose, and her glossy lips were formed into a permanent pout.

'Amanda,' continued Simons as he rose from his seat and stood next to her. 'I want you to answer me truthfully. Will you do that?' Amanda looked at him nervously and nodded. 'Good,' he said. 'Now, there are, let me see, seven young men in the room apart from myself. Have you ever had sex with any of them?'

The girl swallowed hard. Her expression was a picture of embarrassment and shock. 'What do you mean?' she said, her voice wavering.

'It's a simple question,' replied Simons, resting a hand on her shoulder. 'Have you ever had sex, have you ever been fucked by any of the men here?'

'I, I –' she stuttered. Karina felt sorry for her, wondering why Simons appeared to be intent on humiliating her.

Simons circled his arm around her shoulders. 'Come on, Amanda,' he said, gently. 'We're all friends here. Have any of the young men here in this room ever had sex with you?'

There was a short pause. Karina could see that the poor girl's hands were trembling. 'Yes,' Amanda said suddenly, her face colouring immediately.

Simons patted her on the shoulder and then resumed his seat. 'Right,' he said. 'Now, Amanda, I want you to point to any of the men here, anyone at all, but not someone whom you have had sex with.' The young girl looked around the seated group and nervously held out her hand and indicated one of the men. 'Come and stand next to Amanda,' ordered Simons in a tone that demanded obedience. The young man that she had pointed to grinned at the others and got to his feet. 'That's it,' continued Simons. 'Come and stand next to her. Don't be shy; she's a very pretty girl.'

Amanda laughed nervously and hung her head in embarrassment. The youth stood next to her, still grinning broadly, his smile a clear attempt at bravado. He was about six feet tall, with short ginger hair and a pale freckled complexion. To Karina's eyes, he looked like the archetypal student.

'Do you find this young man attractive, Amanda?' asked Simons. She smiled and nodded, then looked down at the floor. 'Come on, Amanda, look at him. Don't be shy.' She raised her head and looked directly into the young man's face. 'Now, Amanda,' continued Simons. 'Tell us. Tell us all. Would you like to have sex with him?'

Amanda gasped and looked at Simons with a shocked expression. 'I – I don't know. I mean, I think I would like to,' she said in a voice that could barely be heard.

Simons slapped himself on the knee triumphantly. 'Of course you would,' he said loudly, rising once more to his feet. 'He's a good-looking lad. You would like him to fuck you; in fact, you would *love* him to fuck you, wouldn't you?'

Amanda looked down at the floor again. Her face was flushed and she was trembling visibly. 'Answer!' commanded Simons.

'Yes,' she replied.

'And you, young man: what is your name?'

'Ian,' answered the grinning student.

'You would like to fuck Amanda, wouldn't you?'

'Definitely,' he replied, turning to face his friends, who were seated on the floor, and smirking like a schoolboy.

'Kiss her,' ordered Simons. The boy shrugged and took Amanda in his arms. Their mouths met and they kissed, the girl's arms remaining at her sides throughout the short embrace. The couple stood apart again and awaited further instruction. 'Touch her breasts,' barked Simons. Karina expected the young girl to rush from the room but she stood her ground. The boy's grin disappeared from his face. 'Touch them,' repeated Simons. 'They're big, and I can see that she's not wearing a bra. She wants you to touch them – don't you, Amanda?' The girl said nothing and just stood there, as if frozen to the spot. Ian raised a hand nervously and cupped one of Amanda's large mounds. 'That's it,' continued their tormentor. 'Take hold of the other one as well and squeeze her ripe young flesh. Feel her nipples hardening under your palm.' Ian did as ordered and Amanda closed her eyes and clenched her fists. She started to breathe deeply. It was evident that she was enjoying the sensation.

'Now, Amanda,' said Simons. 'Take off your T-shirt.'

Karina gasped. This was going too far. There was no way that the nervous young girl would do it, of that she was certain. To her astonishment, however, the girl grasped hold of the hem of the garment and quickly wrenched it over her head and threw it on the floor. Murmurs of surprise and approval echoed around the room. If anything, her breasts were even fuller than Sandy's and her dark nipples were as long as thumbnails. Ian stood transfixed for a moment, gazing at her superb mounds of flesh, his eyes wide and his mouth open. Amanda gave a slight smile. She was obviously proud of her impressive physical attributes.

'Feel them,' said Simons. 'Feel those magnificent tits.' The young man was not about to refuse. He reached out with both hands again and clenched the soft flesh tightly. 'Right, Amanda,' continued Simons. 'Stroke him. Stroke him between the legs.' Amanda began to reach forward with her hand and then stopped. She looked across at Simons.

'I don't think I can,' she said.

'Is it because all these people are watching? You wouldn't worry if you were alone with him, would you?'

'No,' she replied, her voice trembling. 'It's just that everybody's looking at us. Can't we go into another room?'

Simons leant forward with an earnest look on his face. 'You mean that you want to touch him? You want to have sex with him? You want to stroke his hard cock? I expect that it's already as hard as steel.'

The young girl's breathing was becoming short and stilted. She was clearly highly aroused. 'Yes, yes,' she gasped. 'I do.'

'Then do it.' Karina saw Amanda swallow hard and then watched as she tentatively reached forward again until her fingertips touched the front of Ian's trousers. She stroked his bulge and her breathing became shallow.

'It feels very big,' she said.

'You want him to fuck you, don't you? You would like nothing better than to feel that huge rod slipping inside your soaking wet cunt. It *is* wet, isn't it, Amanda?' The young girl merely nodded as she continued to stroke Ian's erection through his trousers. 'Take off your jeans, Amanda,' said Simons. 'He's going to fuck you, here and now, in front of everybody.'

Amanda pulled her hand quickly from the young man's trousers. 'Oh, no,' she protested. 'I couldn't! I just couldn't!'

Simons stepped forward again and slipped his arm comfortingly around her shoulders. 'But why not, Amanda,' he said in a gentle, caring tone. 'You want him to fuck you; he wants to fuck you; and everybody here wants to see you being fucked. So why not?'

Amanda glanced nervously around the room, took a deep breath and reached down and unzipped her jeans, then unclasped the belt and undid the top button. Kicking off her shoes, she peeled the tight denim from her body and cast the jeans to one side. Now all she wore was a pair of tiny blue panties. 'The panties too, Amanda, take them off.' She paused for a moment and looked nervously around at the seated group of onlookers again. She bit her bottom lip and hooked her thumbs under the sides of her panties.

Karina leant across and whispered to Sandy. 'He's going to make her go all the way,' she said, 'and she obviously doesn't want to.'

'Trust me,' breathed her friend. 'I think that I know what's going on. Just watch.' Amanda slipped off her panties quickly and then stood completely naked in front of Ian. The thick bush of hair between her legs was glistening and matted as a sure sign that, despite her nervousness, she was very aroused.

'Now, my dear,' continued Simons in his authoritative tone of voice. 'Kneel in front of him and take out his cock.' Karina glanced at Ian and noticed for the first time that the young man was looking decidedly uncomfortable. Amanda knelt in front of him and reached for his zip. She drew it down slowly and then reached inside his trousers. After a few fumbling seconds, she eased his penis from within his clothing. It was soft, which surprised Karina.

'Suck him.'

Amanda moved her face forward.

Suddenly, Ian moved back and brushed her hand from his limp cock. 'I'm sorry,' he said quickly. 'I can't do this: not in front of everybody!' He forced his flaccid flesh back into his trousers and pulled up the zip. 'I'm sorry,' he said again.

Amanda stood up and moved to stand next to Simons and clutched him by the arm. She grinned broadly as Ian resumed his seat on the floor, his face bright red.

'What you have just witnessed proves my point,' announced Simons, once more taking centre stage. 'Amanda here has been working for some time with me on my project. I brought her along tonight to demonstrate the problem that Western cultures have with sex. Our friend Ian was no doubt highly aroused by her appearance and her apparent reticence to submit to him but, when the time came, when he was actually about to have oral sex with this beautiful girl, he backed off. If they had been alone, he would have been fucking her by now. The Atca people have no such inhibitions. They have sex openly and at any time that suits them. They choose their partners at will. Either sex simply presents him or herself to the other and nature invariably takes its course. There are no recriminations, no thoughts or worries about infidelities and no jealousies. Theirs is a perfect world.'

'I'll fuck her.' The voice came from a young man seated next to Karina. He stood up and walked over to face Amanda. Karina recognised him as one of the men who had pleasured Usha the night before and knew that he would have no qualms about taking the naked girl completely in front of everybody. She was also aware that Simons would know this also.

'I think not, my friend,' he said. 'Ian must have another chance.' He turned to face the ginger-haired student. 'You do want to fuck her, don't you, Ian? Come on; she's waiting for you.'

All eyes turned to look at Ian. He swallowed hard and then struggled to his feet once more.

'Go on, Ian,' said one of his friends encouragingly. 'You can't miss a chance like this. Just look at those tits!' Amanda's other suitor moved reluctantly out of the way and Ian took his place, facing the now confidently smiling young girl. She put her head to one side and regarded him coyly.

'Would you like me to make love to you?' he said hoarsely.

'Of course she does!' snapped Simons. 'Haven't you heard a word that I was saying? Fuck her! Fuck her, now!'

Ian looked nervously around the room again and then seemed to gather up all his resolve. He wrenched his T-shirt over his head and quickly struggled to remove the remainder of his clothing. Once naked, he stood before Amanda and took her hands in his. Karina saw that his cock was thickening rapidly. Amanda let go of his hands and reached out. She gripped his rising stalk and moved close to him. Their mouths met. Amanda circled his neck with her free arm and Ian once again cupped her massive breasts in his hands.

Karina leant over to Sandy. 'Did you know this was going to happen?' she asked.

'I just had a feeling,' replied her friend. 'It was the way she took her T-shirt off earlier. She seemed too willing.'

Amanda broke free of Ian's embrace and turned her back to him. She bent forward slowly and rested her elbows on the chair on which Simons had been sitting, presenting her big bottom to Ian's hungry gaze. He moved to her and stroked the fleshy globes, then slipped his fingers between them. Amanda moaned softly. Ian stood behind her and bent his knees. From her position seated on the floor, Karina could see every delightful detail as the young student slipped his hard cock into the girl's pussy. There was a cheer from the audience as he plunged fully into her. Simons held his hand up for silence, clearly anxious that Ian should not be put off. It didn't seem to affect him, however. He began to thrust rapidly in and out of the voluptuous girl, her breasts swinging heavily beneath her as he fucked her with an urgency that could only have come from being teased so unmercifully.

He slowed his movements slightly and developed a steady rhythm while leaning over Amanda and grasping hold of her breasts. Somebody started to clap in time with his movements and soon everybody had joined in, encouraging him. Ian looked round and grinned at them. Simons moved away and smiled proudly as he sat on another chair at the edge of the room. The clapping increased in tempo and Ian matched the pace. Faster and faster, the rhythm goaded him to thrust ever more rapidly until, with a groan, he came. He rammed his cock deep into Amanda's welcoming hole and held himself still for a second, then began pumping in and out of her at a furious rate as he filled her with his sperm. A roar of approval went up from the crowd. Karina laughed and clapped her hands loudly. It had been a most worthy demonstration.

Following Simons' prolonged discourse, the gathering once again developed into a light-hearted party atmosphere. Usha produced a seemingly never-ending supply of wine and beer and Karina relaxed on a sofa, chatting once more to her old friends and some new ones. Amanda joined her and soon they were getting on with each other famously. She turned out to be an amusing and intelligent conversationalist rather than the shy, retiring little virgin that she had pretended to be at the start of the evening, and Karina quickly warmed to her. At first, it had seemed strange talking to her so soon after witnessing her making love with Ian, but Karina soon realised that it was her own inhibitions that were holding her back. Simons was right, she thought. People these days have far too many hang-ups.

'Where did you meet Charles?' Karina asked her.

'I met him shortly after coming down from Cambridge,' replied Amanda. 'I'd been studying philosophy and we met in the British Library, where I was working towards my master's degree. He told me about the Atca, and said that he was going to South America to meet with them and to study their beliefs. He asked me if I wanted to go with him. It was amazing. I'd only been chatting to him for about an hour and here he was, suggesting that I accompany him to the other side of the world! It was strange. There was something about his manner that I couldn't resist.'

'I think that I know what you mean,' said Karina.

'He's got the most amazing eyes,' continued Amanda. 'There seemed to be an instant attraction between us. It wasn't necessarily sexual but, I have to admit, I found him to be rather dishy.'

'Have you slept with him?'

'Oh, God, yes: lots of times. We ended up in bed together on the same evening that I met him. It was an amazing night, I can tell you!'

'Why? What happened?' Karina was genuinely interested. The young girl's casual attitude to sex intrigued her, and she wanted to know more. She glanced across at Sandy and saw that she was talking heatedly to a group of four young men. For a brief moment, she felt annoyed with herself. She was the one who desperately wanted to lose her virginity and yet it was Sandy who was talking to men, while she sat chatting to another girl. Nevertheless, Amanda fascinated her greatly. 'Go on,' she said. 'Tell me what happened. Tell me all the gory details.'

Amanda grinned. 'OK,' she said, 'you asked for it. It was really weird. I was staying with a boyfriend at the time, in his flat. Phil, his name was. He was at Cambridge with me and we just sort of drifted together. It wasn't the big romance or anything, but the sex was good.

'I invited Charles to come back to the flat for something to eat and to meet my boyfriend. I knew that Phil wouldn't mind; he was studying psychology and I considered that what Charles might have to say could be of interest to him. I rustled up a simple snack for the three of us and then we sat down to talk. Phil found Charles fascinating, as did I. All through the evening, however, Charles kept looking at me and giving me the most enigmatic of stares, which made my skin cover with goosebumps.

'The conversation was about sex, of course; that's what the Atca people are all about. Charles has the most persuasive way about him. He convinced us that fidelity was pointless, and that we should search for hedonistic pleasure wherever and whenever we could. He suddenly asked Phil if he agreed and he said that he did. "All right," he said. "Prove it. Let the three of us go to bed together. Let's give Amanda the fucking that she deserves."

'I couldn't believe it! I looked across at Phil, expecting him to jump up and thump poor Charles in the face, but he just sat there, thinking. I realised that he was actually considering the option and my pussy suddenly began to ache. Right at that moment, I knew that I wanted it and that I was desperate for Phil to agree.

'He looked at me. His expression was really serious. I just shrugged my shoulders, not knowing what to say. "D'you want to try it?" he said, all of a sudden. I pretended to think about it for a minute and then said, "Yes, please!" I remember the look on his face. He was really up for it, I can tell you!

'I excused myself and went off to take a shower, leaving the two men to talk. I remember standing in the bathroom, drying myself and looking in the mirror thinking to myself that I was about to be fucked by two men at the same time! It had never happened to me before and my pussy was dribbling, I can tell you! I was a little apprehensive, of course. After all, Charles was obviously a very experienced man and I wondered what sort of strange and kinky things he might want to do to me. I suppose the not knowing made it even more exciting.

'I didn't bother to dress after my shower. I walked nervously into the room, stark naked. Phil and Charles looked round when I entered and both of them smiled. "I've come to be fucked," I said, in a hushed and sultry way, trying to sound sexy. Both of the men stood up and walked over to me. I felt vulnerable and slightly nervous but also extremely aroused. I always get very, very wet when I'm turned on, and I could feel my juice trickling down the insides of my thighs.'

'I get like that sometimes,' interrupted Karina. In truth, she was already becoming extremely damp between the legs.

'Do you? It's a nice feeling, but it can be a bit embarrassing sometimes, especially if it happens when I'm wearing light-coloured, tight trousers or shorts and it begins to show. Anyway, on with the story. Phil slipped his arm around my shoulders and Charles hugged my waist. It was an incredibly erotic moment. I think it had to do with the fact that I was naked, sandwiched between two fully clothed men. Charles said something like, "You have a very beautiful girlfriend," and Phil said, "Yes, I know, I'm very lucky." I wrapped my arms around Phil's neck and kissed him passionately. For a brief moment, I forgot that Charles was even there until I felt his hand stroking my bottom. I pulled my face away from Phil and looked over my shoulder. Charles was gazing at my backside with an expression on his face that made it appear that my bum was the most beautiful thing that he'd ever seen in his life.

'He ran his fingers down my crease. I jumped when he touched my anus and he tickled me there for a second, then pushed his hand between my thighs. I pushed my bottom out a little and felt his fingers sliding against my pussy. I closed my eyes and I remember shivering. Phil kissed me again and cupped my breasts – he'd always had a thing about my tits. Charles wormed his fingers in and out of me and my juices flowed like they never had before. He crouched down behind me and kissed my bottom, then started to finger-fuck me quite rapidly. There were the most obscene, wet sounds coming from between my legs. Both Phil and I laughed; the noises were disgusting!

Charles said, "Your lady badly needs to be fucked." He stood up and dragged his wet fingers back up the crease of my bottom, then patted one of my buttocks.

'Charles moved away from me and began to remove his clothing. I carried on kissing and cuddling Phil for a while, enjoying the way that he was kneading my breasts and pinching my nipples. I'm very sensitive there, and it was doing wonders for me. My nervous feelings were gone; all I wanted was to be given a good hard fuck.

'Phil moved me away and took off his shirt. I knelt down in front of him and unbuckled his belt, pulled down his zip and wrenched down his trousers and shorts. He already had a full hard-on. I kissed the tip and then took his cock into my mouth. I rubbed my tongue backward and forward under the shaft. I knew that he liked that. "Easy, Amanda," he said, pulling my head away from him. "You'll make me come before we've even started!"

'I didn't want that, so I stood up, gave his cock a squeeze and then turned to face Charles. He was naked, sitting on the sofa and rubbing himself quite openly. I suppose that it was then that the full realisation of my situation really hit me. There was no going back: I really was going to be fucked by two men at the same time!'

'One would be nice,' muttered Karina, wistfully.

'Pardon?'

'Oh, nothing. Go on.'

'I sat next to Charles and he immediately wrapped his arms around me and kissed me, forcing his tongue deep into my mouth. I fumbled for his cock and rubbed him slowly. It was very similar to Phil's, except that the head was slightly larger. His fingers slipped into my pussy again and I felt him rubbing his knuckles against my clit. I was already close to coming and that final touch brought me over the edge. I gasped into his mouth and gripped his prick tightly. He stirred his fingers inside my hot wet cunt, making those awful noises again. Phil sat beside me and he circled my waist with his arm, while he fondled my tits with his other hand and kissed the back of my neck. I pulled from Charles and turned my head. Phil's lips met mine and we kissed. He pinched my nipples again and I sensed Charles slipping his fingers deep inside me. I reached down and grasped Phil's cock with my free hand. The three of us sat back and I just lay there between them, casually fondling two cocks. I was in heaven!

'After a moment, Phil leant over and began to suck one of my nipples. Charles followed suit, taking my other tit into his mouth. They put their hands between my thighs almost simultaneously, and I felt them both pawing at my pussy at the same time. This went on for quite a while until Charles slipped down to kneel on the floor between my legs. Phil moved his hand away from me and Charles replaced it with his mouth.

'As Charles lapped and suckled me, Phil stood up on the sofa and presented his cock to my face. I opened my mouth and took it in, careful not to lick around the stem too much in case I made him come. Charles worked on me with his tongue brilliantly. One minute he would be sliding it in and out of my cunt, tongue-fucking me, and the next he would be flicking it over my clit. He certainly knew what he was doing! I grasped Phil's bum with my hand and pulled him towards me, taking as much of his stiff stalk into my mouth as I could.

'Charles moved from me and, the next thing I knew, I felt his cock slipping effortlessly into my pussy. I was so wet that he slid into me completely with one gentle push. The feeling of having one cock in my cunt and another in my mouth was truly amazing! He fucked me slowly, with long deliberate strokes, while both he and Phil fondled my breasts and I continued to suck Phil's incredibly hard erection. I sensed Phil's cock throb in my mouth and he pulled quickly from me before it was too late for him. He sat down on the sofa next to me and I left him alone to cool down, concentrating instead on the beautiful way that Charles was gently fucking me. He had such a cool, practised style. None of my previous lovers had ever been so smooth in the way that they took me, even Phil. I could feel every inch of his thick cock as he slid it in and out of me. All the time that he was fucking me he was gazing into my eyes in that strange hypnotic way that he always looks at a girl. I honestly don't think he knows that he's doing it, but at the time it made me feel as if I was the most important person in the world to him.

'I glanced at Phil. He was watching what Charles was doing avidly, and his cock was sticking up from his groin like a flagpole. I reached out and grasped it, then kissed him lightly on the lips. "I want some," he breathed. Charles must have heard him, because he slipped out of me and sat back on his haunches. I rolled over Phil's body and his cock was inside me in an instant. He tried to thump in and out of me rapidly, but I forced myself down on him hard and crushed my breasts against his face, smothering him. After a moment, he forced his head up and gasped for breath, then nuzzled his mouth against my tits as though he was about to devour them.

'I began to move myself up and down slowly. Phil tried to match my movements, but I asked him to allow me to make the running, which he was more than happy to do. Charles moved behind me and I felt him stroking my bottom with his fingertips. He gripped one of my buttocks tightly and coaxed me to raise my body until just the head of Phil's cock was held inside me. "Hold still," he said. "Neither of you move." I sensed him fumbling between my legs and then, suddenly, I felt him begin to enter me. He gripped my thighs and forced me to sit down on Phil's lap so that I took the full length of my boyfriend's cock in my pussy, then Charles carefully eased his thick stalk into me as well. Two cocks in my cunt at the same time! I couldn't believe it and, from the look on Phil's face, neither could he. I'm not sure to this day whether he liked the sensation of pressing his stalk against another man's cock or not. I know that I loved the incredible feeling of fullness. They were stretching my poor little pussy to the limit! Charles began to fuck me, slowly, just as he'd done before. Phil matched his movements, while I just squatted there, sandwiched between them.

'Suddenly, Phil's expression changed from one of passive ecstasy into a grimace. "I'm coming!" he groaned. Charles immediately pulled out of me and Phil began to thrust up at my body wildly, his throbbing cock filling me with his cream. There was a deep groan from behind me, and suddenly I felt Charles' hot juice splattering over my bottom. It was all too much for me. I came with a yelp and rammed my body down hard on Phil's wilting cock. Charles pressed his groin against my bum and rubbed his stalk between my buttocks, while reaching round me and grasping my breasts firmly.

'Eventually, we fell apart. I knelt on the floor and smoothed Charles' juices over my buttocks, while the two men sat back on the sofa, exhausted. Their cocks hung flaccid between their legs, glistening in the candlelight. We didn't speak for quite some time; I don't think any of us knew what to say. We dressed and I made some coffee, which we drank in virtual silence. Charles left soon after, but I knew that I had to see him again. Phil was about to travel abroad, so there were no sad goodbyes or anything like that. Charles had taken a note of my phone number when he was in the flat, and he rang me about a week later. I've been seeing him ever since.'

'Doesn't it worry you if he makes love to another girl, or bother him if he sees you doing it like you did tonight?'

'Not at all. That's what the Atca beliefs are all about. I get a thrill when I see Charles fucking someone, and it really excites me when he watches me. Believe me, Karina, the Atca have got it right. It's only sex, after all.'

The party was beginning to flag and a number of people had already gone home. The young men whom Sandy had been chatting to had gone, although she had remained. She was sitting on the sofa next to Karina, sipping her glass of wine thoughtfully. Amanda had left with Charles and Piers, and Karina had wondered if the two brothers were going to be enjoying the delights of her new friend's voluptuous body. Usha had disappeared into one of the bedrooms with a couple of young men and, apart from Karina and Sandy, only a handful of rather inebriated people remained in the room.

'That Amanda told me a hell of a story,' said Karina, breaking the relative silence.

'She seems to be quite a girl,' replied Sandy. 'I don't know if I'd ever have the nerve to do what she did, in front of a crowd of people.'

Karina laughed. 'Oh, I think you could,' she said.

Sandy looked at her watch. 'Come on,' she said, rising from her seat. 'I've got a surprise for you.'

'What d'you mean?' asked a rather bemused Karina.

'You'll see,' replied Sandy mysteriously. 'Come on, or we'll be late.'

Karina got to her feet and retrieved her bag. 'Late for what? What's going on?'

'I can't tell you; it'll spoil the surprise. Come on.' Karina followed her out of the door. Soon, they were walking quickly down the street. Despite the lateness of the hour, people were still milling about the area. Karina clutched Sandy's arm as they hurried along. She hated London at this time of night. They passed two scantily clad girls who were standing in a shop doorway, clearly plying their nefarious trade. Karina glanced at them and the girls glared back at her. She considered that they looked younger than she was, and yet would probably have had more men during the previous evening than she was ever likely to have in her life. For a brief moment, she felt envious, but quickly dismissed such selfish thoughts from her mind. It was well known that the life of a whore in Knightsbridge was not all sex and champagne.

Sandy and Karina reached the doors fronting a large hotel. A uniformed attendant opened one of the plate glass doors and Sandy led the way in. 'What are we doing here?' asked Karina breathlessly. Sandy put her fingertip to her lips to hush her. They moved quickly through the elegant lobby, past the reception desk, and headed for one of the lifts. Sandy pressed the call button. 'I wish you'd tell me what is going on,' said Karina sharply.

'You'll find out, in a couple of minutes,' replied her friend. 'Just be patient. You're going to have a lot of fun.'

Karina shrugged and they stepped into the lift.

Reaching floor eleven, the girls stepped out into a long brightly lit hallway. Sandy checked the direction sign on the wall and led the way towards a door at the end of the corridor. Room 119. 'This is it,' she said. She knocked gently on the door. Karina heard the sound of shuffling inside and the door was unlocked and opened. A young man stood facing them, wearing a pair of tight denim shorts and little else. Karina immediately recognised him as one of the men who had been talking to Sandy earlier, at Usha's flat.

'Hi, ladies,' he said cheerily. 'Come on in.' He stood to one side and ushered them into the room. They walked through a short hallway, past the bathroom and into the main bedroom. Three other men were in the room, all dressed in a similar way to the first. Two of them were lying on one of the pair of large beds and the third was standing by the window, speaking on the phone.

'This is Karina, guys,' announced Sandy.

One of the men lying on the bed whistled appreciatively. '*This* is Karina?' he said, rising from the bed and walking over to them. 'My God, you didn't tell us that she was so gorgeous!' He took Karina's hand in his and kissed her fingers gallantly. 'Pleased to meet you, Karina. My name is Sam.'

'And this is Pete, Steve and Bob,' said Sandy, indicating the others. 'They invited us back for a late drink.'

Karina looked around at the four young men, feeling a little cross with her friend. She had already had more than enough to drink at Usha's place and would rather have gone back to her bed than sit up all night chatting to a group of strangers.

'That's a lovely dress that you're nearly wearing,' said one of the men, the one she thought Sandy had introduced as Pete.

Karina had chosen to wear a short black number, which clung to her slim body like a second skin. She nodded a 'thank you' for the man's inane comment. The men were all quite attractive, but he was, without doubt, the most handsome. He was tall, with a shock of near-black hair that cascaded over his shoulders. His complexion was heavily tanned, giving him the appearance of being of Mediterranean origin, but his accent was distinctly English.

'What are you drinking, ladies?' asked Sam as he opened the door to the fridge under one of the dressing tables.

'White wine for me,' answered Sandy, kicking off her shoes and sitting on the edge of the vacant bed.

'Just a mineral water,' said Karina. She sat next to Sandy and looked again at Pete. He grinned at her, his teeth flashing white against his dark skin.

'Sandy tells us that you live in Devon,' said another of the men. It could have been either Bob or Steve; she wasn't certain which.

'Yes,' she said. She took a sip of the water handed to her.

Sandy gulped down her wine in one go. 'Well,' she announced, 'I've gotta be off. See you tomorrow.' She headed quickly for the door.

Karina jumped up and followed her. 'Where are you going?' she demanded, panic rising within her. 'You're not leaving me alone with this lot, are you?'

'They're nice guys,' answered her friend.

'Oh, come on,' said Karina, gripping her friend by the shoulders, 'what are you doing?'

Sandy looked hard into her eyes. 'Karina,' she said slowly. 'Lighten up. Enjoy.' She turned and marched swiftly out of the door, slamming it behind her before Karina could say another word. Karina stood facing the blank panels of the door, her mind racing.

'Come and join us.' It was Pete who had spoken, his voice sounding warm and tender in its tone. Karina turned to face them. The four men stood in a row, each clutching a glass and smiling at her. She walked slowly back into the bedroom and sat down again on the edge of the bed. Pete sat down next to her and slipped his arm around her shoulders. 'Sandy tells us that you're a virgin,' he said, softly, 'and that you're not happy about it. Is it true?'

'She shouldn't have said that,' protested Karina. 'She really shouldn't have.' She was angry with her friend and her first thought was to run from the room, but Pete's closeness was having a profound effect upon her.

'She was worried for you,' he said, hugging her tighter.

She pulled away from him slightly. 'I'd better go,' she said nervously. 'Sandy shouldn't have done this.'

She turned to face Pete and she felt the colour

draining from her cheeks. His eyes bore into hers, sapping her of her will. He moved his face closer and gripped her tightly with his arm. She knew that it was wrong, but she wanted to feel his lips pressed against hers. They kissed, and her feelings of nervousness evaporated like dew in strong sunshine. He put his hand to her breast, covering it with his palm and squeezing it gently. Her nipple hardened against his touch, the thin material of her skimpy dress being the only barrier between them.

Their lips parted and he looked meaningfully into her eyes. She could sense that she was trembling, but the attraction that she was feeling for the young man was making her head swim. Pete stood up and began to remove his shorts. 'What are you doing?' she said in sudden panic.

Pete said nothing but merely allowed his shorts to fall to his ankles. He was now virtually naked, apart from his lightweight shoes. He kicked the shoes and his shorts off and then stood before her with a wide smile on his handsome face. The other three men followed suit. Karina's heart began to thump inside her chest. So this had been Sandy's surprise! She cursed her friend mentally, but knew in her heart that this was exactly what she wanted. The past couple of days had been a kind of hell for her, watching other people enjoy each other's bodies without once experiencing the same pleasures herself. Her pussy began to ache as she surveyed the scene of lusty manhood before her.

Karina sat on the edge of the huge bed, feeling more nervous than she had ever done before in her young life. The four men stood before her, naked and aroused, waiting for her to make the next move. She looked into their faces and knew that her moment had come. This time, she would not be denied complete fulfilment. She looked from one to the other slowly. Pete's physique was superb. He evidently worked out in a gym on a regular basis; his muscular torso was a picture of perfection in her eyes. Sam was shorter and slightly broader, but his erection was far longer than any of the others that were displayed for her to enjoy. Steve and Bob were quite unremarkable in appearance, but were nevertheless attractive, and the sight of their firm cocks was a joy for her to behold.

Karina made up her mind. Sandy had taken the trouble to arrange this little surprise for her, so why shouldn't she enjoy it? She stood up and gripped the hem of her dress. She eased the garment slowly upward, gradually revealing her body to the men's leering eyes, until she pulled it over her head and tossed it on to the floor. All that she wore now was a tiny black thong and her shoes. She stood for a moment, regarding the men haughtily. From the expressions on their faces, she could see that they were impressed. Pete stepped forward and slipped his arms around her until his hands cupped her bottom. They kissed again and she pressed her body against his in total submission.

She felt him hook his thumbs under the sides of her thong and he began to ease it down. She sat back on the bed and raised her legs, allowing him to remove it completely. He looked down at her and smiled kindly. 'You are going to be fucked, little virgin girl, not by one, but by four nice big cocks. What d'you think of that?'

In response, Karina slipped back until she was lying fully on the bed and lay her head on the pillow, her legs slightly apart.

Pete crawled on to the bed and knelt between her thighs. He pushed them wider apart and moved his head close to her pussy. He breathed in deeply. 'Such a beautiful scent,' he said.

Karina closed her eyes. Seconds later, she felt the warm wetness of his silky tongue playing across her sex-lips. He wasn't as good at it as either Sandy or Michelle had been – no man could equal a woman in that respect – but nevertheless she was soon aroused to the point of orgasm. She came quietly, her pussy throbbing and her juices flowing to soak his face.

Pete sat back and smiled at her. His face glistened with the evidence of her release. He moved to one side and Sam took his place. His tongue was soon worming its way inside her in the same way, delving within the folds of her succulence while he suckled her juicy flesh. Steve and Bob came and stood on either side of her, then knelt on the bed and presented their hard cocks to her face. She reached up with both hands and grasped them, then drew them towards her mouth. She licked the tips of each one in turn while gently rubbing the thick stalks, then took Steve's offering between her lips. She suckled him carefully, lapping her tongue around the spongy flesh of his knob, then let it slip from her mouth. Turning her attention to Bob, she performed the same oral magic on him, until she felt his cock throb between her lips and she tasted the saltiness of his arousal.

She drew her face back, not wanting to make him come. Gripping the two erections tightly, she moved them together until the heads touched, and then she snaked her tongue over them both. She opened her mouth wide and managed to slip both of the bulbous heads between her lips. If only Sandy could see me now! she thought. All this time, Sam continued to suckle and lap at her pussy, while Pete seemed content to merely stroke her breasts and her soft, flat stomach.

She sat up suddenly, almost knocking Steve and Bob from the bed. 'I want someone to fuck me now!' she declared, astounded at her own words.

Pete took hold of her hand and squeezed it. 'May I have the honour of being the first?' he said. She smiled, amused by the charming way that he had phrased the question, and she nodded, then lay back again on the bed. Steve and Bob took hold of her ankles and raised her legs, drawing them back until her thighs rested against her arms. Sam gave her one last kiss on her pussy and moved out of the way. Pete moved round to stand before her at the foot of the bed. She looked down at his stiff cock and at first prayed that he wouldn't come before he'd entered her; then she smiled inwardly at the thought. Even if he did come, there were three other men there, ready to impale her. Surely one of them would manage it. She was definitely going to lose her virginity this time.

Pete knelt on the edge of the bed and gripped his cock by the root. Karina watched as he inched forward until the head touched the tender lips of her pussy. She looked into his eyes deeply. 'Are you ready?' he breathed.

'Please fuck me,' she said imploringly. He pushed forward and she watched as the head disappeared into the pink, wet folds of flesh. It felt different to the rubber phallus that Michelle had used on her. It was harder, and more insistent in the way that it was forced slowly but surely inside her. She sensed the tip touch her cervix and gasped with delight. At last! At long last she was a woman!

Pete held himself still for a few moments, allowing her to become used to the wonderful feeling of having a stiff cock deep inside her. Karina clenched her inner muscles in order to savour every inch, every contour of his bone-hard rod within her fleshy sheath. 'Mm, that's nice,' he breathed.

'Is it?' she asked, with genuine interest.

'Yes, but don't do it too much. You'll make me come and I don't want that yet.'

Karina flung her arms around his neck. 'Neither do I,' she exclaimed. 'I want to be fucked and fucked until I can barely walk!'

'You will be, girl,' said Sam, who was standing at her side, witnessing the proceedings. 'Make no mistake about that.'

Karina grinned at him. She reached out and grabbed hold of his big cock, just as Pete began to move steadily in and out of her. She began to shake with lust and started to thrust her hips back at him.

'God, you're a wild one,' he groaned. 'Are you sure that you were a virgin?'

'I'm not now, and that's what counts,' she replied happily. Pete began to move with far more urgency, hammering his stalk in and out of her with practised finesse. She grasped hold of his long hair with her free hand and forced his mouth against hers, their darting tongues twisting and circling and their lips suckling each other. Suddenly, he pulled from her and withdrew his stiff erection from inside her. 'God, I nearly lost it,' he gasped, moving back from her.

'My turn,' laughed Sam. He moved quickly to position himself between her outstretched legs. His huge cock jutted forward from his body, the head seeming, to Karina's eyes, to be almost as big as a peach. She moaned softly as he entered her. It was far thicker than his friend's weapon and the size caused her a little discomfort, but she said nothing as he ploughed on until over three-quarters of his length was inside her.

'Jesus, you're big,' she gasped.

'So they say,' he replied proudly. 'Just relax. You'll get used to it.' He began to circle his hips, his cock probing and prodding her tender sheath, opening her up and relaxing her. Gradually he eased more and more of his superb rod inside her, until she was able to accommodate the full length.

'That's it, babe,' he grunted. 'You've got the lot! Ten inches of hard cock up your virgin cunt!' His obscenities thrilled her and the thought of something that size inside her made her head swim.

She reached out and managed to grasp both Steve's and Bob's erections in her hands. Pete, meanwhile, moved to squat behind her head. He leant forward and forced his hard stalk down so that she was able to take it into her mouth. It slipped over her tongue and touched the back of her throat. Gagging a little, she swallowed hard and found that her unusual position allowed her to take his cock further until her lips pressed against his hairy groin. She sucked and swallowed heavily until, suddenly, Pete roared and she felt his thick stem throbbing against her tongue and knew that he was coming down her throat.

His release seemed to signal something to Sam, because he, too, groaned loudly and pulled from her, rubbing his monstrous cock rapidly as his sperm jetted from the angry head and streaked over her sweating body. Pete eased his wilting cock from her mouth and she looked down. Her stomach and breasts were covered with streams of creamy fluid.

The two men moved from her and flopped on to the other bed. Karina released her grip of Steve and Bob's erections and attempted to sit up.

Bob put his hand on her shoulder. 'Not so fast, young lady,' he said. 'It's time for our little party trick.'

He got her to move to one side and then lay on his back on the bed and guided her to squat over him with her face close to his. Karina was so aroused by this time that she would have agreed to anything. She lowered herself down, thrilling as Bob's thick cock slid inside her already well-oiled pussy. She sat down on his groin and leant forward. She pressed her mouth against his and he circled his arms around her lower body and gripped her bottom. She wriggled her body against his, rubbing her hard little bud against his pubic bone. She was close to coming, and she knew that this one would tear her apart.

Suddenly, she felt Steve kiss her bottom and knew that he was kneeling behind her. She sensed him run his tongue over her buttocks and then sighed as his tongue slipped down the cleft between them to her anus. She held herself still and Bob began to thrust his hips up at her, driving his hard shaft in and out of her. Steve prodded her tight sphincter with the tip of his tongue and then licked wetly over and over again against the puckered little hole. The heat began to build up within her loins.

Bob was moving steadily, fucking her like an expert while Steve continued to pay oral homage to her arse. She felt him ease a finger into her, and then she felt the coolness of some sort of cream being rubbed into her. It reminded her of the baby oil, and she suddenly realised what they were going to do. The thought delighted her. He pushed two fingers into her and then what felt like three. Her inner muscles relaxed almost immediately to allow the insistent intrusion. After a moment, he removed his fingers and Bob stopped pumping into her and tugged at her buttocks, pulling them apart for the benefit of his friend.

Karina waited for the inevitable with bated breath. She tensed herself as she felt Steve's cock-head touch her anus and then forced herself to relax. She felt the pressure of him pushing against her, almost forcing her off her pleasurable perch. The head entered her and she gasped. Slowly and carefully, Steve eased more and more of his length into her anus until his stomach pressed against her bottom. Karina sighed with joy. Less than an hour before, she had been a virgin; and now three men had fucked her pussy and a fourth had his hard cock firmly embedded in her arsehole!

The two men began to move in unison, clearly well practised at such a pleasurable diversion. All Karina could do was kneel there and take it, and she loved it. They thrust into her faster and faster until, with a loud squeal, she came. Her juices flooded from her, soaking Bob's groin, and the muscles of her anus felt as though they were contracting and dilating rhythmically in time with the spasms within her loins. Almost on cue, Steve came with a gruff moan and she sensed his stiff rod throbbing, deep inside her bottom. As if adhering to some carefully scripted piece of choreography, Bob followed suit and pumped his cream into her aching cunt.

The sensation of having two men empty their seed inside her at the same time was too much for her and she came again, the nerve endings of her sex-lips seeming to be alive with feeling. She gasped over and over again and rubbed her groin against Bob's, in an effort to prolong the release but, at last, the spasms faded to nothing and she fell across him, exhausted.

Karina got very little sleep during that short but eventful night. As she ambled stiffly back from the hotel towards Sandy's apartment building, she remembered something she had said to Pete: something about wanting to be fucked and fucked until she could barely walk.

She had got her wish.

Seven

After gleefully listening to Karina's ribald tale of her wonderful night of lust with the four young men, Sandy had left her friend to doze on the couch while she went out clothes-shopping with Usha. Karina lay there, neither awake nor asleep, half staring at the ceiling and recalling every delightful detail of the previous night's excesses.

Her daydream was interrupted by the sound of the door to the flat being unlocked. She sat up quickly and rubbed her eyes. The door opened and Michelle, the French-Jamaican maid, entered.

'Good morning!' she said cheerily. 'Is it all right for me to clean the rooms?'

Karina rose stiffly to her feet. 'Sure,' she said. 'D'you want a cup of tea or something?'

'That'd be nice,' replied the maid as she tidied up some magazines and pushed them on to a shelf under the coffee table. Karina walked slowly towards the kitchen. Her limbs still ached and her mouth felt dry.

'You look like death!' Michelle laughed. 'Did you have a busy time last night?'

'You could say that,' replied Karina as she busied herself filling the kettle with water from the filter-jug. For no apparent reason, she pictured Michelle kneeling naked on the bed with Rogers whipping her lovely bottom with his belt. 'I'm sorry that I got you into trouble yesterday,' she said guiltily.

'No problem,' she heard the other girl say. Michelle began to sing as she worked and Karina retrieved two mugs from the sink, rinsed them and dropped a teabag into each. She leant heavily against the unit as she waited for the kettle to boil. She conjured up a mental image of Rogers pumping his stiff cock in and out of the lovely maid as she'd knelt in front of him. It had been a sight to behold.

'Is Rogers your boyfriend?' she called.

'No, just my boss. I live with a nice man in Peckham.'

The casualness of her response surprised Karina. She wondered how Michelle had managed to conceal the evidence of her recent infidelity from her lover's eyes. The strap had left clear marks on her beautiful ebony bottom.

The kettle hissed and spluttered as the water boiled. She filled the mugs, squeezed out the teabags and placed the drinks on to a tray, along with a jug of milk and a bowl of sugar. Still feeling a trifle woolly-headed, she carried the tray carefully into the other room and set it down on the table. Michelle was dusting the window-ledge, still humming some obscure tune to herself. Karina watched her working for a few moments, her eyes drawn to the curvaceous swell of her thrusting buttocks under the tight white uniform.

Michelle set her duster down and sat next to Karina on the sofa. 'So, what did you get up to last night?' she said as she stirred sugar into her drink. 'Did you go clubbing?'

'No,' replied Karina. 'I saw some guys.'

'Guys?' said Michelle, her eyes sparkling with excitement. 'More than one?' Karina nodded with a grin. 'How many?'

'Four.'

'Four?' cried Michelle excitedly. 'You lucky girl!' She

paused for a moment, then leant forward and spoke in a conspiratorial tone. 'Did you . . .?'

Karina nodded again, her grin becoming even wider. 'I'm not a virgin any more,' she said proudly.

Michelle cried out gleefully and slapped her hands together. 'Brilliant!' she said. 'Good for you! But *four*? That must have been quite – how do you say – quite an initiation!'

Karina nodded. 'Sandy arranged it,' she said. 'I felt like killing her, at first, but it was worth it in the end.'

Michelle sat back and took a sip of her tea. Her face showed a look of bemusement. 'Four,' she repeated enviously. 'I haven't done anything like that for years.'

'Do you like having sex with more than one person at the same time?' asked Karina, pretty certain of the reply.

'Yes; who doesn't? Paul – he's my boyfriend – loves to watch me getting fucked by other guys. We often have threesomes, sometimes with guys and sometimes with girls. You'll have to come and meet him. I know that you'd both get on very well.' Karina could tell from the salacious expression on the maid's face exactly what she had meant by that last remark.

'I'd like that,' she said genuinely. The thought of once more enjoying Michelle's gentle caress thrilled her, let alone the idea of having her boyfriend there as well. 'Does your boyfriend know what you do with Rogers?'

'Of course.' Michelle seemed to be astonished at the question. 'We tell each other everything. Why hide things like that? What's the point?'

Karina shrugged. 'I suppose you're right,' she said.

Michelle gulped down the rest of her tea. 'I'd better get moving,' she said. 'If Rogers catches me chatting, I'll be in for another thrashing.'

'You seemed to enjoy it,' said Karina. 'He really whacked you with his belt, and yet you hardly made a sound.'

Michelle smiled and stood up. Gathering up her cleaning implements, she turned and faced Karina with an earnest expression on her face. 'Pain can be quite delightful, under the right circumstances,' she said. 'You should try it.'

While the maid quickly dusted the room, Karina sat and sipped her tea thoughtfully. The look on Michelle's face when she had been lashed with the belt still haunted her. She thought back to her time at St Jennifer's College. The paddle had been used sparingly, and never by the teachers. She had only received such a punishment once, when she'd been caught by one of the senior prefects smoking what was to be her first and last cigarette. At St Jennifer's, such a misdemeanour was considered to be a cardinal sin.

The girl had ordered her to bend over one of the desks in the prefect's study. Her skirt had been pulled up to her waist and her panties had been wrenched down to her ankles. There had been two other sixth-form girls there and she'd felt acutely embarrassed at being put in such a humiliating position. At the same time, however, in a strange way she'd felt somewhat aroused at the thought of them looking at her bared bottom. The strokes had been quite severe and had stung her buttocks considerably but, as she'd walked back to class, she had been surprised to find that her earlier feelings of mild arousal had grown into an overwhelming desire for more of the same. Unfortunately, it was not to be. The college outlawed corporal punishment soon after her first taste of the paddle, and she was never again to experience the delights of its exquisite kiss.

Michelle left the flat and soon Karina heard the sound of the vacuum running in the hallway outside the front door. She made a sudden decision. She rushed to the door and opened it. Michelle was bending over the machine as she worked, the shape of her perfect thrusting buttocks clearly outlined under the thin material of her short white uniform. It was plainly obvious that she wasn't wearing any panties. Karina licked her lips. The urge to rush up behind the maid, raise the hem of her uniform and run her tongue between Michelle's ebony globes was almost overpowering. The maid turned and noticed her standing there. She smiled and switched off the vacuum cleaner. 'Is there something else?' she said sweetly.

'I really would like to meet your boyfriend,' Karina said quickly. 'I'm sure that it'd be fun.'

Michelle's smile turned into a lascivious grin. 'How about this afternoon?' she said. 'I get off in about an hour and Paul's not working today; he'll be home and I know that he'd be delighted if I brought you to meet him.'

'OK,' said Karina. 'Give me a knock when you're ready to go.' She went back into the flat and closed the door. She rested her hands against it and took a deep breath. In truth, the thought of enjoying the delicate, sensuous touch of Michelle's studded tongue lapping against her pussy was the driving force behind her sudden resolve, although the idea of having her boyfriend there at the same time filled her with nervous anticipation. She moved over to the sofa and sat down. She conjured up an image of Michelle's delightful bottom as Rogers had lashed her with his belt and once again wondered what the sensation would feel like. The expression on the maid's face had been one of total joy – and yet the pain must have been severe.

She heard the sounds of the door being unlocked again and hoped that Michelle had returned. Instead, it was Sandy who entered the room. 'You're up, then,' she said as she dumped a number of brightly coloured bags on to the floor. She moved quickly into the kitchen and Karina heard the kettle quickly begin to boil. 'D'you want another drink?' called her friend.

'Yes, please.'

The drinks were brought through and Sandy sat opposite her on one of the armchairs. She noticed the two mugs on the tray. 'Have you had company?' she asked.

'Yes. Michelle, the maid, was here.'

'Oh, her,' said Sandy. 'She's quite a girl.'

'I like her. She's invited me to go to her place and meet her boyfriend.'

'You know what that means,' said Sandy with a grin. 'They're into threesomes, you know.'

'I know. She told me.'

'Are you up for it, then?'

Karina nodded. 'Why not?' she said, trying to sound nonchalant. 'Actually, I'm going back to her place this afternoon.'

Sandy laughed. 'You've really got the bug, haven't you?' she said.

'I've had the bug, as you call it, for years. I'm just beginning to find the cure.'

'Are you going to see those guys you met last night again?' asked Sandy.

Karina shrugged. 'I've got their phone numbers,' she answered, 'but I don't know. I mean, they were really nice and the sex was fantastic, but I think I'd rather meet other people; you know, have different experiences.' She paused for a moment, then spoke again. 'Do you know anything about spanking and things like that?' she said.

Sandy nearly choked on her drink. 'Karina!' she exclaimed. 'You've only just lost your virginity and now you're talking about S and M!'

'S and M?' queried Karina, although she had a fair inkling as to what the term meant.

'Sado-masochism. Bondage; whipping; all that kind of stuff.'

'Oh, I'm not sure that I want to be tied up and

whipped or anything like that. Just maybe spanked hard or something, I suppose.'

A sudden look of realisation spread across Sandy's face. 'Of course,' she said. 'You watched Rogers giving the maid a taste of his belt! I've seen them do that a few times. She loves it.'

'So it appeared. She was talking to me about it just now. She says I should try it.'

'So, do it,' said Sandy with a shrug.

'Have you ever done anything like that?' asked Karina.

'Not really. There was one time, when I was at college, messing about with this guy behind the sports pavilion. He dragged me across his knee, yanked my skirt up and slapped my bare bum about six times. It stung a bit, and I must admit that it turned me on, but I wouldn't want to be whipped or caned. That would put me right off. I wouldn't mind doing it to the bloke, though.'

'Really?' said Karina, intrigued at the thought. 'You'd really like to whip a guy?'

Sandy nodded enthusiastically. 'Yeah, it'd be fun.'

There was a short pause. 'I think that I'd prefer to be the one taking the punishment,' Karina said, after a minute or so.

'So, do it,' repeated her friend.

'But how? It's not the sort of thing that you bring up in conversation with a guy, is it?'

Sandy thought for a moment. 'There are places,' she said eventually. 'Clubs where people of similar interests meet. There's one not far from here. Solomon's, I think it's called. I've never been there myself, but I know that Usha is a member.'

Karina laughed. 'That doesn't surprise me for a minute,' she said.

'You'd have to wear all the right gear,' continued Sandy. 'Stockings, leather, all that kind of thing. Look,

I tell you what: I'll give Usha a ring and see if she can sort something out.' She looked around the room. 'Where's the phone?' she asked.

'Oh, I think I left it in the bedroom,' said Karina uncertainly.

Sandy got to her feet and headed for the bedroom. 'Bloody cordless phones,' she muttered. 'I keep losing the damn thing.' She disappeared through the door, closing it behind her. Karina sat back and considered what her friend had said. She'd heard of such places, of course, and had seen pictures in magazines of women dressed in the most exotic and erotic of outfits. The thought that she might wear something like that herself had never entered her head before but now she found the idea to be quite appealing.

Sandy returned after a few minutes. 'Usha says that she'll take us to Solomon's tonight, if you want.'

Karina looked at her in surprise. 'D'you want to go?' she asked.

'I'm not sure if I want to go the whole hog,' her friend replied. 'But, well, what the heck; it'll be a laugh.'

'What about the outfits?' said Karina suddenly. 'I've got nothing –'

'Usha's got all the gear,' interrupted Sandy. 'We've to go round to her place first to get kitted out. Now, what's for lunch?'

As Michelle unlocked the rather shabby door to her flat, Karina felt a sudden pang of nervousness. Throughout their short journey on the train, their conversation had centred on the subject of sex, and she was feeling decidedly aroused: but the fact that she was about to meet a total stranger with the intention of going to bed with him and his girlfriend was disconcerting, to say the least.

'Paul? Are you home?' shouted Michelle as she pushed the door open. There was no reply. 'He must have gone out for something,' she said. 'Don't worry, I'm sure that he'll be back soon.' She led Karina into a small, sparsely furnished room, which doubled as both the lounge and the bedroom. It looked rather sad compared to the opulence of Sandy's apartment. Michelle turned to face her, a broad smile on her lovely face. 'We can get warmed up while we are waiting,' she said, holding her arms open invitingly. Her Gallic tone sounded like music to Karina's ears. The maid slipped her arms around Karina's waist and cupped her pert buttocks. Karina hugged Michelle around the neck and their mouths met. The kiss was long and passionate. Karina ran a hand down Michelle's back and caressed her superb rounded bottom as their tongues slipped wetly against each other. She heard the door opening but Michelle held her in the tight embrace.

A distinctly male voice broke the silence. 'Hey, man, it must be Christmas!'

Karina broke free of Michelle's arms and turned round to face the man who had spoken. He was tall, probably about six foot two with a complexion that was, if anything, slightly darker than Michelle's. His handsome features were accentuated by his large brown eyes and full mouth which, at the moment, was formed into a wide appreciative grin.

'This is my friend, Karina,' said Michelle as she walked over to him and kissed him lightly on the cheek.

He held his hand out towards Karina in greeting. 'Pleased to meet you, Karina,' he said. She stepped forward and shook his hand politely. His grip was strong but his expression was gentle and warm. 'You seemed to be getting on very well with Michelle,' he continued with a wry smile.

'Karina is a very sexy young lady,' said Michelle as she hugged his arm tightly. 'She couldn't wait to meet you, when I told her about you.'

'Really?' he said. He reached his hand up and stroked

Karina's breast with the backs of his fingers, making her shiver with delight. She sensed her nipple hardening to his insistent touch. He cupped her firm mound and she moved closer to him, all the time gazing into his eyes. Their lips met. Karina opened her mouth slightly and felt his tongue snake between her teeth. She responded in a similar manner and curled her arm around his neck. His hand slipped around her waist and he stroked her bottom through the thin material of her tight jeans. She pressed her body against his and felt Michelle nuzzling against her cheek with her pouted mouth. Paul squeezed her bottom tightly and then patted it and pulled away.

'I'm going to take a shower,' he said, moving across the room. 'You two can make a start without me.' Karina was impressed by his somewhat blasé attitude to the situation. It was more than evident that the two lovers made a habit of enjoying such encounters.

Michelle put her arm around Karina's shoulders. 'Come on,' she said. 'Let's get naked.'

Karina wasted no time in stripping off her jeans, shoes and T-shirt and quickly lay on the bed, watching Michelle as she slowly and tantalisingly unzipped the front of her crisp white uniform. As she had expected, the maid wore nothing underneath. Her superb ebony body was displayed to her in all its glory and the gold rings that pierced her long black nipples glinted in the warm afternoon sun. Karina glanced down and once more savoured the sight of Michelle's beautiful shaven cunt, the pierced pouting lips already showing signs of dampness.

Michelle lay next to her on the bed and, for some moments, the two women merely gazed at one other, while caressing each other's bodies softly. They could hear Paul humming happily to himself as he showered. Karina felt a twinge of excitement run through her, knowing that not only was she about to enjoy the delights of the beautiful French-Jamaican's body once more, but she was also going to be fucked by her remarkably handsome lover.

Michelle slid her hand between Karina's legs and her fingers slipped between the lips of her pussy. 'You're very wet,' she said. 'Paul likes that.'

'I can't believe that I'm doing this,' said Karina with a slight chuckle. 'I mean, lying in bed with a naked girl, waiting for her boyfriend to join us.'

'Lick me,' breathed Michelle suddenly. 'Please lick me.'

Karina wasn't about to refuse. She slipped quickly down and knelt on the foot of the bed with her bottom in the air. Michelle pulled her legs back and gripped her ankles with her hands. Karina gazed at the dark promise of her succulent cunt for a moment, and then bent her head and kissed the pouting lips passionately. Michelle groaned happily. Karina lapped hungrily at the wet lips, occasionally drawing them into her mouth and sucking them, swallowing the sweetly scented fluids as though she were enjoying a fine vintage wine.

Suddenly, she felt the warm wetness of a tongue sliding down the cleft of her upturned bottom and knew that Paul had joined them. She carried on sucking Michelle but paused momentarily and gasped as his tongue slipped between her own sex-lips. He lapped her for a few seconds and then moved away from her. 'God, you're soaked!' he exclaimed. 'I've just got to fuck you.'

Karina raised her head and looked over her shoulder at him. He was naked. His smooth sable skin was still wet from the shower and his cock was jutting hugely from his bushy groin. She turned her face and returned to the pleasurable job of tongue-fucking his girlfriend. She felt the tip of his cock touch her bottom and thrust out her buttocks in blatant invitation. His thick stalk slipped into her hot cunt with one slow easy movement, until the entire length was clasped within her welcoming sheath. She groaned, the sound muffled by Michelle's lush sex-lips. He felt incredibly large inside her, a thick, stiff rod of bone-hard flesh that seemed to fill every part of her. He began to fuck her slowly and, each time that he thrust forward, the tip of his cock pushed against her cervix, which sent mind-numbing waves of pleasure coursing through her body.

Michelle suddenly moved from her, turned herself and then managed to wriggle under Karina so that her mouth was directly under her groin. Karina once more pressed her lips against the dark lushness of the maid's cunt and thrilled as she felt Michelle begin to lap the hard bud of her clitoris from beneath her. The sensation of being fucked and licked at one and the same time brought her rapidly to the point of orgasm. She raised her head and her breathing became laboured. 'Oh, yes, oh yes!' she gasped. 'Fuck me! Lick me!'

As if sensing her impending release, Paul began to hammer his thick cock in and out of her, while Michelle suckled the fleshy lips of her pussy voraciously. Karina had no doubt that she was lapping against Paul's ebony rod at the same time. She came with a shout and another gasp of joy. Paul slammed into her again and again, his fingers gripping her waist tightly and his groin slapping noisily against her bottom. Michelle raised her legs and wrapped them around Karina's neck, drawing her face back once more between her thighs. Karina licked the top of the succulent flesh and fluttered the tip of her tongue against the prominent bud. Michelle followed her in blissful release within seconds and tightened the grip of her strong legs, almost smothering Karina's face within her oozing sex-flesh. Paul thrust against her hard and forced her forward, so that she collapsed on top of Michelle's body and his cock sprang from inside her.

Almost immediately, Michelle forced her to roll over on to her back and once more began to suckle her pussy avidly, while pressing her shaven mound hard against Karina's mouth. Karina nipped a couple of the tiny gold rings that pierced Michelle's sex-lips between her teeth and tugged against them, then once more lapped her tongue between the honeyed lips of her cunt. Paul moved to kneel on the bed behind her head. He gripped Michelle's bottom and raised her slightly, then moved forward, his long cock aiming directly at her lush opening.

Karina fluttered her tongue over Michelle's clitoris as she watched him slide his gnarled rod into her, his thickness forcing more of her juices from her to soak Karina's face. Karina arched her neck and managed to lick his tight sac, then traced the shape of his balls with the tip of her tongue. He thrust fully into Michelle and held himself still. Karina moved herself slightly and allowed her tongue to lap wetly over his anus. Suddenly, he pulled from Michelle and aimed the head of his cock towards Karina's mouth. She parted her lips and took the huge knob into her mouth. She heard him groan and felt his cream jetting to the back of her throat. She forced her head up and took as much of his length between her lips as she could manage and swallowed rapidly, feeling his rod throbbing against her tongue. This sensation, coupled with the fact that Michelle still seemed intent on devouring her aching pussy-lips, brought her over the edge once more. She almost bit into Paul's softening erection as the waves of orgasm tore through her and she dug her fingernails painfully into his thighs.

It was all over too soon. The three lovers lay in each other's arms on the bed for a while, recovering from their mutual pleasure. 'You must come and see us again,' said Paul eventually, his deep voice seeming to fill the room.

'I will,' promised Karina. 'I will.'

'Are you sure that you two want to do this?' asked Usha as the three friends sat together in the lounge of her flat, sipping wine.

'Why not?' said Sandy. 'It'll be fun.'

Usha looked at them both intently. 'Many of the members of Solomon's take these things very seriously. You mustn't tease them. You go the whole way or not at all.'

'Do we have to be whipped?' asked Sandy, looking a trifle concerned.

'No, not if you don't want it. Nobody does anything to anybody without his or her consent. I'm not sure that it's the sort of place that you think it is. It's just a social club, really. People dress up; that's all part of the fun. But, sometimes, nothing happens apart from a few friendly like-minded people having a drink together.'

'But things do happen sometimes, don't they?' said Karina, with a tinge of disappointment in her voice.

Usha smiled. 'If you want them to,' she answered enigmatically. She stood up. 'Come on, let's go into my bedroom. I'll see what I can find for you both to wear.'

Karina had been astonished at the amazingly erotic collection of clothing that Usha had presented to them. There were garments made of leather, others of rubber and even PVC, together with chains, buckles and an assortment of boots of varying lengths. Fortunately, both girls' shoe sizes were similar to Usha's, so they had no problem in slipping into her footwear. Sandy was only able to try on garments made of rubber on her lower body, due to the size of her breasts, as Usha was that much slighter of build.

The girls laughed and joked as they tried on the various items of apparel but Karina found herself becoming more and more aroused as time wore on. It wasn't just the thought of going to the club that excited her. With each different outfit that she tried on, thoughts of displaying herself in such a provocative and exotic way made her feel quite light-headed.

At last, the most suitable sets of clothing were

selected. Karina stood before the full-length mirror, scarcely believing the image that was reflected within its ornate frame. She was wearing a tight leather basque that was festooned with small steel studs, together with a matching skirt, which had a slit up one side that stretched almost to her waist and made it plainly obvious that she was wearing nothing underneath. Her stomach was bared, and Usha had fixed a length of thin steel chain around her waist, drawing it tightly to accentuate her curves. A good two feet of the chain hung at her side, almost to her knee. Round her neck she wore a broad leather collar studded with short, but very sharp, spikes. Her outfit was completed by a pair of high-heeled leather boots, which reached up almost to the tops of her thighs, finishing just below the hem of her short skirt.

Karina tried to imagine what her somewhat old-fashioned parents would say if they saw their innocent little girl dressed in such an erotic manner. The idea amused her. She turned to look at the others. Sandy had chosen to wear a simple rubber body-suit, which moulded itself around her sumptuous curves perfectly. Every detail of her body, from the contours of her superb breasts to the outline of her pouting pussy, was clearly defined. Her entire torso was swathed in the sensuous black material. The only other things that she wore were a pair of black fishnet stockings attached by rubber suspenders to the upper garment and a pair of remarkably high-heeled shoes.

Usha's choice of clothing was by far the most outrageous. She wore a black PVC mini-dress, which had holes cut in it to reveal her breasts, bottom and genitals. A pair of simple patent leather shoes completed her outfit.

'How will we get to the club, dressed like this?' asked Karina as a sudden thought struck her. There was no way that they could walk down the street dressed in this way, no matter how near the club was.

'I'll call a cab,' replied Usha simply.

Karina looked bemused. 'Are you sure that'll be all right? Won't the driver mind?'

Sandy laughed. 'This isn't Devon,' she said. 'There's nothing that London taxi-drivers haven't seen.'

Sandy was right. When the cab pulled up outside the club, the driver took the fare with scarcely a glance at the three scantily clad young ladies. They trooped up to the unmarked doorway and Usha rang the bell. An intercom crackled into life and she gave her name. Moments later, the door was opened electronically and they entered a small, dimly lit hallway. Another door opened and a tall young man wearing a formal evening suit joined them. He smiled broadly when he saw Usha standing there. 'Miss Khan,' he beamed. 'It has been some time. Welcome to Solomon's.'

'Thank you, Geoffrey,' she replied courteously. 'These are my friends. I trust that you will permit them to enjoy the facilities of the club, as my guests?'

'Of course, Miss Khan. Please, come this way, ladies.' The tall man led them through the other door, down another short hallway, and then drew back a pair of red velvet curtains.

Karina gasped. Ahead of them was a large room, sumptuously furnished in the style of a Victorian boudoir. There were a number of people sitting on the various plush chairs, sofas and chaises longues. All the women were dressed in outfits that were similar to those of the three newcomers and appeared to be mainly in their twenties or early thirties. The men were soberly dressed, their ages ranging from young to middle-aged.

At the far end of the room was a huge four-poster bed set on a raised dais. It was quite large enough to accommodate at least half a dozen people in comfort. There was only one occupant, however: a young girl wearing nothing but a pair of black rubber shorts. She was lying on her front, her arms and legs spread-eagled and her wrists and ankles firmly bound by thick leather straps to the four corners of the bed. There was no other person near her, and it seemed to Karina that she was there merely for decoration.

The three friends walked into the room and found seats round a small table in the corner of the room. The other women regarded them for a few moments, then carried on with their own conversations. The men, however, glanced repeatedly over at their table and, from the appreciative expressions on their faces, seemed to be quite impressed by their appearance.

Drinks were ordered and served. Karina sat back, hugging her glass and looking around at the other members. It had hardly seemed worthwhile, spending all that time selecting outfits and dressing themselves in such an erotic fashion. For all the attention that they were getting, they might just as well have been sitting in their local pub. In fact, she thought, if they *had* gone to the local that night wearing their exotic clothing they would probably have been surrounded by hordes of lusty young men within moments.

She was about to suggest to the others that they might as well leave, when the lights suddenly dimmed. A gruff male voice boomed out from the PA system. 'Ladies and gentlemen,' said the voice. 'Welcome to Solomon's. Let the entertainment commence!'

There was a ripple of applause and a single bright spotlight shone on the prone figure of the young girl lying shackled to the bed. Karina saw her wriggle momentarily, as though she were making a last effort to escape from her bonds. The girl turned her head to face her. She was beautiful. She had cropped blonde hair and elfin-like features, piercing blue eyes and a full sensuous mouth. Her smooth back was narrow and her bottom, its shape accentuated by the tightly hugging material of her shorts, was pert and boyish. Karina noticed for the first time that there was a zipper on the back of the shorts, as though they had been put on the wrong way round. It ran from the waistband, traced the line of the cleft between the girl's buttocks and disappeared between her slim thighs.

A gong was sounded and Karina almost jumped from her seat. The figure of a man appeared. He was wearing nothing but a small posing pouch fashioned in shining red leather, a long, red cloak and a matching cowl. He was tall and extremely muscular and the pouch was bulging noticeably. He stood at the foot of the bed and bowed to the assembled group of people.

A similarly dressed young woman appeared from the shadows and handed him something. Karina saw immediately that it was a tawse, two strips of thick hide bound together at one end. The only time that she'd seen such an implement before was during a visit to a museum of medieval torture, but she knew its purpose. The man slapped it across the palm of his hand, his action bringing murmurs of approval from the crowd. She noticed the girl on the bed struggle again and felt that she heard her whimper.

The man walked to stand at the side of the bed, facing the trembling girl and the audience beyond. He raised the tawse high above his head. 'Esteemed members,' he announced suddenly in a voice that boomed around the room. 'This young lady is my wife. I ordered her to give oral service to three of my male friends today, but she refused!' There were further murmurs from the crowd, this time of abject disapproval. 'What would you have me do with her?'

'Punish her!' said a voice in the audience.

'Thrash her!' said someone else. Karina glanced quickly around at the seated guests. Both the men and the women were leering at the form of the shackled girl, their eyes blazing with unconcealed lust. She heard the girl whimper again and looked back at the stage.

'No, my husband,' pleaded the girl. 'Forgive me! I will suck them all, I promise!' Her speech was stilted and her acting was terrible. Karina could easily tell that it was all a show, but nevertheless the atmosphere was filled with an ambience of pure sexuality. The dim lighting, the scent of leather and rubber and, above all, the sight of the huge man standing by the bed, his arm raised high and his hand clutching the wicked-looking tawse, all served to present an incredibly arousing scene.

She glanced across at Usha and saw that her friend was openly fingering her bared pussy through the conveniently cut hole in her dress.

'How many strokes shall I administer?' boomed the man on the stage.

Usha was the first to cry out. 'Ten!' she shouted.

Sandy giggled, clearly amused by the situation, but Karina sat stock-still, her mouth dry and her pussy beginning to feel damp between her thighs. The man bowed his head in deference to Usha's command. There was a long pause. The crowd fell silent. The only sound that could now be heard was of the prone girl's quiet sobbing.

Suddenly, without warning, the man brought the tawse down. The leather lashed against the girl's rubber shorts with an ear-splitting crack, which caused Karina to jump in her seat. The girl yelped with pain and struggled vainly against the straps that secured her wrists and ankles to the bed. A second stroke was administered, then a third and a fourth. Karina found that her eyes were drawn to the sight of the girl's quivering bottom. The tawse was brought down again and again and, with each resounding snap, Karina found her arousal increasing dramatically. She lost count of the number of times that the tawse lashed across the poor girl's rubber-clad bottom, but it was certainly more than the ten strokes demanded.

Karina glanced again at Usha. Her friend was

standing now and was rubbing herself between the legs rapidly, the expression on her face showing that she was close to orgasm. Karina looked quickly around the room. It seemed that everybody was fondling themselves or each other. She took a deep breath. If anything, the scent of the rubber and leather was stronger, enhanced by the delicate but unmistakable aroma of feminine arousal. She allowed her hand to slip under her short skirt and her fingers quickly found the wet, puffy lips of her cunt. She looked back at the girl on the bed and knew that she wanted to *be* that girl. She wanted to be tied up and bound. She wanted to be helplessly shackled to the bed and whipped soundly by some faceless, nameless person.

The man handed the tawse back to his assistant and then Karina watched as he slowly drew down the zip on the back of the prone girl's shorts. He peeled back the rubber to bare her bottom completely and then, gripping her by the hips, raised her backside as far as the constraints of her bonds would allow. Karina peered hard at her. Even from this distance, she could see that the girl's bottom glowed a deep red. She may have been acting her part but, the pain had been real enough.

The man bent over and licked the girl's bottom wetly between the cheeks of her buttocks. Karina heard her whimper again but, this time, it was clearly with pleasure. He was handed a small jar of cream, the contents of which he liberally applied to her cleft. At first, Karina thought the purpose was to soothe the girl's pain but, when the man's assistant handed him two large dildos, the real reason for his ministrations became apparent.

The girl moaned softly as he carefully slid one of the phalluses between the lips of her pussy. He eased it slowly into her until just the base was visible. That done, he took the second dildo, smoothed some more of the cream over its length and then deftly inserted it into her bottom until it, too, all but disappeared. He stood up and held out his hand. The other girl placed the tawse once more in his grip. He raised his arm and quickly brought the leather down hard on the prone girl's bottom, this time on her bare skin.

She felt the kiss of the tawse four more times and then, suddenly, threw her head back and gasped loudly. 'Oh, my God,' she cried. 'I'm coming! I'm coming!'

The crowd cheered and applauded wildly as the girl shuddered and trembled on the bed, clearly in the throes of a genuine and uncontrollable release. The spotlight went out and the stage was plunged into darkness. The applause grew into an uproar of cheering and clapping that went on for some minutes. Eventually, the lights were raised again and Karina saw that the bed was unoccupied and all the participants in the show had gone.

The voice echoed again through the speakers. 'Ladies and gentlemen. The management of Solomon's hopes that our little demonstration has served to inspire you. Enjoy the remainder of the evening.'

The voice was replaced by the gentle sounds of some light orchestral music. Three waitresses entered the room, clad in the briefest of costumes and each carrying a large tray. The trays were set down on tables in the centre of the room. They contained numerous items that were clearly intended for sexual gratification – whips, straps, dildos, beads and many other implements that Karina could only guess the purpose of.

Most of the members calmly helped themselves to one or more of the items. Karina watched one man, a pleasantly dressed and handsome person in his early thirties, take up a vicious-looking whip with numerous strands of leather splaying from its phallic-shaped stock. He examined the lash and ran his fingers almost lovingly through the thin strands, as though he were caressing the hair of a lover's head, and then walked back to rejoin a woman who was seated on one of the sofas. She was dressed in a similar way to Sandy, except that her rubber outfit covered her body completely, even the boots forming part of the catsuit. The woman smiled and took hold of the whip, evidently pleased with his choice.

Karina wondered if he would beat her while she was wearing her erotic garment, or whether he would force her to strip before administering her punishment. To her surprise, however, it was he who began to remove his clothing. Within moments, he was naked. The woman whispered something in his ear and he moved to lie prostrate over the back of the sofa, with his backside presented to her. She lost no time in whipping him, the lashes flying across his bottom and leaving thin red stripes across his skin.

Karina heard a crash of glasses falling to the floor close to her. She swung round to see another girl, naked except for a black hood that completely covered her head, lying on her back across one of the tables with a young man rapidly thrusting his stiff rod in and out of her shaven pussy.

Karina turned to Sandy. 'God, what a place,' she said.

Usha brushed past them and was immediately grabbed by two men who were sitting alone at another table. In less than a minute, she was sitting astride the lap of one of them, his cock firmly inside her cunt while the other man fed her mouth with his own hard length. Soon, it seemed as if everybody was involved in some sort of sexual deviation. The air was filled with the sounds of the crack of whips, the hiss of canes or the happy groans of women and men as their bodies were plundered by various instruments of delight.

Karina watched the scene unfold with a look of disbelief on her face. Never in her wildest fantasies had she imagined that people would do such strange but incredibly exciting and arousing things to each other.

She felt someone tugging at the zip of her basque and realised that it was her turn. She turned her head to see who it was that was touching her. To her surprise, she discovered that it was the man who had administered the severe punishment to the girl on the bed. He'd removed his cowl, and she could now see that he was distinctly handsome, with deep-brown eyes and angular features that reminded her of a comic-book hero.

'What do you think of our club?' he asked as he eased her zip slowly down her back.

Karina stopped him and pushed his hand away. 'Don't,' she said simply.

'Oh, come on,' he replied, once more attempting to tug at the zip. 'Nobody refuses anybody anything at Solomon's.'

She pulled away nervously. 'I don't want to do anything in front of all these strangers,' she said quickly.

'OK,' he said. 'We'll go into one of the private rooms.'

'What about your wife?'

The man looked around the room and then pointed. 'You mean her?' he said. Karina glanced in the direction that he was indicating and saw the young girl with the close-cropped blonde hair sitting on the lap of one of the customers, thrusting her body up and down as his cock slipped in and out of her oiled pussy. Karina looked back at the girl's husband and then glanced down at his lap. It was obvious that he had an erection. The red leather pouch was being pushed upwards ludicrously and she could plainly make out the shape of the bulbous head of his cock.

The man stood up and took hold of her arm. 'Come on,' he repeated.

Karina rose to her feet and looked at Sandy, who merely smiled and shrugged her shoulders. Karina was led through the mêlée of writhing bodies and out into the hallway.

'My name's Joseph, by the way,' he said as he guided

her along the corridor. It seemed strange to Karina that the man who had performed in such an enigmatic and commanding way on the stage should possess such an ordinary name.

'I'm Karina,' she replied quietly. He opened a door and led her inside. She stopped short when she entered the room and swallowed hard. Apart from a large bed, the only other furniture in the room was a small chest of drawers and a large wooden frame, similar in design to an artist's easel but far more substantial in construction. Its purpose was obvious, even to her inexperienced eyes. She turned and faced him. 'What are you going to do to me?' she said nervously.

'What would you like me to do?' His tone was subdued, almost caring.

'I – I don't know,' she answered. 'I mean, I don't think I want you to hurt me, at least not too much.'

He slipped off his cloak and threw it across the bed. He was naked, now, apart from the bulging pouch. His physique was superb, like one of the body-builders that she'd admired on television. She turned and walked over to the frame and ran her fingers over its rough surface. 'What's this for?' she asked, feigning innocence.

'I'll show you,' he replied. He caught hold of her hands and turned her so that she faced the frame. Raising her arms, he quickly drew a strap that was fixed to the apex of the construction and fastened it around both of her wrists. She tugged her arms but found that the thick leather held her securely.

Kneeling behind her, he grabbed one of her ankles, forced it to one side and stretched another strap around it and buckled it tightly, then repeated the action with her other leg. He stood up, and she felt him fumbling with the waistband of her skirt. Within a moment, he tore it from her. Now she was naked, save for her short basque and her thigh-length boots, and she was feeling deliciously vulnerable.

Joseph walked round the frame and stood facing her. His expression was stern and she was unsure as to whether he was play-acting again or not. 'I think you have to be punished,' he said in a low, husky tone. 'You're a very naughty young lady, coming to a place like this dressed in such a provocative manner. Do you agree that you've misbehaved?'

Karina nodded. It seemed to be the right thing to do. She could feel her juices slipping down the insides of her thighs. She was totally at this stranger's mercy. He could do absolutely anything that he wanted to her and she knew that she was in no position to refuse. 'Not too hard, please,' she begged. 'I've never done anything like this before.' She sensed him stroke her bare bottom with his strong rough hand. A finger snaked between her thighs and the tip pressed against the soaking lips of her pussy. She closed her eyes and sighed gently.

Suddenly, he slapped her bottom hard with the palm of his hand. Karina gasped, although the pain was slight. 'Naughty girls must be punished,' he said. His voice was trembling slightly, a clear indication to her that he was as aroused as she was. He slapped her again, harder this time, and then clutched her buttocks with his big hand, the fingertip once more slipping between her open sex-lips. 'You like that, don't you?' he breathed.

'Yes,' she replied.

'Yes, *master*,' he said firmly.

'Yes, master,' Karina answered dutifully.

He slapped her bottom three more times in quick succession. Her skin was beginning to sting by now, filling her loins with a delicious warmth that she'd never known before.

'Would you like to try something a little more painful?' he asked.

Her pussy twitched at the thought. She turned her head and looked at him through wide, watery eyes. She nodded slowly. Joseph moved quickly over to the chest of drawers and took out something that looked similar to a table-tennis bat but with a longer handle. He brought it to her and held it up for her to examine. Its surface was covered with pale chamois leather.

'I use this on girls who have been particularly naughty,' he said with a leering grin. Karina glanced down and saw that he had pulled his cock out from within the tight confines of the pouch and that it jutted upward hugely, his bulging sac supported by the garment.

'I have been very naughty,' she whispered, happy to join him in his game. She looked down again pointedly at his cock. 'And I'm going to be even naughtier later.' She watched him as he raised the bat high and then turned her head away and pushed her bottom out in readiness for the first stroke. It came with a resounding slap and stung terribly. Karina gritted her teeth and waited for the second blow. It came quickly, followed by three more. The heat within her lower body grew more and more with each stroke, building up towards a crescendo. One more thwack of the bat against her hot bottom was enough to take her over the edge. She came with a squeal of joy, her shuddering body causing the heavy frame to creak under her weight.

As she calmed down, she sensed him stroking her stinging buttocks gently with his fingertips. He put the fingers of his free hand under her chin and turned her face to his. 'I think you're ready to return to the other room,' he breathed.

'Are you going to tie me to the bed in there?' she asked, her eyes imploring him to do just that. He nodded and she smiled happily. She was more than ready to do whatever he asked of her. He unbuckled her restraints and led her, still half-naked, back into the main room. The bacchanalia was still in progress, and it took them some moments to struggle through the mêlée to reach the great bed. He shackled her quickly until she was held in exactly the same position to that which had been assumed by his wife. That done, he stood and faced the crowd. He clapped his hands loudly.

'Can I have your attention, please?' he shouted. His words made little difference. 'Silence!' he bellowed. A sudden hush descended on the mass of half-naked people littered around the room. From her prone position, Karina managed to notice Sandy, sitting between two young men on a nearby couch. Her rubber body-suit had been removed so that all she now wore was the pair of fishnet stockings and her shoes. Her hair was dishevelled and she was holding both men's cocks in her hands. Clearly, she hadn't wasted any time in joining in with the fun. 'This lovely young lady has just been introduced to the pleasures of pain,' continued Joseph, 'and she has asked that her initiation be continued in the sight of you all.'

He moved to stand beside the bed and snapped his fingers. Immediately, Karina felt the heat of the spotlight on her back. She looked over her shoulders and saw that he was holding the tawse, the same one that he'd used to chastise his wife. Her bottom already stung from the beating that she'd received from the bat, but she knew that this was going to be much worse. She felt both nervous and overwhelmingly excited at the prospect. He raised the scourge high above his head. The room remained in total silence. It was as if the people were reluctant to breathe, lest they ruin the ambience of the moment for her.

Karina heard the crack of the leather against her skin and the pain seared across her bottom. The sensation was like nothing that she could have imagined. It hurt, it hurt a lot, but the stinging pain seemed to mingle with the euphoric spasms of delight that were coursing through her loins. She knew that she would come again, very soon. It took just one more lash of the tawse against her tortured flesh to bring her to the point of no return. Her juices flowed from her cunt to soak the bed beneath her and waves of pain and joy swept throughout her body, tearing at every nerve-ending and filling her mind with total bliss. The crowd roared its approval and she began to sob tears of joy.

Satisfied that he'd done his job well, her tormentor threw down the tawse and knelt on the bed behind her. Karina felt him stroking her aching buttocks again and then felt the now familiar touch of a cock-head to her open sex-lips. He slid into her with ease, filling her throbbing sheath with his thick length. She thrust her buttocks up to take him as deep as she could and he began to pound into her like a man possessed. His groin slapped against her hot little bottom over and over again until, with a low moan, he suddenly pulled from her and she felt his warm, creamy sperm spraying over her buttocks. He smoothed the fluid over her bottom, which had a soothing effect on her still-stinging flesh, and then he bent over her and kissed her lightly on the back of her head. 'Welcome to Solomon's,' he said.

For a few minutes, Karina couldn't remember where she was and then it came to her. She was still at the club, and was still lying on the huge bed, although her wrists and ankles had been freed from their bonds. She opened her eyes slowly and blinked in the fierce light. It was morning, and someone had drawn the curtains back to let in the daylight. The heat of the sun was already making the room feel unbearable. She raised her head and looked around her. There seemed to be naked bodies everywhere, limbs entwined and fingertips caressing soft smooth skin. She looked at a young man who was lying next to her and realised, to her horror, that she couldn't even remember his name.

She pulled herself stiffly up to a sitting position.

Sandy was still fast asleep, lying at the foot of the bed, her head cushioned against a naked man's groin with his limp cock resting against her lips. Karina swung her legs over the bed and pulled herself up to a standing position on the floor. She suddenly felt dizzy and clutched one of the bedposts for support. 'God, how much did I drink last night?' she said to no one in particular.

She staggered across the room, urgently needing to find a bathroom. She was met at the door by the man who had admitted them to the club the night before. He appeared to be remarkably fresh, considering that he had probably been awake all night.

'Bathroom,' she managed to say hoarsely.

The man indicated a door at the end of the hallway with a wave of his hand. Karina rushed down the corridor and tried the handle. It was locked. She leant heavily against the wall, the urge to pee becoming more and more pressing. Thankfully, the door opened after a moment. Usha appeared from the bathroom. She was naked, and looked exhausted. She smiled weakly when she saw Karina standing there.

'You look as bad as I feel,' she said.

Karina sleepily waved her away and almost fell into the bathroom, locking the door behind her. She sat down on the toilet, desperate to take a pee. Her bottom stung, but it was nothing compared to the throbbing ache that she felt between her legs and she wondered just how many men had entered her newly deflowered little hole during the previous night. Any inhibitions that had remained within her had disappeared forever as she'd enjoyed one stiff cock after another, until her exhaustion and the effects of the wine had forced her into a deep slumber.

She flushed the cistern and stood up to look at herself in the long mirror on the far wall. She looked a wreck. The basque had long been ripped from her body and all that she now wore was the pair of thigh-length boots.

She smiled to herself. Two days previously she had been a virgin, desperate to savour the delights of sex. Today, she felt as if she never wanted to be fucked again.

Eight

Karina managed to stay true to her vow of celibacy for close on three days. During that time, she and Sandy spent most of the days scouring the Knightsbridge shops for bargains and the evenings visiting numerous clubs and pubs in the area. The subject of sex was never far away from their conversation, of course, and Karina took immense, if envious pleasure in hearing about Sandy's many conquests. It appeared to her that, while she had been busy studying for her examinations or participating in team games on the college playing field, her friend had been constantly indulging in far more entertaining and salacious pursuits.

It was on the morning of the third day that Karina woke from a fitful sleep with an incredible ache of desire between her legs. She had had similar feelings before – many times, in fact, but this time the urge was altogether more powerful than anything that she had previously experienced. She opened her eyes and looked across at Sandy, who was lying sound asleep on her back next to her. Her friend's large, firm breasts rose and fell with a gentle slow rhythm and her nipples looked enticingly suckable. Karina reached over and gently stroked Sandy's cheek, but the other girl merely murmured something incoherently and turned over to lie on her stomach. It was evident to Karina that further attention from her would be unwelcome.

She lay on her back and stared at the ceiling. The powerful surge of desire and the feeling of emptiness within her loins were becoming unbearable. She couldn't understand it. She had spent years of excited innocence, wondering what it would feel like to be fucked and now, after at last enjoying the ultimate delights of sexual awakening, her craving for more was becoming uncontrollable. She allowed her hand to slip down between her legs. Her fingertips touched the fleshy lips of her pussy and she was surprised to find how wet she was. She couldn't remember dreaming any erotic fantasies, and yet she was as aroused as if she had been licked for hours by the most expert of tongues.

The moist hole opened for her and she slipped all four fingers inside the soft purse of flesh, while pressing her thumb hard against the stiff bud of her clitoris. A sharp thrill akin to an electric shock shot through her lower body, causing her to gasp aloud. She glanced quickly across at her sleeping friend, but Sandy remained soundly asleep. Confident that her activities would not cause a problem, she rubbed the tip of her thumb against her bud, while probing as deep inside herself as she could with her fingers. The urge for deeper penetration grew by the second.

Raising her legs high into the air she bunched her fingers and thumb together and pushed hard. Her hand slipped gently into the soaking sheath until her outer lips gripped her wrist. She lay still for a moment to savour the delightful sensation of fullness and then began to move her hand slowly up and down, imitating the insistent penetration of some unseen lover. She licked the fingers of her free hand and then slipped it under herself. She eased her middle finger into her anus, the ring of muscle relaxing immediately, welcoming the now familiar intrusion.

Forming her other hand into a fist, she forced it deeper into her pussy as she felt the heat of her arousal growing to a climax. She managed to worm a second finger into her bottom and suddenly the spasms of release tore through her. Unable to control herself, she cried out as the orgasm took hold of her senses and she rammed her fist in and out of her cunt as fast as she could. For a few, blissful seconds, she forgot that Sandy was lying next to her as she fist-fucked herself until, at last, the feelings of joyous release began to subside.

Sweating profusely and panting for breath, she relaxed back on the bed and once more glanced across at Sandy. Her friend was well and truly awake now, and grinning broadly at her. 'Did you enjoy that?' Sandy asked with a slight laugh. Karina nodded.

'I needed that,' she said, her voice trembling with emotion.

Sandy looked down and watched as she eased her hand from inside herself. 'So I see,' her friend said. 'D'you want me to do anything for you?'

Karina shook her head. 'No, I'm fine,' she said, raising herself to a sitting position and swinging her legs out of the bed. 'I'm going to take a shower.' She pulled herself awkwardly to a standing position and clutched the bedside table for support for a moment. Her pussy was throbbing and her inner thighs were soaked.

'Shall we go to Usha's place, tonight?' asked Sandy, her meaning blatantly clear from the tone of her voice.

Karina nodded. 'I think we'd better,' she said with a weak laugh.

Charles Simons opened the door to Usha's flat. He kissed Sandy lightly on the cheek and stood aside as she entered, then turned and regarded Karina coldly. 'We thought that you must have returned to Devon,' he said sharply.

Karina was taken aback by his tone. 'No,' she replied. 'Sandy and I have been busy.' She made to push past him but he caught her by the arm.

'I don't think that you should join the group tonight,' he said.

'What's the matter, Charles?' asked Sandy. 'Aren't we welcome?'

Simons responded to her question without turning to face her, his piercing eyes continuing to hold Karina's gaze. 'You are welcome, Miss Harrison, but I feel that the proceedings will not be to Miss Devonside's liking.'

Sandy moved forward and rested her hand on his shoulder. 'Why so formal, Charles? And why shouldn't Karina enjoy it?'

Simons let go his grip of Karina's arm and turned to face Sandy. 'The group has been studying the ways of the Atca in some detail over the past two days. All inhibitions have been lost. This is no place for a virgin.'

Sandy glanced at Karina knowingly. 'You have no need to worry about that any more,' she said with a grin.

Simons looked genuinely surprised. 'Really?' he said.

'Really,' said Karina firmly.

Simons allowed a slight smile to play across his lips. 'Nevertheless,' he said after a moment, 'you are still inexperienced. You will find that some of the indulgences practised by your peers may not be to your taste.'

Karina pulled herself to her full height and regarded him haughtily. 'Allow me to be the judge of that,' she said.

Simons shrugged and motioned for the girls to enter the lounge.

A few flickering candles dimly lighted the room and all of the furniture had been moved against the walls. A group of about twenty young people was sitting in a wide circle on the carpet, all of them completely naked and with their heads bowed, as if in prayer. 'What are they –' began Sandy.

Simons gripped her shoulder. 'Silence!' he hissed.

'The group is meditating, preparing for the pleasures to come. If you wish to stay, remove your clothing and join them.'

Karina looked anxiously at Sandy, who appeared to be considering the matter carefully. As far as Karina was concerned, the thought of stripping her clothing off and joining twenty or so naked young people on the floor excited her immensely. She began to unbutton her blouse. Sandy shrugged her shoulders and followed suit, and soon the two girls were as naked as their seated friends were. Only Simons remained fully clothed. He moved to stand in the centre of the circle, while Karina and Sandy sat on the plush carpet between two young men who had shuffled to one side to accommodate them. Karina looked quickly around at the circle of nakedness. Usha was sitting almost directly opposite her and, although her eyes were open, she didn't appear to see her. Her eyes were glazed, as though she were held in some sort of trance.

Simons stood silently, his hands clasped together and his head bowed. To Karina, he looked for all the world like a high priest at some unearthly coven. She began to feel uncomfortable, but at the same time she sensed an aura of sexuality that pervaded the very atmosphere of the room. She glanced at the young man who was seated next to her. She'd seen him before at one of Usha's parties, but hadn't yet spoken to him. He was about twenty years of age with a smooth, slim body and short-cropped hair. She looked down. His cock was in a state of semi-erection and was lying heavily on his thigh. Resisting the sudden temptation to reach out and grasp it, she turned her head and once more looked up at Simons. In the flickering candlelight, he looked even more handsome than ever before. She remembered the feel of his stiff cock against her tongue and the taste of his sperm and the ache returned between her legs to plague her thoughts.

Suddenly, Simons raised his hands high into the air. 'It is time,' he said in a hushed voice.

As if snapping out of some sort of mass hypnotic trance, the members of the group all raised their heads and looked up at him. He smiled benevolently and then stepped out of the circle and took up a small high-backed chair. He returned to his position at the centre and placed the chair in front of him. He stood for a moment, resting his hands on the back of the chair and looking slowly around at the seated group. Karina could see that they were all waiting in eager anticipation.

'We have a newcomer to our esteemed gathering,' began Simons in a sombre and authoritative tone. 'Come forward, Anna.'

Karina was somewhat relieved that he hadn't been referring to her. She hadn't cared for his disdainful greeting and wasn't ready to submit herself to further humiliation. She watched as a young girl got to her feet and walked slowly to stand before him. The girl was probably a couple of years younger than she was, small-built with tiny breasts but remarkably long dark nipples. Her hair was white-blonde and very long, cascading over her narrow shoulders and almost reaching her waist. Her legs were long and slim and her small bottom was boyishly pert.

Simons placed his hands on her shoulders and turned her so that she had her back to the chair. 'Anna is another student of mine,' said Simons as he motioned to her to sit down. 'She is a little shy, so you must be patient with her.' Now seated, the young girl gazed up at him through wide adoring eyes. He reached down and caught hold of one of her legs and then raised it until she rested her heel on the edge of the chair-seat. He did the same with her other leg and moved her knees apart so that the lips of her sex were fully exposed.

He moved to stand behind the chair once more.

Those of the group who were sitting behind him shuffled quickly round to kneel in front of her.

Karina looked around and saw that every single one of the males present was now sporting a full erection. She looked back at the girl on the chair. Apart from a small tuft of hair at the top, Anna's pussy was completely shaven. It looked so tiny. Karina could hardly imagine any of the dozen or so stiff cocks managing to slip into it without causing the young girl intense discomfort, but she also knew that if Anna was one of Simons' students, then it was highly likely that she was very experienced in matters of the flesh.

'Now, Anna,' began Simons slowly. 'I want you to masturbate. I want you to show the others how proud you are of your tight little pussy and to demonstrate what happens when you come.' He looked at the assembled audience. 'Come closer if you wish, but do not touch her in any way.'

A couple of the men present moved forward and crouched on their knees to gaze at the lovely sight between Anna's widely splayed legs. They were so close that it became necessary for Karina to sit up straight, in order to savour the same view. Anna licked her fingertips and then began to caress the shaven lips of her cunt. She closed her eyes and let her head loll to one side, clearly enjoying her self-stimulation. Karina watched in amazement as her sex-lips became more and more prominent, swelling quite remarkably to become cushions of wet inviting flesh.

Anna used the fingers of her other hand to tug the lips apart, displaying her most intimate treasures to the gaze of the others. Karina could plainly see her juices beginning to flow, the cream glinting in the candlelight as it trickled from the open hole and slipped down the crease of her bottom. Karina touched herself between the legs and found, with little surprise, that her own pussy was already becoming very moist. She licked her lips, feeling a compelling urge to throw herself on the carpet between Anna's legs and to suckle the juicy prize that seemed to be getting more succulent by the second.

Anna began to groan quietly. She delved two fingers between her sex-lips and started to finger-fuck herself while, at the same time, continuing to stimulate her clitoris with her other hand. Suddenly, she threw her head back and moaned loudly, a long, guttural sigh that sounded almost ethereal. Karina stared at her pussy. The lips had become bright pink and the girl's clitoris could easily be seen through the blur of her fingertips. Anna gasped again and her juices seemed to squirt from within her, spraying over the faces of the two shocked young men who were kneeling in front of her.

Karina could never have imagined that such a thing was possible, that so much passion and pent-up emotion could be released in such a beautiful way. Anna continued to plough her fingers in and out of herself until, without warning, she came again, once more showering the faces of the two men with her lush cream. Karina involuntarily grasped the shoulder of the young man squatting next to her, so shocked was she that anything so wonderful could happen. The boy looked at her and grimaced. She glanced down and saw a stream of sperm jet from his rigid cock. Evidently, the demonstration had been too much for him.

Anna allowed her legs to slip down and sat forward on the chair, panting heavily. Simons stroked her head gently and then kissed her lightly on the forehead. 'You may not believe it,' he said as he stood up to face the others, 'but that was the first time that Anna has done such a thing in the presence of an audience. Such is the power of the Atca teaching. You saw how much pleasure she enjoyed from losing her inhibitions entirely, but it has taken her a long time to reach this stage. This is how it must be for all of you. Imagine what a wonderful, happy world we would be living in if everybody developed the same, relaxed attitude to sex. There would be no jealousies, no envy, and no agonising infidelities. Just pure enjoyment.'

'But, what of marriage and children?' ventured one of the women in the group.

'Polygamous marriages work perfectly well in some parts of the world,' replied Simons. 'Children are not affected if they see that their parents are happy.' He looked down at Anna, who was relaxing back in the chair and was once again fingering herself. 'I think that Anna would like a little more,' he said. 'Who would like to taste her?'

Karina was about to rush forward but Sandy beat her to it. Her friend flung herself on to the floor in front of the seated girl and immediately buried her face between Anna's outstretched thighs. Karina watched enviously as Sandy's head bobbed up and down, the sounds of her tongue lapping against the other girl's sex-lips plainly audible. A heavily-built young man moved to kneel behind Sandy and stroked her upturned bottom gently. Sandy looked over her shoulder, smiled and then returned to her pleasurable task of stimulating Anna's pussy with her mouth.

The man took this as a sign of approval and he grasped his cock in his hand and slid it quickly into the welcoming succulence of Sandy's cunt. A second man rose to his feet and moved to stand next to Anna. She grasped his thick stalk and pulled it towards her face, then took it into her mouth. The young man who was fucking Sandy leant across her until he was squatting on the balls of his feet and began to plunge heavily in and out of her.

From her seated position, Karina could see every detail of his wonderful assault on her friend's lovely body. He was using virtually every inch of his superb length with each stroke, thrusting powerfully against her, his belly slapping noisily against her bottom. Every so often he would slow down, clearly anxious to prolong the event before building up once again to a rapid, jabbing rhythm.

Usha moved to kneel behind him and Karina soon realised, from the way her head was moving, that she was licking his bottom while he fucked her friend. Seconds later, another man joined the chain and rammed his stiff rod deep into Usha's pussy from behind. A girl whom Karina hadn't seen before managed to wriggle under him on her back and promptly started to lick his balls, while holding her own legs wide apart in blatant invitation. It was only a matter of seconds before she too was impaled by yet another male member of the group and she began to enjoy the rhythmic plunging of a hard, thick cock inside her young body.

Karina watched in startled amazement as the chain grew and grew. Although she was incredibly aroused by the scene of total bacchanalia going on before her eyes, the thought of joining in didn't occur to her. She was happy merely to witness the sight. The sounds of skin slapping together and the groans of delight filled the room.

Simons was standing by the chair, watching the proceedings. He noticed Karina, who was now sitting alone on the floor. He walked over to her. 'Aren't you going to join in?' he asked sternly.

'No – yes – I . . .' she answered, not sure what to say.

'I warned you that you might not like what you saw,' he continued. 'I don't believe that you are ready.'

'I am,' she protested. 'It's just that I was watching!' Simons shook his head sadly and walked away. Karina wanted to rush over and tell him about her night at Solomon's, to prove to him that she was just as uninhibited as the rest of the group, but he strode quickly out of the room, slamming the door behind him. Angry, she struggled to her feet and rushed after him.

She found him in the hallway, speaking on the phone. She felt stupid, standing there naked, waiting for him to finish his call.

Simons set the receiver down and turned to face her. 'Is there something that you want?' he said dispassionately.

'I *am* ready,' she pleaded.

Simons smiled a cruel, shallow grin. 'We will see,' he said. 'I have made a special arrangement for you. We will soon see how ready you are.' He pushed past her and re-entered the lounge before she could make any further protest. Karina sat on a chair by the telephone table, feeling utterly wretched. She remained there for what seemed like an age, feeling both angry with Simons and furious with herself. Why was he doing this to her? Why was he treating her in such a disdainful manner?

Eventually, she summoned up her courage and returned to the lounge. She would show him, she thought. She would have every man in the place, if necessary, to prove that she was no innocent little virgin.

The orgy that had begun in such a wild and frenzied manner had, by now, turned into one of sated exhaustion. The participants lay in groups on the carpet, gently stroking and nuzzling each other in a state of post-coital bliss. It was plainly evident to Karina that her feelings of sexual frustration were not going to be eased, at least for the moment.

She searched for her clothes among the pile of discarded garments on the floor. Finding her skirt and blouse, she began to dress herself.

'I'd rather that you didn't do that,' said Simons suddenly from behind her.

Karina stopped short, her little skirt pulled halfway up her long legs. 'What d'you mean?' she asked.

'I told you,' replied Simons. 'I've made an arrangement for you. It is necessary that you remain naked.'

'Just what have you arranged?' she demanded,

nevertheless allowing her skirt to fall to her ankles once more. Before Simons could answer however, she heard the sound of the doorbell.

'It seems that our guest has arrived,' he said with an enigmatic smile as he went to answer the door. Karina watched him go, her curiosity fired. Whatever it was that he had arranged, surely it couldn't surpass the excesses that she had just witnessed?

Simons returned after a moment accompanied by a tall man in his early thirties. Karina found him passably attractive, but felt uncomfortable standing before a total stranger completely naked. She automatically put her hands in front of her bushy mound and looked to one side, desperate to hide her embarrassment. Simons walked over to her and took hold of her wrists. He drew her hands away from her crotch and held them against his chest, while staring meaningfully into her eyes.

'Karina,' he said. 'I would like you to meet Robert, a very good friend of mine. I told him about you on the phone and he's rushed over to meet you.' He released his grip of her fingers and moved to one side. Robert stepped forward, took hold of her hand and shook it politely. It seemed decidedly odd to Karina that, despite the fact that she was totally naked, this stranger was greeting her in such a formal manner. She glanced nervously at him and he gave her a slight smile.

'You are very beautiful,' said Robert, his voice tinged with a slight European accent. 'Far more lovely than Charles suggested.' Karina found herself warming to him as he clutched her hand gently. He looked down at her naked body. 'Very beautiful,' he repeated.

She glanced away coyly, feeling her nipples hardening under his gaze.

'Ladies and gentlemen,' said Simons suddenly as he addressed the group. 'Karina wishes to be readmitted to our little circle. I have asked Robert to join us tonight to give her the ultimate test.'

Robert gripped her hand tightly as Simons uttered those final words. She looked into his eyes and felt her heart beginning to race. He wasn't especially handsome but the events of the previous hour or so had left her feeling incredibly aroused and she was ready for anything. After all, she thought, what could this stranger do to her that she hadn't already experienced during her long and eventful night at Solomon's?

The group quickly formed itself once more into a circle surrounding Karina and the newcomer. Robert made her sit on the chair and removed his jacket and shirt. His torso was remarkably muscular, suggesting that he spent most of his time working out in a gym. He knelt before her and rested his hands on her thighs, while gazing between her legs.

'You have a beautiful little pussy,' he said.

'Thank you,' she breathed, unsure of what else to say.

'I am going to kiss you there,' he continued, still staring at her moist flesh. 'I am going to lick you, suckle you and swallow your come. I am going to turn you and lick your bottom, then I'm going to tongue-fuck your arsehole.' He looked up at her. His obscenities made her breathless with desire for him and she could feel her entire body trembling. He grinned, clearly aware of the effect his words were having on her. 'I am going to take you across my knee,' he continued, 'in front of all your friends here, and I'm going to spank you until your little bottom stings. Would you like me to do that?'

Karina nodded slowly. Her mouth felt dry. His mention of the others reminded her of their presence, but she was unconcerned. The dull ache in her loins needed to be sated.

Robert bent his head forward and kissed her lightly on her pussy. She jumped with the suddenness of the unexpected touch of his mouth to her tender flesh. He looked up at her again. He appeared more handsome to her now and infinitely desirable. 'After I have spanked you, I am going to fuck you, and it will be the most memorable fuck of your life.'

His apparent conceit didn't trouble her. 'Do it,' she said in a voice that was barely audible.

He leant forward again and she closed her eyes. She sensed his hot breath playing over her sensitive sex-flesh and wanted to grasp his head, in order to ram his mouth against her. Instead, she remained passive and waited for him to take the initiative. The first touch of his silky tongue to her cunt made her gasp. It was as though nobody had ever done such a thing to her before. She felt him trace the line of the wet crease and sensed her sex-lips opening to his tender but insistent probing. His tongue slid into her and he pressed his mouth hard against her mound, engulfing her pussy entirely. She felt him lapping hungrily at her hot flesh; his tongue seemed to be as long as any cock that she'd accommodated in the past.

She raised her legs high into the air and spread them as wide as possible, while arching her back and forcing her groin against his suckling mouth. The mixture of her juices and his saliva slipped between the cheeks of her bottom. She knew that she was going to come. Nothing could stop the mounting surge of pleasure that was building up inside her. She opened her eyes and immediately saw the grinning faces of Sandy and Usha, who were sitting close by and watching the proceedings avidly.

'Oh, yes!' she shouted suddenly. 'Oh, God! I'm going to come!' Robert took her cries as a signal and immediately began to lap his tongue rapidly over her hard bud, which brought her instantly over the edge. 'Yes! I'm coming! I'm coming!' she squealed. The orgasm ripped through her as powerfully as anything that she'd known before and she grasped his hair and forced his face hard against her pulsating sex-flesh.

It was over too quickly, but she knew that it was only

the beginning. Robert sat back on his haunches and looked up at her. His face was soaked, glistening in the candlelight. She gazed into his eyes, her feelings for this complete stranger an ambiguous mixture of love and lust. Her pussy was still throbbing and the seat beneath her felt uncomfortably wet.

Robert got to his feet and took hold of her hands. 'Stand, Karina,' he said quietly. She obeyed immediately. He turned her gently until she had her back to him. 'Rest your hands on the chair, Karina,' he continued, 'but keep your legs straight.' Karina did as instructed, knowing what was coming next and thrilling to the idea. She gripped the edges of the seat tightly and purposely curved her back to force her bottom out in what she considered to be an erotic pose. She heard an approving comment come from one of the males in her audience and felt justifiably proud.

She looked under herself between her thighs and could see Robert kneeling behind her, gazing at her bottom. He shifted forward and gripped her thighs, and then she felt his tongue slowly trace the shape of her buttocks before the tip touched her at the top of the cleft. Slowly, agonisingly slowly, he drew it down, inch by inch, getting ever closer to the spot that she so desperately wanted it to touch. He teased her, however, deliberately avoiding her little sphincter and lapping once more around her pert buttocks until he again rested the tip of his tongue at the base of her spine. Karina shivered as he licked slowly downward. He paused, the tip of his tongue touching her just above her little hole. She waited with bated breath. He had to do it this time or she would scream.

She gasped aloud as his wet tongue at last tickled her arsehole and felt the delicious ache of desire returning to her pussy. He licked up and down and around her sphincter, then prodded the tip of his tongue into her. At first, her flesh resisted his intrusion but quickly surrendered to his insistent and expert ministrations and she felt his long tongue slide deep into her bottom. She came without warning, a sudden gentle orgasm that caused her juices to flow from within her, once more soaking her inner thighs. Robert gripped her buttocks tightly and pulled them apart, then pushed his tongue in and out of her rapidly. It felt like a soft wet cock penetrating her most intimate place.

She reached under herself and began to caress her soaking pussy, rubbing hard at her clitoris with her fingers. Robert continued to tongue-fuck her bottom as she quickly brought herself to yet another delicious release. This time, the waves of joyous pleasure were far stronger and she cried out with a sharp resounding yelp of shocked rapture, followed by a long gasp of complete satisfaction.

Robert moved from her and helped her to stand erect. Karina was shaking visibly and felt that her legs might give way. She clutched his arm tightly.

'You are a very naughty girl,' he said. She looked at him questioningly. His expression could only be described as a leer. He took her in his arms and their mouths met. Karina tasted her delicate scent on his lips and this only served to arouse her even more.

Robert pulled from her and sat on the chair, then motioned to her to lie across his lap. She happily assumed the submissive position, thrilling to the thought that twenty or more pairs of eyes were watching her subjugation. He stroked her buttocks gently and ran the tips of his fingers between them. 'A very naughty girl,' he repeated breathlessly. Karina closed her eyes and waited eagerly for the pain.

The first slap was dove-like, barely hurting her at all. The second was equally bland, although the sound of skin against skin resounded around the room. 'Harder!' she breathed.

'Harder?' he questioned.

'Yes! Harder!'

The next slap was delivered across both of her buttocks and stung sharply. Karina wriggled against him, rubbing her pussy along his thigh. 'Harder!' she demanded again. The fourth stroke smacked hard across her right buttock and was immediately followed by a fifth across the other quivering globe of flesh. She felt her juices flowing yet again, and knew that she was soaking his trousers, but couldn't care less. The stinging pain in her hot bottom was giving her the most intense pleasure.

She felt him slip a finger deep into her anus. She allowed him to move it in and out of her for a few seconds, but her need was for more urgent ministrations. 'Spank me!' she ordered. 'Spank me again! I want more!'

She heard somebody in the crowd laugh but felt no embarrassment. Robert eased his finger from her tight little hole and slapped her again across her bottom, this time with such a force that a number of the watching group gasped with surprise. The pain seared through her tortured flesh and waves of arousal coursed throughout her lower body.

'More?' he asked.

'Yes! More! More!' It took three more whacks of his hard hand to her poor bottom to make her come yet again. Karina surrendered herself to the surge of joyous delight, not caring who was watching as she gasped and moaned with pleasure. Robert bent his head and kissed and licked her sore buttocks, then allowed her to slip gently from him until she knelt on the carpet at his feet.

She looked up at him. He had done everything that he had said he would. Now he was going to fuck her. The thought of his – or, in fact, any – cock impaling her excited her beyond measure. She would show Simons; she would prove herself worthy of joining the circle.

Robert got to his feet and helped Karina to stand.

She was still feeling rather shaky, having experienced numerous orgasms in such a short time, but she was ready for whatever he wanted to do to her. He made her sit back on the chair. Turning his back to her, he quickly removed his shoes and socks and then began to unfasten the belt of his trousers.

This is it, Karina thought. Simons is going to see me fucked in front of the group. Surely that will be enough to make him accept me? In her heart, she knew that she wanted Simons himself to take her, to ravage her, to do absolutely anything that he wanted to her. His magnetic personality and his almost hypnotic eyes drew her to him like a bee to a flower.

She watched hungrily as Robert slipped his trousers down and kicked them off. Now, all he wore was a rather over-large pair of boxer shorts. Still with his back to her, he removed them slowly. Those members of the circle who were sitting in front and to the sides of him gasped in unison.

He turned slowly and Karina saw the reason for their expressions of surprise. His cock rose from his bushy groin like a rod of iron, far, far bigger than anything that she had seen before. A foot in length and thicker than his wrist, it jutted forward threateningly as he moved towards her. She glanced across nervously at Simons. He was smirking. This, then, was the ultimate test.

Robert moved towards her until the head of his monstrous erection was inches from her face. She swallowed hard as she stared at the thing. There was no way that he could get inside her without causing her great pain. It was simply just too big. She looked up at his face. He must have seen the concern on her face because he smiled kindly. 'Don't worry,' he said. 'I'll be careful.' Obviously he was well used to such a reaction from a prospective lover.

She looked again at the thick fleshy rod. The head

was easily as large as a peach and the stalk was gnarled with prominent veins. She reached forward with her hand and clasped it in her grip. Her fingers could in no way encircle its girth. She clutched it with both hands held together and, if anything, it seemed to thicken under her touch. Although aroused by the very sight of the monster, she knew that she could not accommodate him.

'Lick it,' he said.

Karina bent her head forward and ran the tip of her tongue around the huge bulbous knob. She decided to try to make him come.

Rubbing the long stalk with both of her hands, she lapped the head with her tongue, in the hope that his obvious arousal and their previous experiences would cause him to ejaculate quickly. She parted her lips and attempted to take it in her mouth, but it was far too big. Accepting this, she licked up and down the stem, while continuing to rhythmically masturbate him. Suddenly, he grasped hold of her wrists, forcing her to stop.

'Careful,' he said. 'You'll make me come before I fuck you.'

She looked up at him. 'I don't mind,' she said. 'You can come in my mouth, if you want.'

'I don't want that,' he replied earnestly. 'I want to get inside you.'

Karina shook her head. 'I don't know,' she pleaded. 'It's so big.'

Robert stroked her head lovingly. 'You'll like it, I promise, when you get used to it.' The temptation to try and accommodate the huge thing was very strong but so was Karina's fear of the discomfort that it might cause. She tried to rub his stalk again but he held her wrists firmly.

'Come on, young lady,' he said in a patronising tone. 'Open your legs. I want to fuck you.'

She looked up at him again imploringly, in a last

attempt to persuade him to change his mind. 'I want you to,' she said, 'but it's just too big.'

Robert smirked and turned away from her to face Simons. 'You were right,' he said in a cruel, almost vindictive tone of voice. 'She is not ready to join the circle of the Atca.' He grabbed up his clothing from the floor and stormed from the room.

Karina sat back on the chair, feeling both stupid and afraid. She looked round at the others. Most of the group were regarding her sympathetically but Simons was glaring at her, clearly furious. Suddenly, she grabbed her clothes and shoes and scurried from the room, through the hallway and out of the front door to the apartment.

She paused on the landing and leant back against the wall. Her heart was racing and she could feel the blood pounding in her temples. For a moment, she considered returning to the flat and allowing Robert to take her, to prove to Simons that she was worthy, but then thought better of it. It simply couldn't be done. She dressed herself and then hurried out of the building, not sure where she was going and not really caring.

It was still relatively early and the pubs and inns in the area were still open. Normally, Karina wouldn't have gone into such an establishment alone, but she felt that she couldn't go back to Sandy's empty flat – at least, not yet. The Lion and Cross beckoned to her, a small but quiet inn that she had frequented with Sandy during their breaks from their shopping trips during the day. She opened the door cautiously and was pleased to see only a handful of people inside – three or four couples seated at tables and a solitary young man straddling a stool by the bar. She walked over to the bar, sat down on the only other stool and ordered a double vodka with ice. She downed the drink in one go and ordered another, this time with cola. This time she sipped from the glass slowly, as her breathing became steadier and her heart ceased to thump in her chest.

'You looked like you needed that.' It was the young man at the bar who spoke. Karina looked at him and smiled politely. 'Are you working or do you live round here?' he asked.

She had a good idea what he meant by the term 'working', but wasn't offended. Knightsbridge at this time of night was often busy with young ladies plying their nefarious trade. 'I'm staying with a friend,' she replied simply, not really wishing to get in conversation with him, despite the fact that he was particularly good-looking. The young man wasn't having any of it, however. 'My name's Sam,' he said, holding out his hand in greeting.

Karina shook his hand loosely. 'Nice to meet you, Sam,' she said.

There was a short pause. 'Aren't you going to tell me your name?' said Sam eventually.

'Karina.'

'Nice. I bet you get called Katrina all the time.'

'No,' she replied haughtily. Sam looked glumly at his glass and she felt a little guilty about the off-hand way that she had spoken to him. This was precisely the attitude that Sandy had cautioned her about. 'D'you live in this area?' she asked, trying to sound interested.

He looked back at her and smiled. It appeared that he was simply glad of someone to talk to. 'No,' he said. 'I'm here on a management course. All the others are in the hotel bar, talking about nothing but work. I just had to get away.'

'What do you do?'

'I'm just a boring old civil servant. Nothing special. What about you?'

'I've just finished college and I'm waiting to go to university.'

There was another pause. Karina tried hard to think

of something to say but it was difficult. All her thoughts were still centred on the events in Usha's apartment. She could still see Robert's monstrous cock in her mind's eye and the thought of it was making her very wet between the legs.

'I went to see Pink Floyd at Earls Court, the other week,' said Sam, quite evidently finding it as difficult to make conversation as she was. 'It was superb – awesome.'

'I don't know much about them.'

'They're really something. It's strange: I mean, they're all old enough to be my dad, and yet their music transcends the boundaries of age. There were people of all ages there.'

'They must be very good.' Karina considered that the conversation was going nowhere, but at least they were talking and she found Sam's attitude towards her to be warm and friendly.

'I've got a tape of one of their concerts, back at the hotel. D'you fancy coming back to listen?'

Karina almost laughed out loud at the weakness of the young man's chat-up line, but she was feeling so desperately aroused that she felt that she should respond positively. Besides, the very idea of being picked up by a stranger in a seedy London bar quite excited her. It was something that had never happened to her before, that was for certain.

'I'm not sure,' she said. 'I hardly know you.'

'I told you. My name is Sam and I'm a civil servant. Come on; it's a big hotel. You'll be quite safe. We can have a drink in the bar and you can meet the others, if you want.'

He seemed so genuine that Karina put her fears to one side. She gulped down the remainder of her drink. 'No; let's go and listen to your tape,' she said.

The two of them lay on the bed in Sam's hotel room and listened to the recorded concert. Karina found the music quite intoxicating, despite the themes at times being a trifle depressing. She occasionally glanced at him but he seemed to be mesmerised by the electronic sounds that wafted from the small speakers of his portable stereo. He made no attempt to touch her, which at first she considered to be quite charming but after a while she found somewhat frustrating.

The tape ended and the machine clicked off automatically. Sam turned his head to face her. 'Did you like it?' he asked.

Karina nodded. 'It was good,' she answered.

There was another maddening pause. He kept looking at her anxiously, as if he were trying to pluck up the courage to say something. Karina decided to take the initiative. 'Would you like to kiss me?' she asked in a soft sultry tone.

He didn't answer. Instead, he moved his face towards hers and their lips met. He kissed her nervously, as though he were still unsure as to how far he could go. She liked that, remembering how awkward she had felt during similar, earlier encounters in her innocent past. She slipped her arm around his neck and pressed her mouth harder against his, then traced the shape of his lips with the tip of her tongue. He responded immediately, delving his tongue into her mouth and moving his body until he was almost lying on top of her.

Karina pushed his shoulder and forced her face away. 'Steady on,' she said, in a mock display of innocence.

Sam looked devastated. 'I – I'm sorry,' he stuttered. 'It's just – it's just that you are so beautiful and I thought . . .'

'You thought that, just because I came back to your hotel room to listen to your tape, that I'd automatically go to bed with you?' Karina spoke the words deliberately harshly, thoroughly enjoying the game. Sam moved from her and sat on the edge of the bed with his back to her. She wanted to drag him back and tear every strip of clothing from his body, but she wasn't going to tell him that: at least, not yet.

'I'm sorry,' he said glumly. 'I didn't mean to push you. I'm really sorry.'

Karina slid from the bed and stood up. 'Pass me my bag,' she said. 'I need to use the bathroom.' Sam retrieved her handbag from the floor and handed it to her. He looked at her through sad doleful eyes but she regarded him with disdain.

Taking her bag, she strode quickly into the bathroom and closed the door, locking it behind her. Karina stripped off her clothing and washed herself, paying particular attention to her pussy, which was still moist from her earlier encounter with Robert. After drying herself, she stood in front of a long mirror and ran her brush through her long auburn tresses. Her firm breasts bounced provocatively as she brushed her hair. She looked down at her groin. Her sex-lips were still puffy and very prominent, and she knew that they were likely to remain so until she had received full sexual satisfaction. She touched her silky flesh with the middle finger of her free hand. She slipped the tip along the full length of the creamy crease until she touched the bud of her clitoris. Taking a deep breath, she was tempted to continue her erotic caress, but decided that Sam had waited long enough.

Karina unlocked the bathroom door and opened it slowly. Sam was still sitting on the edge of the bed with his back to her and his head bowed. She took a couple of steps into the room and adopted a sensuous pose, with one leg slightly in front of the other, her stomach drawn in and her breasts thrust high. 'Sam,' she said in a voice that was barely above a whisper.

The young man turned to look at her. The sad expression on his face changed immediately to one of shocked delight. He stood up quickly and almost toppled over a nearby armchair. 'Karina!' he gasped as he moved swiftly round the bed and stood facing her. 'Oh, Karina, I . . .'

She put the tip of her finger to his lips to hush him. 'I want you to make love to me,' she said simply, the use of more coarse expressions somehow seeming inappropriate this time. She started to unbutton his shirt. Sam stood stock-still, as if frozen to the spot with terror. Karina removed his short-sleeved shirt and let it fall to the floor. His torso was lightly tanned and his chest was completely free of hair, something that she had always found especially attractive in a man.

Karina ran her hands over his firm pectoral muscles and caressed his hard nipples under her palms. She bent her head forward and licked one of the nipples, then took it between her teeth and bit it gently. Sam stroked the back of her head lovingly. Karina turned her attention to the other nipple and sucked and nipped it, while slowly unzipping the front of his trousers. The room seemed uncommonly silent, the only sound being that of Sam's shallow laboured breathing.

She reached into his trousers and found, to her delight, that he wasn't wearing underwear. Her fingers circled his stiffening erection and she looked up into his eyes. 'You're so very beautiful,' he repeated. Their mouths met and their tongues darted playfully against each other as their lips became crushed together in a passionate and yet tender kiss.

Karina eased his cock into the open and rubbed it gently until it had hardened fully. It was big; nothing like Robert's, of course, but quite enough for her needs. She broke from his embrace and sank to her knees. She took hold of his stiff flesh with both of her hands and gazed for a moment at the mushroom-shaped head as though it were the first one that she'd ever seen. She looked up at him and smiled. Sam was biting his lower lip nervously. Karina pushed out her tongue and playfully licked the tip under his glans, then circled the head with her tongue before moving her face forward and enveloping almost half of his length inside her mouth. She heard him groan and she drew back quickly, anxious not to make him come too soon. She kissed the tip of his cock and stood up.

Karina looked meaningfully into his eyes. 'Take me to bed and fuck me,' she said. This time, the profanity seemed apt, although she said it in such a way that it could have been heard as a whispered prayer.

Sam led her the few steps to the side of the bed and she slipped on to the sheets and lay on her back. She watched with mounting excitement as he quickly stripped off the remainder of his clothing. In her eyes, his body was perfect in every detail. He was sturdily built, though not over-muscular, with a fair complexion and masculine but gentle features. His long cock rose superbly from his bush of neatly clipped pubic curls and his sac hung heavily beneath the thick root. Karina held her arms open wide, beckoning to him to join her. Sam clambered on to the bed and knelt by her side.

For some moments, he just gazed down at her, his expression one of total wonderment. 'I can't believe this is happening,' he said eventually. 'One minute, I was sitting in a bar, bored out of my head and the next I am here with you, the most beautiful girl that I have ever seen.'

Karina smiled and flung her arms around the back of his neck. 'Shut up and kiss me,' she said. Their lips met and, once more, their mouths became locked in a fervent, almost frenzied kiss. Sam lay down and pressed his body against hers. He ran his hand down the gentle curve of her back until his fingertips touched her bottom. Karina reached down and grasped his cock, then squeezed the rigid shaft tightly. Sam responded by moving his hand down over her buttocks until she felt his fingers slipping against the soft flesh of her pussy.

He drew his head back. 'God, you're soaked!' he said.

'I want you,' she replied breathlessly. 'I need you.' There was no need for further foreplay. That could come later. What Karina wanted more than anything else was to be fucked by this handsome young man. As if sensing her desire, Sam moved across her until he was lying fully on top of her. Karina could feel his big cock pressing against her groin. She raised her legs high and spread them wide. Sam shifted upward slightly and she reached down and grasped his stalk, then guided the head to her aching opening. He slid into her with ease, his thickness stretching her wonderfully. Their groins crushed together. Karina ran her hands down his back and gripped the tight globes of his buttocks with her fingers, digging her nails into his taut flesh.

Sam began to thrust in and out of her lush sheath rapidly. Karina held him firmly against her. 'Slowly, darling,' she breathed. 'I want it to last.'

Sam slowed his movements, allowing the full length of his stiff shaft to slide gently back and forth. She could feel every wonderful inch of him inside her. Her inner flesh seemed to be alive with sensation. He fucked her steadily for what seemed like an age. Karina wanted it to go on forever. It was perfect, utterly perfect. She had neither a yearning to be spanked or whipped, nor any desire to be bound and shackled to the bed. All she wanted was to be made love to in this gentle, caring way.

He began to move faster. His cock felt harder and longer inside her silky sheath. She gripped his bottom tighter, and then slipped one of her fingers down the crease between his buttocks until the tip touched his anus. He gasped as she wormed it inside the tight sphincter, and plunged harder and faster in and out of her. Karina responded by thrusting her hips upward.

'Oh, God, you're big!' she cried.

'Yeah?' he panted.

'Yes. Oh, yes! I love it! Fuck me! Fuck me hard!'

Their groins thrashed together and the bed shook and complained noisily. 'More! More!' she yelled. 'Give it to me! I'm gonna come!' No sooner had the words left her lips than her release hit her, causing her to gasp and cry out incoherently.

Sam's expression turned into a grimace. 'I can't hold back!' he moaned.

'Come over me!' Karina demanded. 'I want to see it!'

Sam pulled from her and gripped his cock by the root with one hand, while rubbing the long stalk rapidly with the other. Karina gazed at the plum-coloured head hungrily. Suddenly, his cream jetted from him and sprayed over her face and breasts. Karina forced herself forward and grasped the throbbing rod, then engulfed the spurting head inside her mouth. She felt the velvety texture of his juices against her tongue and swallowed hard, taking as much of his length into her mouth as she could in her awkward position. Letting go of his shaft, she gripped his balls tightly and squeezed them, as if trying to draw more of his cream from his body. The thick rod continued to throb heavily against her lips, the sensuous rhythm slowing gradually until, at last, it stopped.

Karina lay back and wiped her mouth with the back of her hand. Sam knelt between her legs, his body covered in sweat and his cock hanging limply from his groin. The silence returned to the room.

Nine

Karina opened the door to Sandy's flat slowly and noiselessly. It wasn't particularly early – well past ten o'clock, in fact – but she had no idea what time her friend had returned from Usha's apartment and didn't want to wake her. She needn't have worried. As she entered the lounge, she heard the distinctive sound of the shower running in the bathroom.

'Hi, Sandy,' she shouted, in case her sudden appearance might startle the other girl.

'Hi, Karina,' came her friend's cheerful voice. 'What happened to you last night? Where did you get to?'

'Oh, I met a friend and we had a few drinks.' Karina would tell her the truth, of course, but not now. She was tired and needed to rest. She and Sam had made love for most of the night and had fallen asleep in each other's arms when it was almost daybreak. Were it not for the fact that she'd had to leave the hotel with him when he'd set off for his training course, she would have gladly remained curled up in the big bed in his room for the rest of the day.

She walked through to the bedroom, dropped her handbag on to the floor and slumped down on the bed. Sandy appeared from the bathroom, wearing nothing but a small towel tied around her waist. 'You look shattered,' her friend said.

'Heavy night,' was Karina's exhausted response.

Sandy took the towel from around her body, sat on the edge of the bed and started to dry her hair. Karina watched her lazily, admiring the way her large breasts bounced and jiggled as she rubbed her head with the towel. 'You shouldn't have gone off like that,' said Sandy. 'We had a really great night.'

'That guy was just too big,' answered Karina. 'God knows what damage he could have done to me.'

Sandy stopped towelling her hair and turned to face her. 'Oh, Karina,' she said. 'Didn't you realise? It was all a put-up job. It was a test, to see just how far you were prepared to go.' She leant forward with a conspiratorial grin on her face. 'Shall I tell you something? Robert is a virgin!'

Karina's eyes widened with surprise. 'You're kidding!' she said. 'Surely not?'

'Honest. Believe me. Like you said, he's far too big. No woman could comfortably take something that size. Mind you, a couple of us tried.'

'Did you?'

Sandy glanced coyly down at her lap. 'I had to,' she said. 'It was hopeless. He managed to get the head inside me but that was it. It wasn't the length of it – I think I could have managed that – it was the thickness. God, I can still feel it!'

'So, this test. What was I supposed to do?'

'Submit. The Atca teaching is clear. Nobody refuses anybody anything. Once you had offered yourself to him, that would have been enough. Robert wouldn't have tried to fuck you. He's well aware of what could happen. He only agreed to let me and Usha try because we begged him to. I was surprised that Usha didn't manage it, though. I've seen her take two cocks in her pussy many times.'

'So,' continued Karina. 'If I had agreed to let him do it, that would have been enough to prove myself worthy of joining the group?'

'Exactly. Charles was angry, at first, when you ran off. I think that he's quite taken with you.'

Karina sniggered in disbelief. If Sandy had said that a day or so before, her heart would have leapt. But that was before she'd met Sam. 'I suppose that I've blown it, then?' she asked.

'You mean with Charles?'

'No, of course not,' said Karina angrily. 'I meant with the group.'

Sandy gave her an old-fashioned look and suppressed a smile. 'I'm not sure,' she replied. 'There's another meeting tonight. It's up to you if you want to come.' She got to her feet and threw the towel into the laundry basket at the foot of the bed. 'Are you doing anything special today?' she asked as she sat down again next to Karina. 'I promised that I'd meet Usha for lunch. You can join us if you like.'

'I'll see how I feel later. I'm really tired.'

Sandy leant over her and stroked her face softly. 'You do look bushed,' she said. 'What were you really up to last night?'

'I'll tell you later,' said Karina with a grin.

Sandy allowed her hand to stray to Karina's breast. 'Your nipple's hard,' she breathed. 'D'you want some fun before you go to sleep?'

Karina was about to say no, but her friend's insistent caress was getting through to her. She reached up and cupped one of Sandy's pendulous breasts. Her friend moved over to kiss her gently on the mouth and then ran her hand down her body to her bare thigh. She moved her hand upward, raising Karina's skirt as she did so until her fingertips touched Karina's pussy.

'I see that you've stopped wearing panties,' she said.

'It's a bit of a waste of time, these days,' replied Karina, with a laugh. She took a deep breath as Sandy's fingers slipped inside her.

'You're soaked,' said her friend, 'and I don't think it's just you.'

'I don't know what you mean,' replied Karina sarcastically. Sandy giggled like a child and then slipped down to kneel between Karina's splayed legs. Karina raised her head from the bed and watched as she began to lick her hot sex-flesh, pulling her skirt up high so that she could see every movement of her friend's fluttering tongue. Her orgasm hit her like a thunderbolt, so sudden that it made her shudder involuntarily.

'My God, that was quick,' said Sandy as she sat up and wiped her mouth with her hand.

'I was feeling horny,' replied Karina.

Sandy grinned as she slipped from the bed. 'You really will have to tell me what you were doing last night,' she said. 'It must have been quite something!'

'It was,' replied Karina. She turned over to lie on her side and closed her eyes. Within seconds, she was asleep.

It was nearly nine o'clock in the evening and Sandy had already set off for the meeting at Usha's apartment. Karina had made a pretence of not being sure whether she wanted to go or not and had said she might see her later.

But she was sure. She had never been more certain of anything before in her young life. She would show the Honourable Charles Simons and his friends what she was made of. She would prove herself worthy.

She had bought the outfit from one of those specialised little shops that nestle in the back streets of the West End, the sort of establishment that, until recently, she would never have dreamt of entering. The dress was fashioned from black latex and clung to her superb body like a second skin. Every inch of her sexuality was clearly defined – her long hard nipples, the prominent pouting lips of her pussy and the smooth swell of her pert bottom. The hem of the dress finished slightly below her mound, revealing a couple of inches of bare creamy flesh between it and the tops of her black hold-up stockings. A pair of patent leather stiletto shoes, the heels of which gave her a full four inches extra in height, completed her attire.

She regarded herself in the long mirror in the bedroom. She looked like a whore, which was precisely the image that she wished to portray. The group, and particularly Simons himself would see her as a woman available for – no, *demanding* sex. Karina Devonside, the innocent curious virgin, was no more. She was hungry and insatiable, thirsty for knowledge and salacious experiences. In one respect, the feelings frightened her but, in another, they filled her with delight and excitement.

The doorbell rang, the sound startling her momentarily. She moved quickly through the lounge and into the hallway and then paused for a moment. Whoever was out there would see her dressed in this provocative and exotic manner. She fixed the safety chain on the door and opened it an inch or so. 'Who is it?' she asked nervously.

'Rogers, miss,' came the reply. Relieved, she pushed the door closed, removed the chain and then opened the door wide. Rogers was standing on the landing in full uniform, including his peaked cap. 'Miss Devonside, I . . .' The remainder of his sentence seemed to have become trapped in his throat as he stared at her through wide appreciative eyes.

'What is it, Rogers?' she asked impatiently.

He swallowed hard and then appeared to regain his composure. 'I'm sorry, Miss Devonside,' he continued. 'Is Miss Harrison in?'

'No. She's out at the moment. Is there anything I can do?'

Rogers shifted uncomfortably on his feet and continually looked her up and down. Karina found her eyes drawn to the thick belt in the waistband of his trousers. Her mouth felt dry as she pictured an image of the beautiful Michelle kneeling on the bed, her perfect bottom being mercilessly lashed by the same harsh scourge.

'It's nothing, miss,' continued the doorman. 'I merely called to check if Miss Harrison wished to order any newspapers for next week.'

His excuse was so weak that Karina wondered whether he had seen Sandy leave the building earlier and had come up to the flat with an ulterior motive in mind. 'I doubt it,' she said. 'Would you like to come in for a coffee?' Why she asked that, she wasn't sure; Usha's party beckoned and she didn't want to arrive too late, but there was something magnetic about Rogers' powerful presence.

'Thank you, miss, but I have work to do.'

His response disappointed her. She reached out and grasped his belt buckle. 'Please, Rogers,' she said, 'just for a few minutes.' The situation seemed unreal. By her action, she'd made it clear to him that coffee was not on the agenda. He stepped forward and she released her grip of his buckle and closed the door behind him. She turned to face him and immediately flung her arms around his neck and crushed her lips against his.

Their tongues lapped together, their mouths suckling each other. She felt his strong hands grip her buttocks. Her dress had ridden up and his fingertips were touching the bared flesh of her bottom. She could feel his hardening cock pressing against her belly as she rubbed her body sensuously against his. She pulled her face from him. 'Can your work wait for a few minutes?' she pouted.

Rogers nodded.

She moved from him and he followed her into the lounge. Karina knew exactly what she wanted. She knelt on the sofa with her bottom presented to him and peeled her dress up until it was pulled up to her waist. She looked over her shoulder. Rogers was standing behind her, a confident lustful expression on his handsome face. 'Whip me,' she said breathlessly.

'Whip you, miss?' he questioned.

'You heard me. Do it!' Karina felt surprised at the confidence of her commanding tone. She watched as he quickly unbuckled his belt and withdrew it from his trousers. He folded it in half and clutched the buckle and the other end in his hand, then slapped it meaningfully across his palm. The sound thrilled her and she felt her loins warming in anticipation of the joy to come.

'Why are you dressed like that?' he asked, as he moved to stand at her side.

'I'm going to a party.'

'Are you intending to be naughty?'

'Yes.'

'You have a very pretty little bottom.'

'Thank you.'

Rogers' voice was becoming hoarser with every word that he spoke, while Karina's excitement was growing by the second. 'Are you going to let a man fuck you in the bottom?' he continued, once more slapping his hand with his belt.

'Yes,' Karina replied simply.

'D'you like that?'

'I love it.'

'It's a very naughty thing to do. You deserve to be punished most severely.'

'I know.'

There was a long silence. Karina turned her head away from him and braced herself. She sensed him move behind her. Suddenly, there was a hiss of air and the leather lashed across her buttocks. She yelped with the pain and gripped the back of the sofa tightly. 'Was that too hard?' he asked.

'No,' she gasped. The pain had been severe, but had merely served to heighten her arousal. He whipped her again and she clenched her teeth, determined not to cry out again. Three more cuts stung the hot flesh of her bottom in quick succession, and then she felt him caressing her buttocks and tugging them apart. She looked over her shoulder again and saw that he was now kneeling down behind her, gazing at her backside with a look of abject desire on his face. She turned her head and closed her eyes once more.

The wet feeling of his tongue slipping up and down the crease of her bottom was the next sensation to delight her. She forced her buttocks out and thrilled as his tongue probed and prodded into her anus. It was clear what he intended to do. She didn't have long to wait. She felt him push two or more fingers into her bottom and forced the muscle to relax, to allow him easy entry. Obviously encouraged by this, he eased his fingers out of her and she heard the distinctive sound of his zip being opened.

Karina reached behind herself and tugged her buttocks apart in blatant invitation. Rogers rested one hand on her back and then she felt the head of his cock press against her sphincter. The wetness of his saliva helped but, without the benefit of oil, entry was a little difficult. Despite the discomfort, Karina yearned so much for the ultimate penetration of her body that the tight ring of muscle became relaxed almost immediately and he slid into her. She groaned with pleasure. Rogers began to move slowly and considerately until, at last, her bottom accommodated the full length of his thick cock.

'Is that what you want, you little slut?' he panted.

'Yes!' Karina gasped in reply. 'Fuck me! Fuck my arse!'

Rogers took her at her word and started to ram his stalk rapidly in and out of her anus. Karina reached under herself and clawed at her soaking pussy as he plundered her intimate sheath mercilessly. He slapped her buttock with his hand.

'Do that again!' she demanded. 'Spank me! Spank me hard!' He obeyed her words immediately, the hard stinging slaps raining down on her poor tortured little bottom in time with the constant plunging of his stiff flesh into her tightness.

Suddenly, he rammed deep into her and gripped her waist firmly. After a second, Karina felt the now familiar throbbing of his cock inside her body and knew that he was filling her arse with his cream. The knowledge brought her to an immediate and excruciatingly powerful orgasm as he once again ploughed in and out of her with almost manic force, until he could give her no more.

Rogers eased from inside her and then kissed her lightly on the bottom. 'You are well marked,' he said, with some pride.

Karina turned herself and sat on the sofa, brushing down her dress as she did so. The thought that Simons and the rest of the group would see the evidence of the thrashing pleased her. She watched as Rogers replaced his belt.

'Will there be anything else, miss?' he asked with mock courtesy.

'No, thank you, Rogers,' she replied with a wry smile.

Karina washed herself and then, moving back into the bedroom, she took another look at her reflection in the mirror. A sudden thought struck her. She would not go to the party dressed like a tramp; she would go dressed as a lady! She was the daughter of a wealthy family, people who were well respected in the upper echelons of English society. Her appearance tonight would reflect her position.

She peeled off the latex dress and threw it contemptuously on the floor. Deciding to keep the black stockings on, she complemented them with a pair of black silk panties and a matching bra. After rooting through the wardrobe she selected a pink, floral-print dress. After quickly putting it on, she once again looked into the mirror. The loose-fitting garment hid her shapely curves completely; the elegant line of the dress more fitting for an embassy ball. But there was one more touch that was needed. She reached up in the wardrobe and took a large hatbox from the upper shelf. She had brought it from Devon, not knowing that Sandy's social calendar was to be anything but formal, and it had remained in its box until now.

After brushing her hair she placed the wide-brimmed pink hat on her head. The reflection in the mirror was now of a lady who was about to attend a royal garden party or a day at Ascot Races, not one of a young girl whose bottom was still stinging from the strap and who was intent on enjoying as many sexual diversions as possible that night.

It suited her mood perfectly.

Karina Devonside took a long, deep breath as she stood outside the main door to Usha's apartment. She had no idea what sort of reception she would receive from Charles Simons, but at least she knew that her friends Sandy and Usha would be there and, consequently, he would at least have to treat her politely.

She brushed down her dress and adjusted the line of her hat, then rang the doorbell. After a few seconds, the door was opened by Usha.

'Karina!' she exclaimed when she saw her friend's formal attire. 'You look lovely! Are you going on somewhere?'

'No,' replied Karina as she followed Usha into the apartment. 'I just fancied a change. I'm sick of dressing up like a tart.' She regretted her words as soon as she had uttered them. Usha's mode of attire was anything but ladylike. She was wearing skin-tight PVC shorts that enhanced the firm swell of her superb bottom and a small-netted T-shirt, which did nothing to hide her pert little breasts. Her friend didn't appear to take offence, however, and led her into the lounge.

As usual, Simons was sitting on a chair with the group circled around him, although this time everybody was fully clothed. He was in the middle of some sort of discourse but stopped short when he looked across at Karina. She nodded her head politely in greeting and moved to sit on a chair close to the far wall, facing him.

'Aren't you going to join your friends, Miss Devonside?' asked Simons, with a definite hint of contempt in his tone.

'I prefer to sit here,' she replied, crossing her legs and staring haughtily at him under the brim of her hat.

'This is no place for observers,' he said angrily, glaring back at her.

Karina regarded him with passive disinterest. 'Believe me, Charles,' she said, 'I have no intention of remaining an observer.'

Simons appeared to be a little nonplussed at the calmness of her response. He paused for a moment, as if attempting to think of an effective reply, and then looked back down at his seated students. 'Karina's manner of dress is actually a happy coincidence. It illustrates precisely the one thing that I considered was wrong with the philosophy of the Atca people.' Karina drew a sharp intake of breath and awaited some kind of insult.

'The one flaw in their otherwise perfect existence was boredom,' he continued. 'The people spent all of their days naked and, as I have said, had sex whenever and with whoever their fancy took them. They would play games to try to add some sort of spice to the proceedings, and some of their practices would have made the Marquis de Sade blanch.'

He stood up and held out his hand to Karina, a warm and welcoming smile playing across his lips. 'Miss

Devonside – Karina, would you please come and join me?'

At first, Karina felt that she would refuse, but his insistent gaze and the sudden change in his mood made his request difficult to resist. She rose from her seat and walked over to him, stepping through the circle of young people seated on the carpet.

Simons took her hand and gripped it gently. 'You all witnessed Karina's humiliation yesterday,' he continued. 'However, look at this beautiful, refined young lady standing here before you. Like me, do you find it hard to believe that this is the same woman as the one whom you all saw in this very room, naked, having her bottom spanked and licked?

'When I first met Karina she was dressed in a similar, albeit more sensuous manner. There was subtlety in her appearance, but there was also a hint of promise that even she was probably unaware of. I was captivated by her immediately. I sat looking at her across the dining room table and found it difficult to concentrate on the food or the conversation. I wanted her, as simple as that. Throughout the meal I thought of little else, although I did my best to conceal my true emotions.'

Karina looked at him wide-eyed, astounded by his unexpected revelation. 'After the dinner was over,' he continued, 'I managed to work it that she and I were alone. It was a warm and romantic evening. We went for a walk in the grounds of her home and she took me to a place by a large lake. I felt that she wanted me as much as I wanted her – all the signs were there, but there was also a curious, nervous reticence about her. Soon, she was naked but still managed to maintain an aura of innocence. She told me that she was a virgin. When she said those words, I knew that I was going to have difficulty in controlling myself physically, something that rarely happens to me.

'She gave me oral sex and, watching her do something

like that, knowing that it was the first time that she'd ever done anything remotely like it before, took me past the point of no return. I came in her mouth and, to my amazement and delight, she swallowed my cream as if it were the most natural thing to do.

'I felt ashamed and stupid. I wanted to visit her room that night and take her completely but I considered that I would be unwelcome, in view of my pathetic performance. Instead, I took solace with one of the manor's serving girls.'

Karina squeezed his hand. 'You should have come to me,' she whispered. 'I was waiting for you.'

'I realise that now,' he said softly, looking directly into her eyes. 'I will regret missing that wonderful opportunity for the rest of my life.' He looked back at the students. 'The point that I am making is this. While there is a place for blatant sexuality, and the lack of inhibitions is paramount to enjoying a libidinous sex life, a woman must also maintain her mystery, her allure, in order to seduce her partner into raptures of desire.'

He turned and looked at her again. 'I want to do something to you. I want to do what I should have done that night by the lake.'

Karina gazed into his eyes and felt her heart melt. 'I want you to, Charles,' she breathed. 'I really do.'

'Would you like me to take you to one of the bedrooms?'

'No. I want you to make love to me here, in front of the group, and then I want everybody to take me in any way that they wish. Try not to come, Charles, because when it's all over I want you to fill my mouth again.' She sensed that his hands were trembling and realised that, at last, she had discovered the secret of her true sexuality. Despite his powerful and enigmatic persona, she was in charge. She was dictating the rules.

Simons let go of her hands and then slipped his arms

around her waist, pulling her to him. Their mouths met but the kiss was gentle, an embrace of lovers. He traced the fullness of her pouting lips with the tip of his tongue, which made her immediately anticipate the touch of his mouth to her pussy. Her juices began to flow. The audience of young eager students was forgotten as he slowly drew down the zip on the back of her dress. The garment slipped from her shoulders and she stepped back to allow it to fall to the floor. Simons looked at her, his expression one of clear admiration. She stood still, waiting for him to continue to undress her. This was how she wanted it.

'You are so very beautiful,' he said, his voice sounding dry with emotion. She said nothing. He put his arms around her and she felt him unhook her bra. They kissed again, this time their tongues delving into each other's mouths, as their embrace became all the more urgent. He pulled the thin lacy straps from her shoulders and she raised her arms to allow him to remove the garment completely. He gazed at her breasts as though it were the first time that he'd seen them. Cupping them in his hands, he bent forward and kissed and suckled one and then the other. Her nipples hardened immediately.

'Your breasts are as firm as apples,' he said, moving back from her and caressing the ripe mounds lovingly.

The comment was trite but at that moment it was exactly what she wanted to hear.

He hooked his thumbs under the waistband of her panties and slowly drew them down. For a few, brief seconds she felt like an innocent virgin again, about to be impaled for the first time. He knelt down in front of her and pulled her panties down over her stocking-covered legs and over her shoes. She raised one foot and then the other and he tossed the flimsy garment to one side.

He leant forward and kissed her lightly on the

stomach, then ran his tongue down until the tip touched the wet, tender lips of her cunt. She gasped as the sensations of arousal shot through her loins. He looked up at her.

'You taste divine,' he whispered. He licked her again, a gentle, fluttering touch of his tongue that made her sex-lips throb with desire.

He stood up and kissed her again on the mouth. She could taste her own scent on his lips. His hands roamed down her back and then cupped her buttocks. She pressed her crotch hard against his and felt the unmistakable shape of a very hard cock crushed against her groin. She reached down between them and gripped his stalk tightly. 'Please fuck me now,' she said.

Simons stepped back and Karina watched as he quickly divested himself of his clothing. Moments later, he was standing before her, as naked as she was and with his cock rising stiffly from his bushy groin. She turned and rested her hands on the seat of the chair, presenting her bottom to his eager gaze. She knew that he would now see the welts caused by the thrashing she had received from Rogers and also knew that the sight would delight him. He stroked the cheeks of her bottom softly at first, caressing her tender skin with his smooth palms.

She bent further forward and curved her back to force her arse upward in total subjugation. She looked over her shoulder. He was just staring at her backside, his mouth open and his eyes glazed. She wondered whether she should take the hat off; it seemed strange, to be wearing it with nothing else but shoes and stockings, but she decided to keep it on to maintain the aura of the true English lady. Simons didn't seem to mind. His interest was in a far different part of her anatomy. 'Please fuck me,' she begged again.

He moved forward and gripped her waist. Karina continued to watch him, wishing that she could witness the moment when his hard cock slid into her moist pussy. She felt the touch of the spongy head to her sex-lips and turned her face away, closing her eyes and waiting for that wonderful moment when his stiff shaft would enter her aching sheath.

She was so wet and so aroused that she barely felt the first few inches slip inside her. Only when the head touched her cervix did she realise that she held his rod within her completely. She groaned with satisfaction and he began to move slowly and deliberately in and out of her. She matched his movements with those of her own, forcing her bottom back and forth in perfect rhythm. Simons held himself still and allowed her to make the entire running. The ache inside her was rapidly building up to a crescendo. She gripped the chair seat and slapped her bottom faster and faster against him, gasping with delight every time that the head of his cock slammed against the entrance to her womb.

'Fuck her! Fuck her hard!' said a voice in the audience.

'Yes, fuck me!' echoed Karina. 'Fuck me until it hurts!'

Simons obeyed immediately and gripped her waist even tighter, before starting to slam his groin against her bottom wildly. The sound of skin thrashing against skin filled her ears.

'I'm coming!' she yelled. 'I'm coming! Fuck me!' Simons grunted and panted loudly as she rode the final wave to the pinnacle of ecstasy. 'Yes! Yes! Yes!' she cried. 'Harder! Harder!'

'I can't help it, Karina,' he suddenly blurted out. 'I've got to come!'

Karina immediately pulled herself from him, swung round and fell to her feet. She grasped hold of his wet cock and forced it into her mouth. The head touched the back of her throat and she arched her neck and absorbed as much of his length as she could down her throat. The familiar throbbing of the thick shaft began as she suckled its stiffness within her mouth and she gulped hard, knowing that his cream was jetting down her throat. Moving her head back, she let his cock slip from her mouth and lapped around the spurting head, smoothing his remaining juices over her lips.

Simons grasped her shoulders for support. 'Oh, Karina.' he breathed. 'That was marvellous.' Karina stood up and smiled broadly at him then took his head in her hands and kissed him passionately on the mouth, sharing the taste of his seed with him.

They parted after a few seconds and she licked her lips. 'I've never done that before,' he said. 'The last bit, I mean.'

'Neither have I,' she replied. She turned to look at the others in the circle. 'I want you all,' she said, stressing the last word emphatically. 'Every one of you.'

There was a short pause and then one of the young men rose to his feet and took her in his arms. Karina reached down, unzipped his trousers and pulled out his already hard erection. The boy almost tore his shirt as he wrenched it off and Karina yanked his trousers and underpants down to his ankles in one fervent movement. She clamped her lips around his stiff cock as she dragged his clothing from his ankles and sucked him for all she was worth. He pulled her from him, tugging her hair painfully until she allowed his rod to fall from her mouth and then he lay down on his back and held his stiffness erect.

Karina immediately squatted over him and guided his cock into her soaking cunt. She rammed herself down, absorbing every inch, and then she began to ride him as though he were a wild stallion.

She sensed somebody else touching her bottom and held herself still. Whoever it was raised her slightly until just the tip of the prone man's cock was held inside her slippery wetness. Moments later, she felt the pressure of another hard rod against her sex-lips. She braced herself and felt it slide into her, the two stalks quickly becoming enveloped by her oozing sheath. Two at the same time! Even the boys who had taken her virginity hadn't done that to her!

The entire group suddenly seemed to explode into an uproar of frenzied activity. Clothes were strewn haphazardly all over the place as young men and women threw themselves into an orgy of total abandonment. Sandy knelt at Karina's side and somehow managed to sandwich her head between her upturned backside and the youth who was kneeling behind her and, moments later, Karina felt the silky touch of her tongue slithering over her anus. Two more men knelt on either side of her and she reached out and grasped hold of their proffered cocks, while yet two more crouched before her face and offered their stalks to her mouth. She sucked one and then the other, then managed to accommodate both of them between her lips and tickled the heads with the tip of her tongue.

The boy behind her groaned and ejaculated inside her, his release causing the young man lying underneath her to follow suit. Immediately after they pulled from her, one of the youths that she was masturbating threw her on to her back and dived on top of her, his thick cock ramming into her with a force that almost knocked the breath from her body. Sandy took the opportunity to squat over Karina's face and she pressed her wet pussy hard down on Karina's mouth. Karina lapped hungrily at the juicy little hole until somebody grasped Sandy's bottom and raised her a little, then eased his stalk into her.

Karina lapped the unknown man's balls as he fucked her friend, occasionally allowing her tongue to lick over his anus when he thrust forward. Every now and then, the man withdrew his cock from Sandy's succulence completely and offered it to Karina's willing mouth. The last time that he did it he came, his cream gushing down her throat as he fucked her face.

No sooner had he moved from her than another man replaced him. He could have been anybody. Karina's only view of him was of his backside and his genitals. He fucked Sandy slowly, which allowed Karina to concentrate her oral lovemaking on his anus, the result of which was that the poor young man was unable to last more than a few seconds before filling Sandy's hot little cunt with his juices.

Karina was in heaven. Whether she was fucked by every young man present was of little consequence. She was used and abused for what seemed like an age, the nerve-endings in her body in a constant state of electric arousal. Eventually, it had to end. Sheer exhaustion finally defeated the most ardent amongst the group and, one by one, they fell from her to lie wearily on the floor. Karina raised her head stiffly and looked down at herself. Her body was coated with a thick sheen of sperm and her pussy-lips were reddened and painful.

Simons moved to kneel beside her. He stroked her face gently. 'Karina Devonside,' he began. 'The reluctant virgin is no more. May I welcome you as an honorary Atca.'

She looked into his eyes and knew that this was just the beginning.

The Nexus imprint is the largest collection of erotic fiction published in Britain. The list is as diverse as it is erotic, boasting a wide variety of themes and settings – from classic Victorian erotica to contemporary and cutting-edge SM fiction – while ensuring that only the finest and most arousing stories are published.

If you have enjoyed reading this, and would like a detailed list of Nexus books, please send a large SAE (or two IRCs for overseas enquiries) to:

Nexus
Thames Wharf Studios
Rainville Road
London W6 9HT
UK